RICHARD

Billionaire Boys Club

———————

ELLIE MASTERS

JEM Publishing

Copyright © 2018 Ellie Masters
Richard
Billionaire Boys Club
All rights reserved.

This copy is intended for the original purchaser of this print book ONLY. No part of this print book may be reproduced, scanned, transmitted, or distributed in any printed, mechanical, or electronic form without prior written permission from Ellie Masters or JEM Publishing except in the case of brief quotations embodied in critical articles or reviews. This book is licensed for your personal enjoyment only. Please do not participate in or encourage piracy of copyrighted materials in violation of the author's rights. This book may not be re-sold or given away to other people. If you would like to share this book with another person, please purchase an additional copy for each person you share it with. If you are reading this book and did not purchase it, or it was not purchased for your use only, then you should return it to the seller and purchase your own copy. Thank you for respecting the author's work.

Image/art disclaimer: Licensed material is being used for illustrative purposes only. Any person depicted in the licensed material is a model.

Editor: Erin Toland

Proofreader: Roxane Leblanc

Published in the United States of America

JEM Publishing

This is a work of fiction. While reference might be made to actual historical events or existing locations, the names, characters, businesses, places, and incidents are either the product of the author's imagination or are used fictitiously, and any resemblance to actual persons, living or dead, business establishments, events, or locales is entirely coincidental.

ISBN: PRINT NUMBER

Dedication

This book is dedicated to my one and only—my amazing and wonderful husband.

Without your care and support, my writing would not have made it this far.

You pushed me when I needed to be pushed.

You supported me when I felt discouraged.

You believed in me when I didn't believe in myself.

If it weren't for you, this book never would have come to life.

Also by Ellie Masters

The LIGHTER SIDE

Ellie Masters is the lighter side of the Jet & Ellie Masters writing duo! You will find Contemporary Romance, Military Romance, Romantic Suspense, Billionaire Romance, and Rock Star Romance in Ellie's Works.

YOU CAN FIND ELLIE'S BOOKS HERE:
ELLIEMASTERS.COM/BOOKS

Military Romance

Guardian Hostage Rescue Specialists

Rescuing Melissa

*(*Get a FREE copy of Rescuing Melissa when you join Ellie's Newsletter*)*

Alpha Team

Rescuing Zoe

Rescuing Moira

Rescuing Eve

Rescuing Lily

Rescuing Jinx

Rescuing Maria

Bravo Team

Rescuing Angie

Rescuing Isabelle

Rescuing Carmen

Rescuing Rosalie

Rescuing Kaye

Cara's Protector

Rescuing Barbi

Military Romance

Guardian Personal Protection Specialists

Sybil's Protector

Lyra's Protector

The One I Want Series

(Small Town, Military Heroes)

By Jet & Ellie Masters

EACH BOOK IN THIS SERIES CAN BE READ AS A STANDALONE AND IS ABOUT A DIFFERENT COUPLE WITH AN HEA.

Saving Abby

Saving Ariel

Saving Brie

Saving Cate

Saving Dani

Saving Jen

Rockstar Romance

The Angel Fire Rock Romance Series

EACH BOOK IN THIS SERIES CAN BE READ AS A STANDALONE AND IS ABOUT

A DIFFERENT COUPLE WITH AN HEA. IT IS RECOMMENDED THEY ARE READ IN ORDER.

Ashes to New (prequel)

Heart's Insanity (book 1)

Heart's Desire (book 2)

Heart's Collide (book 3)

Hearts Divided (book 4)

Hearts Entwined (book5)

Forest's FALL (book 6)

Hearts The Last Beat (book7)

Contemporary Romance

Firestorm

(KRISTY BROMBERG'S EVERYDAY HEROES WORLD)

Billionaire Romance

Billionaire Boys Club

Hawke

Richard

Brody

Contemporary Romance

Cocky Captain

(VI KEELAND & PENELOPE WARD'S COCKY HERO WORLD)

Romantic Suspense

EACH BOOK IS A STANDALONE NOVEL.

The Starling

~AND~

Science Fiction

Ellie Masters writing as L.A. Warren
Vendel Rising: a Science Fiction Serialized Novel

Grab the First Book in The Guardian Hostage Rescue Specialists Series for Free

https://elliemasters.com/RescuingMelissa

ONE

Legacy

ROWAN

"Rowan, there's nothing more we can do," Henry Porter said with a weary sigh.

Son of Ralph Porter, Henry might be young for a lawyer, but he led a team of eight lawyers and accountants from the Savannah law firm of Hamilton & Porter. He was being groomed for succession and sat across from me with a serious expression. His job was to deliver news I wasn't prepared to hear. He didn't want to give it. I didn't want to listen to it. But neither of us could deny the truth of it.

Money didn't lie.

The Porter's had managed my family's accounts for generations. Henry, and his father, Ralph, knew where all the bodies were buried, if there were any. My father never shared his business dealings with me, which left me to rely solely on Henry's advice. Unfortunately, he had nothing good to say.

With me, a partnership spanning generations would die.

"Nothing?" I held my hands clasped tightly in my lap. It took every ounce of self-control not to fidget and twist my fingers.

The sadness in his expression spoke more to the truth than any of the numbers and figures printed on the reams of paper littering the desk. I barely glanced at the reports. I didn't need to. I knew.

Heat pricked beneath my lids, but I'd been born and bred to privilege. I was a proud Southern lady, a blue blood of the great South. The women in my family didn't cry—at least, not in public. I could faint. There was that option. A hundred years ago, that would have been acceptable behavior for a young lady of my standing, but I sat in a plush leather chair and had more respect for myself than that. Besides, I was over and done with drama.

No matter what I did, the legacy of my birthright couldn't be erased, escaped, or ignored. I would always have my name—for what that was worth. The Cartwrights had built Georgia into what it was now. We stood proudly alongside the Montagues, Fitzgeralds, and other prominent Southern families. We owned land, companies, and banks. Lots of land and lots of banks. Our money made money. Most of the land was gone though, and there was precious left of the companies my father had run. As for our money? That was why I'd found myself in Henry's office.

"How long?" I asked.

How far can I make our dwindling reserves last? I had a plan but needed more time. I wasn't screwed. I was royally fucked.

There'd been a time when I held my head high and lifted my nose to look down on those beneath me. My family's name might be steeped in the history of the South, but Savannah, Georgia, wanted nothing to do with my family anymore. Cutting stares and harsh whispers had brought crippling social distance until I became a pariah. I hadn't even received an invitation to Adelaide

Montague's annual charity event. That hurt more than it should have.

I'd been looking forward to seeing her daughter, Alexandria, and maybe even my old friend Patrick Fitzgerald. He'd been in the class above me at the academy. She'd been a year or two behind, but they were both ahead of me as far as life plans went. Patrick had finished his degree at Pratt, and Alexandria was well on her way to becoming a lawyer. They'd moved on, chasing their futures and pursuing their dreams, while I had taken several years off to travel the world.

Back then, money hadn't been a problem.

Back then, there'd been no scandal.

We'd had more money than I could count, and I'd had my heart set on seeing the world. One year had turned into two, and two had become three. Patrick and I'd kept in contact after his graduation, and it was because of him I'd finally found my way to the Pratt Institute for Design. I had dreams, too.

My father's sins weighed heavily on my shoulders, suffocating every breath. His crimes had stolen any joy I might have once thought to squander. The Cartwright name should have endured the scandal that had brought my father down, except it hadn't. Not after he'd taken the coward's way out. His actions had affected not only my future, but also the plight of my brother. *What will become of Freddy?*

I sat across from my lawyers, trying to salvage what I could.

No tears fell from my eyes. My smile met the sorrow weighted in Henry's expression. A core of steel ran through me. I drew on that, even as my insides swirled in a blender. The only problem with steel was, it only bent so far before it shattered. I had met my breaking point.

Henry pushed the paper in front of him across the table. I refused to look at it. Instead, I kept my gaze level and fixed on his face. Maybe, if I didn't see what was written in black and white, it wouldn't be true.

"How long?" I repeated my question into the overwhelming silence.

His lips pursed, and those seated adjacent to him shifted in their seats, covering their unease with a cough. The oppressiveness of the conference room affected us all, but they would leave here and head to their fancy homes and fat bank accounts. The same could not be said for me.

"If you make certain adjustments"—he rubbed at his chin—"we can wait to foreclose—"

"How long?" I didn't want the details.

"Rowan, it's not that simple."

"How difficult can it be?"

How long until I'm broke? How long until I have to move Freddy out of the long-term care facility he calls home? How long until we're destitute and on the streets? All these questions flitted through my head, but I held my tongue and waited for an answer.

I needed more time—two and a half years to be precise.

My degree in design wouldn't make much money to start. I had to have enough to cover Freddy's needs until then. Where I slept or what I ate didn't matter, and I had closets of designer clothes to last at least that long.

Henry swiped at his mouth, and he pulled a face, glancing down at the paper. "I can buy you six months."

"Six months!" I slammed my hand down on the tabletop and stood as my anger and frustration rose. "I need more than six months." I needed two and a half years.

Sara Donaldson, the only other woman in the room, cleared her throat. "What about quitting school? The tuition is steep—"

"I can't afford to quit school." I needed the career it would bring. Besides, no one in New York gave a rat's ass about some washed-up Southern belle.

Sara arched a brow. "You can't afford to remain either. You should look into scholarships."

I rolled my eyes. Of course I had. I'd exhausted all my options, but even though I would be bankrupt within six months, I didn't qualify for scholarships, grants, or loans, not enough to cover my tuition, let alone pay rent on my apartment or cover other necessities like food. With the mess of my finances, no bank would extend a student loan.

"I've considered everything," I said, sinking back into my chair with defeat.

Henry rolled his pen over the table. "Rowan, I'm sorry, but there is another option. Have you considered—"

"No," I said, feeling the heat rising. I was going to blow a gasket if someone mentioned that again. I wasn't a whore, and I'd be damned if I sold myself to any man.

I needed a drink and the oblivion of a good fuck. Alcohol to numb the pain and a man who could fuck me until I forgot my name.

TWO

Privilege

RICHARD

No matter what I did or didn't do, the privilege of birth couldn't be erased, escaped, or ignored. There were moments when my birthright smothered me with the weight of expectations I didn't care to meet.

"Richard..." My mother's voice came out smooth as silk and covered in cream.

She had been blessed with an angelic voice, and when lifted in song, it made angels weep. When filled with ire, kings fell to their knees, queens trembled in their shoes, and the leaders of nations took notice. I did none of those things. I met my mother's iron will with the strength she'd instilled in me from my very first breath.

"Yes, Mum?" I said, trying my best to look apologetic.

The fake smile plastered to her face didn't fool me. Her crystalline-blue eyes sparked with anger, and I braced for the harshness that would follow. She, however, wasn't in a rush to lay down her condemnation and seemed content to take her time in dispensing judgment. When pushed past her tolerance of what was right and proper, Her Majesty Mary Margaret Windsor could be a cruel-hearted bitch, but she loved her younger son with the whole of her heart. Of that, I had no doubt. It was how I got away with so much, whereas my brother did not. She was about to attempt to whip me into shape, only I was no longer a six-year-old boy, and she'd never once been successful in the past.

"Are you incapable of self-control?" Her left brow lifted, challenging me to deny the truth.

We knew how this dance would play out. She would be stern. I would be remorseful. I would behave for a time, but we both knew I'd be damned if I ever bowed to the court of public opinion, and she didn't have it in her heart to force me to do anything I truly hated.

"Mum, it's wasn't like that," I tried to explain, but it had been exactly like *that*. There were photographs speeding through the Web that attested to that fact.

My brother, Edmund, gave a snort. "Oh, brother, you have stepped deep in *shite* with this one."

With a narrowing of my eyes, I shot daggers at my elder brother. Edmund had no place in judging my actions. He was worse than me. Unlike me, he'd perfected the art of discretion. He was everything I was not—proud, regal, in control, and ready to take the reins of our country. More power to him. I didn't want that job, the pressure of marriage, or the need to produce heirs as quickly as possible.

Eight years younger than him, my youth stretched before me. Heck, twenty-seven was much too young to settle down. Arranged marriages endured but not because either party found peace or happiness. I knew for a fact that my brother juggled several potential hopefuls. He had no room to judge my actions.

Mother's voice ripped through the room, making me flinch. "Wasn't like what? Are you denying the photographs that are going viral, even as we speak?" She *tsked* her disapproval. "I don't dare go online. I don't want to see my son—*my son!*—exposed like that."

Her Majesty the Queen never went online. She had people for that, very well-paid analysts who scoured the Internet for what she should and shouldn't be made aware of, but I understood why she would shy away from those images. I worked hard to live up to my playboy image, and I'd been caught with my trousers down—literally. She had every reason to chastise me for what I'd done.

Edmund maintained a squeaky-clean image despite his multiple flings, but as the Prince of Wales, and heir to the throne, that was expected of the future king. I would never ascend to the throne, and I was grateful for that small miracle because I didn't want the burden of the throne weighing me down. My position suited me well, and there was no reason not to have a little fun with royal privilege.

I tried to defend my actions, opening my mouth to insert my foot, but Mother lifted an imperious finger and silenced me with her indomitable will.

"In this conversation, you do not speak." She made a pinching gesture, effectively sealing my lips, and leaned back in her favorite chair, looking very much a regal monarch rather than the mother of a recalcitrant son.

The royal family had retired after supper to our private rooms where she was at liberty to execute this conversation and chastise me. Only the servants remained—eyes that saw everything, ears that heard every secret, and mouths that never uttered a single word about any of it to the outside world. They were at once ever present and invisible. One delivered Mum a cup of tea.

She cradled the saucer in her palm and lifted the delicate

china to her lips. Her eyes closed as she took a languorous inhale, and then she reveled in the first taste of an expertly poured cup of the finest English tea.

I waved off the servant who held out a cup and saucer. I was thirsty but not for tea.

Brandy and cigars would come later, and there was no doubt I would need the spirited liquor to soothe my nerves. That was, if I made it out of this conversation alive. Booze and a good shag—that was what I wanted. Alcohol to numb my soul and a girl with compliant flesh strong enough to exorcise my frustrations. What I really needed was time away from the public eye.

"It's time to settle down." She took another sip from her cup as my heart raced to a sudden and profound halt. "I will speak with my advisers, and we'll settle on a suitable match. The obligations of a family will prevent…such occurrences in the future."

Edmund chuckled and shook his head. "Good luck," he said, lifting his cup.

I wasn't certain if he meant that for our mother or me.

"Mum," I said, speaking although commanded to silence—I never was good at following orders—"perhaps some time away?"

I had a buddy in America who lived in New York—exactly the town where a person could disappear, even someone as royally screwed as me.

Her eyes narrowed as she gave my idea consideration. With a slow nod, she granted my reprieve. "That might be a good thing. Let this negative press die down, and gain some distance from this debacle."

I inclined my head, grateful for a chance to escape familial obligations for a little while longer.

"But, Richard," she said, "you have one year to make yourself respectable."

"Mum!"

Her head shook, informing me that her mind was made up.

One year? I wasn't Edmund. I was the spare, the heir who didn't matter.

However, I saw the truth in her eyes. She was giving me freedom, but it came with an expiration date.

THREE

Pratt

ROWAN

A FEW DAYS FOUND ME BACK IN MY APARTMENT IN NEW YORK. IT felt cramped, but I'd been told by my classmates that I lived in the lap of luxury. Manhattan studios went for thousands a month. I had that and more.

The kitchen could be crammed into a shoebox and was probably smaller than a ship's galley. I had a queen-size bed but barely any room to move. My friends had thought this was funny and wondered why I didn't replace the queen with a twin since I lived alone. I had a stove and a dishwasher—luxuries my classmates had insisted were not standard. Not that it mattered. I ate out for virtually every meal. In New York, there was no reason to cook.

All that would change.

I hurried to dress and headed downstairs.

"Good morning, Miss Rowan," the doorman, Tom, greeted

me with a charismatic smile, twinkling eyes, and a face deeply lined with a life full of laughter.

I'd never seen the man frown. Didn't think it was possible.

"Hey, Tom." I lifted on my tiptoes to give him a morning hug and peck on the cheek.

After nearly two years, he still thought that behavior was odd, but I had grown up in the South. Kisses and hugs were a part of our social dance, and I'd be damned if I let the city of cities take that away.

Tom stood stiffly for my hug. "It's a beautiful day." He extricated himself and held the door. Then, he hailed a cab with his shrill whistle and a wave.

"Oh, I'm going to walk today." My voice sounded chipper, like I thought it was a lovely idea. The truth was much different.

Henry Porter and his team couldn't have been clearer. If I downsized to a studio, moved away from Central Park, got a MetroCard instead of using taxis, and cooked all my meals rather than eating out, my money would extend another few months.

I had drawn the line when Henry mentioned roommates—plural, not singular. That wasn't happening even if Henry had said I could squeak by for another two months if I roomed with others. Two months could very well be another two years. There had to be another solution. With the adjustments to my lifestyle in place, I had nearly a year to sort out my financial woes before I was truly broke.

"Are you certain, Miss Rowan?" Tom asked.

If I immediately moved Freddy out of his home, Henry had assured me that my remaining funds would stretch to graduation. That still left me six months short. A quick visit with Freddy before returning to New York had turned disastrous when I mentioned the possibility of a move. Freddy didn't handle change very well. He didn't handle it at all.

Classes were starting again after spring break, and I had my eye on attending the Spring Job Fair at Pratt. I might find my way into an early internship. It didn't need to be much, but I had to find something.

At least the hunt for an apartment wouldn't be on my shoulders. Sara Donaldson had taken over that task, and I waited in limbo for her to make the impossible happen.

A cab pulled to the curb, and I hesitated. *One last ride?*

"Thank you, Tom, but I'm looking forward to the walk." I sniffed and turned into the wind.

He cocked his head and waved the impatient cabbie to move on. I gave a fleeting smile and headed to the nearest metro stop. It wasn't like I'd never ridden the subway before. Not all my classmates could afford the luxury of a cab. I simply hated the press of all the people jammed underground.

Fortunately, it was a beautiful day. The crisp spring temperature chilled the air. Juggling jacket, purse, and satchel, I successfully purchased my first MetroCard and officially became a public transport commuter. I hated it.

School was on my mind and distracted me from the incessant noise, harsh smells, and overcrowded subway. After I emerged from the bowels of the subway, a quick walk brought me to Pratt's campus. Most of my classmates spent their break having fun or visiting family. I'd had one brief afternoon with my brother, Freddy, and three long days with Henry and his team of lawyers.

My two morning classes breezed by as my professors welcomed everyone back. Assignments were turned in, and new ones were handed out. All the while, I kept my attention focused on the clock. The Spring Job Fair was a place to ask questions and make connections. Many graduates of Pratt would return to speak to the student body, providing valuable insights and lessons learned. I was pleasantly surprised to find a friend speaking to the crowd.

Patrick Fitzgerald captivated those gathered as he spoke about his company and explained some of the tips and tricks that had worked for him. I hung in the back of the room, watching him enrapture eager students with his passion for design. A blue blood like me, he was the epitome of a Southern gentleman. His light accent made many hearts flutter, and there was an honest warmth to his personality—something not common to those born and bred in New York, who rarely looked a stranger in the eye.

A couple of inches shy of six feet, he was a handsome man with a trim, muscular physique. He wasn't thick and brawny, but he carried himself with a sense of possession and strength. It gave him an undeniable presence, which won over friends and colleagues. Soft brown eyes brought a measure of peace to those gathered. For me, it felt like coming home. I'd missed my friend. When he noticed me, those brown eyes lit with recognition. I smiled and gave a slight wave. It had been too long since we sat down and talked.

I really needed a friend right now, but what I needed more was someone with contacts in the business. Patrick could give me both, and I didn't feel bad for relying on him. Fortunes were made and lost based upon who you knew.

He concluded his presentation to thunderous applause and slowly made his way to where I waited.

"Rowan!" He approached with his arms open for a hug.

"Patrick, it's so good to see you."

Folding myself into his arms, I welcomed myself home. My hands might have gripped a little harder than normal, but I couldn't help it. Seeing Patrick brought all my insecurities rising to the surface. I didn't want to lose him, and I was afraid of what would happen when he learned about the chaos of my life.

Powerful arms drew me in tight. "Are you okay?" His words fluttered in my ears and reminded me we were in a public place.

I gave a quick squeeze and released him. Tears pricked in my eyes, but a quick blink flicked them away. "I'm good, just glad to see you." I made a sweeping gesture toward the stage. "Looks like things are going well for you."

He gripped my hand and tugged me outside. "They are, but let's talk about you. I haven't seen you in over a year."

Patrick had helped me with my application to Pratt. He'd sat with me while I agonized over what to place in my portfolio for the application review. I wouldn't have been accepted if not for his involvement. I hadn't made an effort to seek him out even though we lived fairly close to each other, but there'd been a good reason for my distance. The mess my father had made distracted me from most things.

"Has it been that long?" I asked.

He gave me a look. "Yes, my dear, it has been precisely that long. Are you free for lunch?"

I was, but my new budget wasn't. "I, uh…"

"No way are you saying no. My treat, and I have the perfect place in mind."

"How can a girl say no to that?"

"You don't," he said, "and you're going to tell me exactly why you're so sad."

"I'm not—" The sternness of his look had me biting my tongue.

"Just let me know where to bury the body," he said, joking. "Man troubles or something else?"

If only I had man troubles.

"Something else," I admitted.

He drew me away from the press of other students, but there were still too many who could overhear. Lies weren't something Patrick and I had ever shared. I owed him the truth but not here.

"Where are you thinking for lunch?" I asked.

FOUR

Lunch

ROWAN

PATRICK'S IDEA FOR LUNCH CONSISTED OF A TINY SHOEBOX DELI wedged between two buildings. He paid, and we found two seats crammed in the back. He opened wide to take a bite of one of the tallest Reuben sandwiches I'd ever seen. I watched as he tore off a chunk. He closed his eyes and leaned back in the chair, thoroughly enjoying his sandwich.

My tuna melt remained untouched. We were about to have a conversation I didn't want to have, and that churned my stomach. There was no good way to explain how far my status had fallen after my father's arrest and subsequent suicide.

"Not hungry?" He licked his lips and then gave me a long, hard stare.

"I thought I was, but now, I guess, not so much."

"You should eat." He took another bite, but this time, his keen eyes remained on me. After he swallowed, he wiped his lips and placed the napkin down on the table. "Are you going to tell me why you look so sad?"

Breath rushed in, and a deep sigh escaped me. "I'm not sad."

"You look sad."

"I'm not."

"Then, what's weighing on your mind, my friend? Why do you look so incredibly miserable?"

I stared at the abandoned tuna melt sitting before me. Then, I took in a breath and asked for a favor, "I need a job."

"A job? What kind of job?"

"One that pays."

He shook his head. "You don't have time for a job. No student at Pratt does. You're halfway to the finish line, but that only means, things are going to get more intense, not less. Besides, it's too soon to be looking."

I pressed my fingers on the tabletop and admired the immaculate French manicure adorning the tips of my nails. That, too, would have to go. Manicures, pedicures, and the massages I loved weren't in the budget Henry had set for me.

"Patrick," I said, dreading the next words, "if I don't find a job, there won't be any graduation."

He slanted his chin down. For a long while, he said nothing. It killed me because I was dying to know what was going on in his head. The silence between us dragged because I sure as hell wasn't going to fill it with any words of my own. Finally, he took another bite. It took forever for him to chew and swallow. But he did, and he put the stacked sandwich down.

"How bad is it?"

"It couldn't be any worse. I have less than a year to come up with enough money for my tuition and pay for Freddy's home."

"How is your brother?"

"Happy. Content. He really loves that place."

"I sense there's a lot more you're not telling me."

I nodded. "My father's embezzlement left us destitute. My lawyer tells me I'll be bankrupt within the year. I don't care about me, but I can't pull Freddy from his home. In order to afford it, I have to graduate from Pratt and find an internship, which leads to a job, but I can't stay at Pratt because I can't pay my tuition, let alone my apartment."

"I see," he said. "I'm surprised no one has swooped in to rescue you."

"Oh, trust me, I've had offers." I had one, the worst possible offer. "The thought of becoming a trophy wife for some man who wants me for nothing more than my name and my looks turns my stomach. Besides, I'm not looking for a savior. I'm looking for a solution, and I'll do whatever it takes to see that Freddy never has to leave his home."

"Anything?" His left eyebrow cocked up. "That leaves the barn door wide open."

"Have you never been desperate?" I asked. "I mean, I'm not sleeping on the streets, and I'm not trying to be insensitive to those who are. There are other people in much worse places. If it were just me, I could make a ton of sacrifices. I'd quit Pratt and find a job that paid enough to put a roof over my head and food in my belly, and I would work my ass off to make things better. But it's not just me. I have Freddy, and I'm not going to do that to him. I won't rip apart his world. So, yeah, the barn door is wide open."

"I'm sorry about your father."

A pang stabbed at my heart. "Thank you."

"I don't get why he did it. Not when Freddy was so dependent on him."

"I think he couldn't deal with everything he'd lost. I've seen the numbers. It's all gone. Maybe he couldn't live with that."

"Again, I'm very sorry."

"Thanks."

"I might have a solution for you." He gave a low chuckle and whispered under his breath, "I can't believe I'm doing this again."

My heart fluttered with hope. "What are you talking about?"

"Eat!" he ordered. "You're going to need it."

"For what?"

"For our talk." Patrick made a show of lifting his Reuben to his mouth real slow, letting me know that question would not be answered here.

His eyes shifted sideways as he chewed, and he placed a finger over his mouth. The bastard was having fun with this. With me. He pointed to my sandwich, giving me another command.

Well, I said I'd do anything. With my stomach in knots and my heart thumping hard, I took my first bite and tasted…heaven.

"Oh my God," I said as succulent flavors coated my tongue. "This is amazing."

"I know," he said. "Have I ever steered you wrong?"

"I just don't know how I've lived here for two years and never known of this place."

The deli was only a few blocks away from Pratt.

"That's New York," he said between bites. "Now, finish up, and we'll go somewhere we can talk."

Our conversation drifted from there, touching on everything, except the one thing I wished he would mention. What did Patrick have up his sleeve?

He showed a lot of interest in my design work, and I showed him some of what I'd been working on.

As a child, I'd built forts for the boys and princess palaces for the girls, both constructing and decorating them. When the decision had come to choose between interior design and architecture, the choice had been difficult. Patrick had encouraged me to pursue architecture, but I still loved decorating the inside. My father had encouraged me to apply for interior design school because it was more appropriate for a woman. I hadn't yet decided which I would pursue.

"There's no way you're quitting. Not with your talent," Patrick pronounced.

"I don't want to quit." I folded my napkin and placed it on my empty plate. "And, if I can get through the next two years, I'll be able to support Freddy."

"What about a husband?"

I shook my head. "I have an offer, one that would solve all my problems, but I'm not willing to settle. Call me foolish, but I believe in true love."

Being dependent on a man made me sick to my stomach. The taste of bile coated my tongue with the very thought of needing someone else. I blame that on my father, who had raised an intelligent daughter to be the son Freddy could never be.

Honestly, there wasn't anything in life I'd failed at when I set my mind to it, and I wasn't ready to start now.

"Pride," my father had said, "will one day cripple you."

I hated to think he might be right. There were many reasons to give up my dreams at Pratt but many more reasons to stay. I had to look beyond the short-term. If it didn't kill me, I would do almost anything to fulfill my dreams.

"I take it, you're only looking for a stopgap measure?" Patrick said. "Something dependable but with an expiration date?"

"If it pays well," I said with a soft laugh.

"Say I knew of people hiring for only a year and the pay would more than meet your needs, is that something you'd be interested in?"

"If it kept Freddy where he is and I could still go to school and finish my degree, then yes. I don't want to give up my future, not when I'm nearly halfway through with my education. If you have something for a year that pays what I need to stay afloat, then I'm all ears."

He grabbed my hand and pulled me from my chair. Once outside the deli, he glanced up and down the street. "Let's take a walk."

"Where?"

"Anywhere, and I have only one request."

"Yes?"

"It's a big one."

"Which would you like? Cross my heart and hope to die? Or is a pinkie swear enough?"

That comment brought a laugh. "Only you would pinkie swear, but no reason to go promising to die. What I am about to tell you can't be shared with anyone, and you have to swear to keep it to yourself."

"Is it legal?"

His tone had my nerves lighting up.

"I might be a lot of things, but a criminal isn't one of them, and if I were, I'd never ask you to..." He waved off my comment. "It's legal. It's safe. It's a privately run, very exclusive company, and I work for them."

"I thought you worked for a design firm?"

"I do that, too. No one says you have to have only one employer."

"Well, I'm all ears."

If Patrick works for this company, how bad can it be?

FIVE

Hrh

Richard

England's beautiful landscapes and rich history flowed in my blood. I loved my country, but I craved the brilliance that was New York. The city pulsed with the vitality of millions; every breath, every step, every moment imbued itself with a lusty, soul-gripping zest. I'd been in New York for two months, and I already knew it would never be enough. The pulse of the city pounded in my veins and whispered to me of sin, sex, and seduction. If I had a mistress, I would keep her in this city, if only to have a reason to return. I craved New York with a fiery hunger, and she spoke to me, whispering her secrets while uncovering mine.

It was easy to get lost within the crowd, and I'd become an expert at evading the flashing lights and invasive lenses of the paparazzi. England wanted to know about their wayward prince, but New York didn't care for royalty. Here, I was but one of countless souls, traveling my path and exploring who I might have been if not for the privilege of my birth.

"You headed out again?" David asked.

David had graciously offered the spare room in the penthouse apartment he shared with his girlfriend of six months, Evelyn Gaynes. That was a marathon event for my friend, who burned through women with nearly the speed and veracity as me.

He and I'd met during our time at Oxford and spent our Uni years carousing the pubs and making headlines. One of the few true friends in my life, he cared nothing about who I was, only that we had somehow managed to form an indescribable fraternal bond.

Edmund might be my brother, but he was a pompous ass and huge stick in the mud. He lorded his birth over me—a constant reminder that he would be king and I would not. It was a palpable force holding us apart. He spilled my secrets to our mother and capitalized on my failures to hide his own indiscretions. My brother was far from a saint.

With David, I could let down the facade get pissed and have a gas, or *shoot the shit*, as Americans called it. There was no jockeying for position or vying over Mum's closely guarded love. With David, I could be the real me.

The private elevator dinged, and the doors slid open to reveal the captivating mystery that was Evelyn Gaynes. The mysterious woman remained a frustrating unknown. I couldn't figure her out. She was the only woman David seemed to be sleeping with, which made her even more of a puzzle. My friend had settled down.

David was a self-made man, so I never expected he would wind up with only one woman. And I'd asked what was so special about her. I'd stuck my nose in it and wound up frustrated by their secretive smiles and furtive glances. Whatever it was, they weren't telling me, which only fueled my curiosity.

"Why don't you come with me?" I asked, trying yet again to get David to join me.

He refused to join my nights on the town unless Evelyn came along.

"You two heading out?" Evelyn asked. Her low heels clicked on the Egyptian marble as she approached David.

Leaning down, she gave him a languorous kiss while he shamelessly palmed her ass.

"Not if you don't want to," he said. "We can kick His Royal Highness out for the night and have some fun."

"Hmm," she said, her tone low and sensuous. "Now, that sounds like fun, but I have bad news for you, my love, though good news for HRH Richard."

She turned and beamed her megawatt smile. Tall and willowy thin, she had the body of a runway model and the brains of a neurosurgeon, which made sense since she was on the faculty at New York-Presbyterian Weill Cornell Medical Center. The woman was wicked smart. What she was doing with David boggled my mind.

"Please stop with all the HRH crap," I begged.

But they wouldn't. Evidently, I was fun to tease and the butt of all their jokes. Having a prince crashing in their place was hilarious as shit to these two. I had a flat, but I hated the emptiness.

"Let me slip out of my scrubs," Evelyn said. "We have a function to attend."

"Of course, dear," David said.

"You really have a thing for her," I said once she was out of earshot.

His cheeks bowed with an honest smile. "You calling me pussy-whipped?"

"Odd phrase and not what I was going to say. I guess I don't understand."

"Understand what?"

"What happened to you?"

"Nothing happened—or rather, something unexpected happened."

"You should tell me about it." I jabbed my thumb in the direction of their bedroom. "I'd kill to have what the two of you share."

"You're a damn prince, Richard. All you have to do is snap your fingers, and hundreds of eligible bachelorettes will come running."

I sighed in exasperation. "That, my friend, is the problem."

"How so?"

"A woman in my bed is too easily found. I want more substance."

He pointed back down the hall. "I've found *more*."

"How? You might have been my wingman at Uni, but you suck at it now. If you have a secret, you owe it to me to share."

His left brow winged up. "Really? Because I don't think you could handle having only one woman."

"I'm not looking for *the one*." I didn't believe in love. I couldn't afford to, not with my mother's machinations in play back home.

"Then, what are you looking for?"

With a shrug, I paced the room. "I don't know." Moving to the bar, I poured a finger of whiskey. "My forever doesn't exist. My mother has made it perfectly clear that I'll marry whomever she approves and none other, but I would give my left nut for my *right now*."

"Is that so?"

I shrugged, realizing how lonely my life had become. It was true though. I could have a new woman in my bed every night, but a mindless shag no longer held any appeal. Even less after watching what David and Evelyn shared.

"Is the whole a-prince-can-only-marry-another-royal thing true?" David asked.

"It's not."

The whiskey burned as it slid down my throat. Damn, it tasted good. I poured another two fingers, knowing I'd need to loosen up before heading out. Evelyn's functions could be interesting affairs, but they were generally well attended by an eclectic crowd. I never knew if we'd be surrounded by doctors, benefactors of the hospital, or a group of artists. Given a choice of heading out alone or being the third wheel to David and Evelyn, it was a no-brainer that I'd go with them.

"I can marry anyone I choose, if I have permission from the Queen," I explained. "It would be helpful if she wasn't Catholic, but other than that, who I can and can't marry isn't tied to their royal lineage. In this, dear old Mum has me over a barrel."

"That sucks. So, you can basically fall madly in love and propose to a girl, but your mother could say no? Is that for real?"

"Unfortunately."

Evelyn returned, wearing a tight-fitting black dress. Basic in design, it was nonetheless stunning on the redhead.

David rose from the couch. "You know, maybe your forever isn't something you can control, but you can have your *right now*."

I scoffed at his comment, and he arched a brow in return.

"You think I'm kidding?" He gestured at Evelyn as she busied herself at the bar, pouring a glass of merlot. "I have an idea."

"You do?"

David had never once steered me wrong. He could be a trickster at times, but when it came to the important things, he was a straight shooter.

"I know exactly what you need," he asserted. "Let me ask Evelyn."

I had no idea why we needed to bring her into this discussion, but he valued her opinion, and therefore, I did, too. I was willing to play along.

What I wanted was something uniquely mine, a woman who belonged to me body and soul, who wasn't afraid to explore darker desires, and who wasn't intimidated by the privilege of my birth. Mostly, I needed someone with whom I could lower my defenses and come out from behind all the walls and the decorum my birth demanded. I needed something true, honest, and real. Above all, I needed something that would never make it into the press. I didn't know if it was possible to have that level of trust with another person. My forever might always be out of my grasp.

"I'm game," I said. "You tell me what you think you know, and I'll give it a go."

"Evelyn," David called, "I think he's ready to hear about Infidelity."

"Infidelity?" That didn't sound like anything I'd be interested in. In fact, it sounded exactly the opposite. "Um, I'm looking to keep a low profile. I don't need to give Mum any reason to be yanking me back home."

Evelyn sipped her wine. "Oh, Richard, just wait while I explain the wonder that is Infidelity."

SIX

Opportunity

ROWAN

I stared at Patrick after he gave me this spiel about a secret, word-of-mouth, backdoor company that basically sold sex. My mouth gaped, and a strangled sound escaped into the space between us.

"You've got to be fucking kidding me!" I shouted.

Not my finest moment, and my words struck Patrick like a slap in the face. He recoiled as my indignation rose. I was surprised there wasn't steam shooting out of the top of my head.

He grabbed my elbow and tried to get me to lower my voice, but I yanked out of his grip and prepared another volley of expletives. I drew stares from the pedestrians rushing by. In New York, people didn't make eye contact, but they found my tirade interesting enough to gawk.

Patrick tried to soothe me and pulled me out of the stream of traffic. "It's not what you think, Rowan." He used my name to get my attention, but I was beyond listening.

"You want me to become a whore?" My screech turned more than a few heads.

One guy even slowed down, twisting his neck in passing to give me a hard once-over from tits to ass.

"You're not listening," Patrick said, tugging me off the sidewalk and into a small alley.

The alley smelled funny, and the walls bowed inward, blocking out nearly all light as they practically touched far overhead. I didn't want to be here, but I didn't want to be surrounded by the press of humanity passing on the sidewalks either.

Patrick cupped my chin and squeezed my cheeks like I was some recalcitrant six-year-old. "Infidelity is not *that* kind of company."

"But you said—"

"You didn't let me finish."

My mind struggled to process everything, but I kept getting stuck on getting paid to be someone's companion.

"And you work for them?"

"I do."

I gulped with that knowledge. *Why does he need to get paid to be someone's companion?* "And you trade sex for money?"

"That's not what Infidelity is about," he asserted.

He released me and leaned against the rough brick wall opposite me. I shook like a leaf. His eyes softened, and warmth returned, reminding me that he was my friend. He wouldn't have told me about Infidelity if he didn't think they could help.

"Then, what is it about?" I asked, more curious than I should be. "Because, no matter how you spin it, that's exactly what it sounds like."

He ran his hand through his hair and vented a deep sigh. "Let me try to explain. Promise you'll let me try?"

"I don't really know if that is for me."

"It might not be, and there's an intake process. There's no

guarantee they would accept you. Even if selected, there's a chance of never getting paired with a client, but you said you'd do anything, and this could solve your problems. One year. That's all you said you needed. Now, you can do anything for a year. Right?"

Sell my body? My integrity? My soul?

My insides twisted in revulsion. I'd told Henry I wouldn't sell myself, and I'd run from an unwanted marriage that could have solved my problems. That would have been a lifetime commitment, but this? Maybe Patrick's solution would be more palatable. I didn't know, but desperation drove me to find out more.

"Then, explain it because I sure as hell don't understand."

"Take sex out of the equation for a minute, and let me use an analogy."

"Okay." But I didn't think any explanation would make a difference.

"When a man and woman date, there are expectations placed upon each party as the relationship progresses. If you follow the stereotype to its logical conclusion, the couple marries, but what happens along that path is what I want you to consider. When dating, there's a belief intimacy will follow—whether it's hand-holding, kissing, groping, or sex. The man *pays* for that privilege by paying for dinners and entertainment. All Infidelity does is turn the intricacies of social dating into a business arrangement, one which is mutually beneficial to both parties."

"Still sounds like selling your body, and I don't think I agree with your statement that the man pays for the privilege of sex."

"When exactly is sex expected these days?"

I didn't have an answer because I hadn't dated in nearly two years, but my friends did. "I don't know." Except I did. Most of my friends had said sex was expected by the third date.

He nodded. "How many guys do you think stop dating a girl if she doesn't put out? I'll tell you, they pay and expect to play."

"You make it sound cheap. When did you become so jaded?"

"When I realized I was gay and saw how easily men traded sex in dirty bathrooms and back alleys. That scene wasn't for me. I wanted something more."

That was something I could agree on. More—whatever that nebulous *more* might be. It was my unicorn. I'd never experienced love. I doubted I'd every really experienced passion, but I envied those who had.

"Not every contract negotiated by Infidelity winds up in a sexual relationship."

"Really?" My brows pulled together as I considered, and that churning in my stomach eased just a bit.

"See, this is where you need to understand what Infidelity is, what they do, and how they accomplish their goals."

"Then, break it down for me because I still don't get it."

"Imagine a gentleman who, for various reasons, has tired of the dating game, or maybe he's looking for simple companionship. Maybe he doesn't want to date but needs a companion for social functions. Maybe he's been burned by scandal and seeks to simplify how his needs are met. There are many reasons clients seek out Infidelity."

"We're talking only single men?"

"Well, the name is Infidelity. They cater to a wide range of clientele. Some are single. Some are married. And some are women."

"That's horrible." I crossed my arms and kicked a heel over my opposite foot. "The married part." Mirroring Patrick's pose, I leaned against the bricks behind me.

"Is it? Say a man is in a marriage that doesn't fulfill his needs, sexual or otherwise. He wants a circumspect partner, a time-limited engagement, and no drama. He could be single, too. Maybe he's a wealthy man, tired of women trying to get at his money, and all he wants is a little companionship. He's not looking for a woman anxious to become his wife. Infidelity's clients are the kind of people who don't want their private business broadcast to the world. They seek discretion above all else. No scandals. That's in the contract, too. They want a clean exit. The contract runs out, and the relationship ends, drama-free. Contracts keep things neat. Each person goes in knowing what is and isn't expected. And, as far as being a glorified pimping service, Infidelity has that covered."

"How?" The whole setup made way more sense than it should, which meant I might very well be considering it.

"They only pair an employee once. There's no revolving door where an employee is matched with multiple clients. You can see why this would be important?"

I thought back to the blue bloods of Savannah and our very exclusive social circle. "I guess it could be awkward if the same woman kept being passed around."

He snorted. "Exactly."

"And the same goes for the clients? Or do they get to keep paying because that would still make Infidelity a skin broker."

"They're limited as well, but as paying clients, Infidelity gives them two chances. If the first contract doesn't work, they initiate a second pairing. If the client is dissatisfied after that, the relationship between Infidelity and the client is terminated."

"If you enter an agreement and things don't work out, you can leave?"

"No, the agreement is for one year."

"How can they guarantee you won't hate each other?"

"Again, this is the brilliance of Infidelity. Their client satisfaction scores are exceptionally high. There are grounds for terminating a contract, but those fall under issues of physical abuse. Like I said, they're selling companionship, not sex. You're becoming a bona fide couple, in private and in public. Couples have good days and bad days. Sex is merely a fringe benefit both parties enjoy. Infidelity won't force you to have sex, but it's on the table."

"That's crazy."

"They have the whole matching system down. I'm telling you, the intake interview is exhausting and doesn't guarantee you'll be placed with a client. They only match individuals they believe will make a successful couple. They even pay for the intake interview."

"How much?" I couldn't believe that question had left my mouth.

"Five thousand."

"That isn't even a drop in the bucket for what I need."

Five thousand would buy one more month. My excitement waned.

"Of course not. But, for some, it's enough of an incentive to apply. I wouldn't have mentioned Infidelity if I didn't think it wasn't a viable solution for you."

"It won't work. I have to think about my future, and that hinges on completing my degree and landing a job that ensures I'd have enough money to pay Freddy's costs for life. And I have to make a living for myself as well."

"But that's the thing." His voice rose with excitement. Pushing off from the wall, he came to me. Clasping my hands in his, he gave them a squeeze. "You can have both."

"How?"

"You specify your requirements. Infidelity understands most people can't stop their lives. They realize you have a life you'll be returning to at the end of the contract. This is a word-of-mouth company. It's in their best interests to have exceptionally satisfied clients and employees with nothing but rave compliments about the company. I made sure I could continue with my studies and listed it as one of my hard limits."

"You did?"

"I was a student when I applied, and I specified that not only would I need the time and freedom to finish my degree, but also that the contract wouldn't prohibit me from working afterward."

"Where are you in your contract?"

"Cy and I are finishing up our second year."

Everyone knew Patrick Fitzgerald had come out of the closet, but I'd had no idea he'd been seeing someone—or rather, had been paid to be seeing someone. Wrapping my head around the concept was not easy.

"Two years? But you said the contracts are for only a year."

"The contracts are renewable annually, and there's a buyout option for those who want to marry or continue the relationship long-term."

"Long-term? That happens?" Then, it hit me. "You're happy with your client?"

"Very. Cy's the best thing that's happened to me. Most of Infidelity's contracts are extended, and a large majority are bought out. Did I mention the high client and employee satisfaction rates?"

Patrick should be a salesman for the company because he had this pitch down.

"I don't know," I admitted. "One year is a pretty long time."

"They pay twenty thousand a month."

My eyes popped at that number. "Twenty?"

"That and living expenses. Everything is negotiable, but the client will pay for your living arrangements—for obvious reasons." He gave a sheepish look. "A monthly stipend is also standard."

"Holy crap!" In one year, I'd have more than enough to pay for Freddy's care and also have time to find a job. Not just a job, but the *perfect* job.

This could be life-altering.

All I had to do was sell my body and lose a little bit of my soul.

"I don't know, Patrick. That's a lot to take in."

"Take your time. I took a few months before I took the leap, but, Rowan…"

"Yes?"

"It took many more months before I got paired with a client. If you're running against a time line, please don't take too long before you decide."

SEVEN

Interview
———————

Rowan

It had taken forty-eight hours of soul-agonizing searching before I made the decision about Infidelity. My gut had screamed that I was a fool. My heart had spoken of being able to give Freddy the security he deserved.

My head had mumbled, *It's not safe. You'll be ruined for life.*

A conversation with Henry had decided the matter.

A patient man, he'd sat with me over the phone and gone over my finances. To help out, he'd offered to take over Freddy's guardianship, but I couldn't do that. He'd insisted, saying it would be difficult to care for Freddy from such a distance.

The five thousand for the interview wouldn't buy a month's reprieve. Freddy's bill was twice that amount. I'd have to take a leap of faith and trust in Patrick's words.

The argument for and against Infidelity had raged between gut, heart, and mind until all sides had been thoroughly weighed and measured. Twenty thousand a month simply wasn't something I could walk away from, and it wasn't like there was an equivalent job waiting for me.

I'd called Patrick several times, and he'd assured me I would be safe. This would begin and end with a contract, and once released, my time with Infidelity would be as if it had never happened. Nobody would know I'd sold my soul and given my body to a stranger in return for cash.

Patrick had introduced me to his partner, Cyrus. Their interaction had seemed genuine and honest, nothing like a business arrangement. If Patrick hadn't been happy, then he never would've signed on for an additional year. Right? And, by the looks of things, those two would be a couple for many years to come.

None of that had made my decision easy. Necessity had driven me.

Patrick had secured an interview, and my feet brought me to the base of a skyscraper made of curving blue glass. That was where they stopped. I stood outside the entrance while my heart hammered away, and my entire body trembled. *Was I actually going to do this?* I glanced at my phone, at the picture of my lovable but severely autistic twin, and I sighed.

"For you, Freddy."

It was only an interview. There was no reason to be nervous. Except this wasn't a normal job interview. I came to sell myself to a man who could afford the privilege of my companionship. Patrick had insisted it wasn't all about sex, but who were we kidding? Sex drove relationships, and I'd be tied to my client for an entire year. *Would I be able to stomach some greasy, bald, overweight man?*

With a deep breath, I forced my feet to move, and I traveled the distance across the lobby without faltering. My finger shook like a leaf as I pressed the elevator call button. Inside, I pushed the button for the thirty-seventh floor. People stepped on and off, joining me for a few floors as we ascended upward. They had jobs. Fancy jobs from a look at their business attire. I felt underdressed in my dress and low heels.

My anxiety level rose with the ding of each floor passed, and I picked at the seam of my red linen dress. Conservative in cut, it had a fashionable business collar, but the sleeves stopped above my elbows. A black belt cinched tight around my waist, and shiny black buttons decorated the front. The A-line skirt accentuated my figure and flared a little at the knees. My knees shook as the elevator paused at the thirty-fifth floor and took on a pair of businessmen. They both gave me a once-over and then turned to face the doors as they closed, making my discomfort rise even higher.

I could pretend I wasn't here for an interview. I could continue to ride past the thirty-seventh floor. I could do any number of things. What I did was step off at my designated floor and into a large lobby with a glass desk and *Infidelity* stamped in beautiful scrolled letters on the wall behind it. For a company that wasn't supposed to exist, the bold company name prominently displayed took me aback.

No going back. I introduced myself to the receptionist at the desk.

"Hello, my name is Rowan Cartwright."

"Yes, Miss Cartwright, Ms. Flores is expecting you. Let me tell her you're here, and she'll be right out."

"Thank you."

I headed to take a seat at one of the expensive leather couches, but a middle-aged woman in a black pin-striped suit emerged from behind a set of doors.

She made a beeline directly for me. "Miss Cartwright," she said, eyes beaming. "Welcome to Infidelity!"

My smile came easily, thanks to years of Southern manners drilled into me since birth. "Ms. Flores?"

"Yes!" She greeted me with a handshake, and I awkwardly took it.

In the South, we greeted strangers with a hug. A kiss if you knew them well. Never a handshake.

"It's nice to meet you, Ms. Flores."

I don't want to be here.

"Please, call me Karen," she said with a nod. "Follow me, if you would."

What choice do I have?

It would be foolish to run. Besides, that would only take me to the bank of elevators where I'd have to wait for a car. I held the smile on my face and followed Karen Flores as she took me through a maze of cubicles and offices. We wound up at a private elevator with a key card for access.

Am I really doing this?

My feet moved on autopilot, and I stepped in and stood beside Ms. Flores. The doors whooshed closed, sealing me in.

"Don't be nervous, dear," she said.

But I jerked as the elevator surged upward. I had no idea how far up we traveled. There were only two buttons inside—*O* and *1*.

After a short ride and complete silence between us, the elevator doors opened to another lobby with a large glass desk, another receptionist, and yet another large Infidelity sign. One door exited the room, and Ms. Flores marched straight toward it. After punching in a security code, she led me into her office.

The sun shone through a full wall of windows overlooking the Financial District. Two chairs faced the desk.

"Please, make yourself comfortable," she said. "Would you like anything to drink? Tea, water, coffee?"

I could use something a whole lot stronger than any of those, but I sensed I would need a clear head for what would come next.

"No, thank you, Ms. Flores."

"Please, call me Karen. So much less formal than last names. Don't you agree, Rowan?"

I did, but it didn't make me feel any less self-conscious. I kept my hands clasped and tried desperately not to fidget.

Karen lowered herself into her seat and gave a flick of her computer mouse, lighting up the screen to her computer. "Patrick has told me many good things about you."

"He did?" *What kind of good things? That I'm broke? That my father lost everything? That I would soon be bankrupt? That I came here, more desperate than was wise? What kinds of things had he mentioned to Karen?*

"Rowan Cartwright." She glanced up. "That's such a pretty name."

"Thank you."

"You're in your second year at Pratt, a little bit older than most sophomores."

"I took a few years off to travel abroad." Years I sincerely regretted. If not for taking that time to play, I would have been a graduate of Pratt and wouldn't be in my current predicament.

"You're majoring in architecture and interior design?" A look of confusion filled her face. "An odd combination."

"I was accepted into the architecture program, but I love interior design. I still have time before I have to pick one."

"Smart, talented, and an artist. Amazing qualities to have in a partner."

Did that make me more marketable?

"I see your grades are in the top of your class, and I assume you'll want to continue your studies?"

"Patrick said that wouldn't be a problem."

"Of course not."

If I sat any stiffer, I was going to tip forward and fall right on my face. My ankles ached from pressing them together. My legs slanted to the side, perfectly poised, and I held my back ramrod straight. I wanted to jump out of my skin with all the nervous energy I had swirling beneath my skin.

"Ms. Flor—Karen," I corrected, "did Patrick tell you about my circumstances?"

"He did," she said with a nod, "but even if he hadn't, I have all the information at my disposal. Infidelity does extensive background investigations before we even get to this point."

All my dirty secrets were out. The Southern belle fallen on hard times. *Could I become even more of a cliché?*

She leaned back and regarded me for a moment. "Are you willing to humor me for a moment, Rowan?"

This woman held my future in her hands; there was very little I wouldn't do.

"Yes?"

"I want you to close your eyes and take three deep breaths. Don't think. Don't worry. Just breathe. Breathe out all your anxiety and unease."

"I'm not—"

"Humor me," she insisted.

My gaze darted to the windows behind her, to the blue sky outside and to the skyline of New York. I bit my lower lip and walked to the windows while she watched. I loved my father, but I hated what he'd done to me and to Freddy. I hated how his greed had forced me to this place. I abhorred how his selfishness had ripped him from us.

A slow inhale filled my lungs while I stared out the window and fought my tears. Closing my eyes, I counted slowly until my lungs burned. I wasn't getting rid of stress but rather gathering my anger and expelling it with each forceful breath. After five of these, my eyes opened, and I took in the scene outside. Somewhere out there, a man was waiting for me.

"Feel better?" she said, coming to place a hand between my shoulder blades.

"I'm not sure about better. Is it like this with everyone?"

"That depends on what you mean."

"Why do people come to you? Is everyone like me?" *Are they desperate and looking for relief from the tragedies of their lives?* I couldn't ask that, not without a flooding of tears.

"Potential employees come to us for any number of reasons. Their reasons, like yours, belong to nobody but themselves. We will maintain your confidentiality, as we do theirs, and even the client we pair you with will only know what you choose to share."

"Is that so?"

"Of course."

I breathed a little easier, but my chest still ached.

"Patrick shared a little of your story and reasons this job would suit your current needs. I'm certain he explained what we do here at Infidelity."

"He did, but I have questions."

"Questions are good. Let's begin with the obvious one—the one he said you might have the most difficult time with."

"Okay," I said, not sure how I felt about Patrick's openness with this woman about such intimate details of my life. But what kind of life was I living if I had to resort to a company like this and barter away my freedom for cash?

"We do not sell sex. First and foremost, get that out of your head. What we sell is companionship. Our clients come to us, looking for a partner with poise and class. They're looking for someone who can go out into the world with them, stand by their side, and be a companion. Someone they honestly enjoy spending time with. We sell compatibility, not sex."

"And yet I'm assuming most relationships wind up there."

"Any good pairing of two individuals has that potential. Compatibility and attraction are potent forces. Our clients trust our track record to find a partner they can share all aspects of their lives with, not just their public face. Intimacy is our specialty, but it's not required."

"Patrick mentioned that."

"We have well over a hundred employees in extremely successful relationships. Our employees are happy. They don't regret their decisions, and you won't either. And we guarantee nothing will ever be disclosed, not about you and not about the nature of the agreement between you and our client."

"I see," I said, understanding a little bit more about Infidelity.

I still had more questions—like, *Why one year?*—and we spent well over an hour talking. Karen answered honestly, never shying away from delicate topics, until I suddenly realized the tension in my shoulders had evaporated, and I was no longer twisting my fingers with unease.

"We broker relationships, Rowan, and relationships take time."

"But are they real?"

"They're as real and enduring as you choose to make them. Have you met Patrick's partner?"

"I have."

"Then, you already know the answer to that question." She leaned back and crossed her arms. "Infidelity reimburses our employees well. The average salary is twenty thousand a month for living expenses, but you'll find our clients' generosity extends beyond that. I understand this would meet your current needs."

More than meet. "Yes. And no one will know how we met? That I'm being paid…"

"No one will know those details, except you, me, your client, your sponsor, and your client's sponsor. No one comes to us without a sponsor, and all sign nondisclosure agreements."

"I assume I'll be tested for STDs, but what about condoms and monogamy?" *Or pregnancy?* I needed to ask about that.

"Not all of our clients are monogamous. You will have a

chance to list your preferences, your limits, and more. Some of our clients insist on condoms, and others insist on not using them. In that case, we provide ongoing monthly testing of both parties. For the duration of the contract, you agree to remain monogamous. No dating. No sexual relations with anyone other than our client. Anything like that can cause a media scandal—exactly the bad press and exposure we're trying to avoid."

Our conversation continued, touching on everything and anything, until I'd exhausted every thought in my head. She reiterated what Patrick had said about being introduced to one client and one client only. Finally, Karen withdrew a folder from her desk and slid it across the table. It was an agreement, one with my name and today's date on it.

"Rowan, once you sign this agreement, you're consenting to a full medical examination and extensive psychological testing. There's one other thing..."

"Yes?"

"Until our intake exams are completed and especially after the physical exams, we ask for abstinence."

"Abstinence?"

Patrick had mentioned it could take months to be paired with a client. *Do they really expect me not to date until then?* With a glance at the expression on Karen's face, I realized that was the case.

"And if I do...date, that is?"

"We strongly advise against it and require that relationship to end. Signing this agreement signals your intent to make yourself available for an immediate pairing once we match you with our client. Being involved in a relationship complicates things."

"Okay." I glanced at the agreement and reached for a pen.

A watery veil rippled across my vision. My palms sweat each time Karen pointed to a line requiring my initials. Three pages. Such a short document to sell my soul, but I made it to that final line. With elegant script, I sealed my fate.

No dating.

It wasn't a hard and fast rule, but Karen had stressed the importance of not getting involved in an outside relationship while the team at Infidelity worked their magic.

I left her office and was ushered into a string of appointments and exams, both physical and psychological.

"To ensure a perfect match," she said along with another reminder about keeping Infidelity up to date on any romantic entanglements I might find myself in until the call came to meet my match.

Now, all there was to do was wait.

That didn't mean I couldn't go out, and the need to blow off a little steam boiled inside me. I'd sold my soul, and in a week, a month, maybe up to a year, I would have to fulfill the whole of that contract. I needed to disappear, lose myself within the crowd, and become something else for a night.

My evening began alone, which was how I planned on ending it. I had every intention of honoring my contract with Infidelity. Without much of a thought for where I might wind up, I ate dinner at a small deli close to home, knowing perhaps it was wise to keep my stomach light. Then, I wandered, letting my subconscious guide me through the city as it came alive for the night. I shouldn't have been surprised when my feet took me straight to Club Infinity. Here, nobody knew me, and I could lose myself and forget.

I wanted to disappear. I needed to breathe. I couldn't believe what I'd done.

EIGHT

Infinity

RICHARD

EVELYN HAD BROUGHT US TO A FUNDRAISER—NOT MUCH OF A surprise there. She hobnobbed with the wealthy to raise money for her hospital. Every time I glanced at her, I struggled to remind myself that the lithe redhead dug around in people's brains for a living. Smart and stunning. David was a lucky man.

The event was well attended by her colleagues from Cornell, and many of New York's elite were also in attendance with their generous pocketbooks on display. The venue for the evening, an art auction, didn't interest me, but I hadn't come to look at art. Instead, I circled among the crowd, rubbing elbows with the rich and powerful, while I stalked fresh meat for a dalliance later tonight.

My self-imposed isolation across an ocean provided many perks. Photographers still snapped my picture, and I played my part, but given a moment to slip away, desire would shape my evening prowls rather than thoughts about decorum. What I saw, the things I learned, left me with an appetite for darker urges, but I didn't risk acting upon those impulses.

The tabloids had already had their fun with my most recent fall from grace. The mags still dredged up the photos of me in the back of that town car while my date's head bobbed up and down between my legs. Not my finest hour and not one that would be repeated anytime soon. My mother would have my head if I dared to bring more shame upon the royal household. There was no question of whether I should be circumspect, which left a dilemma.

How do I feed the dark desires growing inside me yet keep any evidence of it out of the press? One misplaced word by one of my dates, and it was game over.

I ached for something uninhibited, unhinged, and completely free. Rather than feed the growing hunger gnawing in my gut, I circulated among the crowd, restless and on the move. With a smile plastered to my face, I picked out likely candidates who might enjoy a night in bed with a prince. When my selection narrowed on three potentials, my attention snagged on David and his dear Evelyn.

He stood behind her, one arm wrapped around her waist as he tugged her close. His other hand cupped her elbow. His fingers began a leisurely stroll up her arm, danced along her shoulders, and then teased and tickled her neck. Brushing away a ringlet of her hair, he gently kissed the tip of her shoulder. She, in turn, leaned against him. With a flute of champagne in one hand, her other fluttered down to entwine her fingers with his. The two of them carried on their conversation with the couple standing opposite, never once breaking the flow of their intimate dance.

On seeing them, my desires for an evening tryst dissipated, leaving a bitter taste in my mouth. I could have any woman I desired, yet I craved an intimacy similar to what my best friend shared with the woman of his dreams. Deflated, I snagged a glass of champagne and tossed the entire contents down my throat.

It was time to slip into the anonymity only the ever-present throngs of New York could provide. Darkness called, and I wanted to feed the beast snarling in my gut. The polite social dance involved in reeling in one of my three chosen potentials made my stomach revolt. Nice and sweet, a meaningless romp in the sheets held no appeal for me. Not now. Not when I needed something much different.

I headed over to David and spoke low into his ear, "I'm checking out."

"I'm surprised." David swayed back and forth, holding Evelyn tight to his chest. He lifted his glass and gestured across the room, toward one of the beauties I'd scoped out earlier. "She's interested. Hasn't taken her eyes off you since you entered."

"Neither has practically every other woman in the room."

That wasn't arrogance speaking—although I had plenty of that to spread around. I drew stares, always had, and my uniquely royal and single status meant women constantly weighed their chances for significant upward mobility.

With a hand on his shoulder, I told him my plans, "I'm bouncing."

Loved that phrase, very American, and it fit my mood perfectly. With my thoughts for an easy conquest discarded, a spring lit my step. I was on the hunt for something else. The heavy pulsating rhythms of a club called to me, someplace where I could burn off restless energy and forget about everything I didn't have.

The genteel sounds of the fundraiser disappeared behind the closing of the heavy glass doors as I exited the venue. A simple wave of my arm brought a taxi, and I slipped inside the car.

"Where to?" the cabbie asked.

My British accent set me apart from the usual pedestrian, but I'd lived here long enough not to sound like a tourist. The key was to give cross streets rather than an address. Giving a street address was the sure sign of a naive tourist and often resulted in roundabout routes, which added to the fare. But, if this cabbie knew Manhattan, he'd have no problems with my instructions.

"Club Infinity."

An up-and-coming nightclub, Club Infinity catered to an eclectic crowd. The nouveau riche gathered there but only because hard-edged regulars filled out the crowd. Hard-cutting music was Infinity's claim to fame as well as the more risqué stage shows, which drew in those curious about BDSM lifestyles. That was exactly what I needed—a public place where I could be seen without judgment yet afforded exactly the spice my darker side craved.

As expected, a line snaked from the door and around the corner. Eager hopefuls waited hours for a chance to get inside. Dressed smartly in a suit, I loosened my tie for a more casual appearance. Sophisticated and chic, my approach to the bouncer at the door was full of confidence and pride. Before he could tell me to stand at the back of the line, I leaned in, identified who I was, and slipped the man a hundred-dollar bill. He palmed my money and lifted the red velvet rope barring my way.

"Enjoy," he said, eyes still bugging.

A few paces took me through an imposing set of stone doors. Between one step and the next, the primal beat of the club transported me off the streets of New York and into an elaborate reconstruction of a medieval fortress.

Stone stretched floor to ceiling, both real and faux. The walls had been engineered to emulate rough-cut granite. The stamped concrete of the floor had been stained to match the walls, and the ceiling soared four stories overhead, replete with arches crisscrossing overhead. Three levels of balconies circled the walls.

Each tier ascending not into light, but into darkness where clubgoers could escape into their private world.

As far as I could see, gyrating bodies undulated with the hard-hitting beats pounding through the club. The bar sat far to the back, crowded of course, and I made a beeline to procure a drink. There was no easy path. I chose the direct approach and worked my way between those dancing on the floor. Several girls caught my eye, young things with too little experience and far less clothing to keep my attention. One wore a tight dress, which barely covered her ass. The poor thing could barely move without having to tug on the hem, lest her entire dress climbed up to settle around her waist.

My priorities included a drink, and then I would see what came next. As usual, Infinity's stage show drew stares. Against the back wall, on an elevated platform, dancers pushed the boundaries of what city ordinances allowed with rough and aggressive scenes of couples engaged in sensual play.

I paused to watch the intricacies of the rope work a dominant used to subdue his recalcitrant submissive. These images scratched the surface of what I desired, and given a different life, I might have chosen to spend my evenings in a completely different kind of club.

Threading my way through the dancers, my steps faltered when I spied a woman standing still within the sea of moving flesh. Long strawberry-blonde hair cascaded down her back to pool in soft curls at her waist. A form-fitting red dress encased her well-toned body. She was a petite beauty, and my hands could nearly encircle her waist. Her hips flared outward from there, drawing my eyes down to her tight ass and fabulously sculpted legs, taking my mind on a completely different path. I wanted her bound to my bed, completely at my mercy, and mine to do with as I pleased.

For a woman of her stature, I expected high heels, but she

wore low ballet flats, perhaps more concerned about comfort than beauty. Her dress hid very little of what lay underneath, and I had no problem imagining every sweep and curve. As my gaze roamed her body, the need to possess overwhelmed my senses. Not possess. That wasn't the right term for what stirred in my gut. Something awakened deep inside me. I didn't yet have a name for it.

Her exquisite form might be enough to enrapture any man, but the attention she paid to the dancers on that elevated platform intrigued me. The rapid rise and fall of her chest and how she ignored everything around her caught my eye. In the few moments I spent watching, she dismissed two men who had dared to approach. And, while many women in these clubs danced alone, she held herself completely still, all her focus on that stage.

Considering how quickly she'd dismissed the others, it might have been foolish to think I would have better luck. The thing was, I enjoyed a challenge.

When I stepped behind her, she didn't notice my approach.

I took note of which pair of dancers held her attention and bent down to whisper in her ear, "There's beauty in surrender, don't you think? Strength such as that is incredibly sexy."

She stiffened but didn't turn around. Odd, I'd expected at least some acknowledgment of my presence.

"You think submission is strength?" she asked.

The pair of performers twirled onstage, the man clearly in charge. His hand gripped the girl's hair, much like I imagined doing to the beauty before me. Shifting her left and then right, he ran her through a series of dips and twirls, their dance seductive and powerful, erotic yet sensual. The man pressed his hand flat against the woman's chest and yanked her head back, swooping in to brush his lips against her exposed throat. She bent before him, her entire body controlled by his strength.

"Don't you?" I asked.

She spun and lifted her chin when she realized how much I towered over her. Those on the dance floor moved around us, letting the rhythms of the club carry them away, while she and I stood perfectly still, encased in the privacy of our moment.

"I—" Her mouth gaped with the struggle to complete her thought.

Meanwhile, she took a moment to take in the width of my shoulders and the expanse of my chest. I knew what she would find because I worked hard to maintain my physique. I also allowed her the time she needed to gather her thoughts because, while she'd enraptured me from behind, seeing her angelic features nearly made my heart stop.

Brilliant eyes the color of bluebells skittered across my body. Her gaze darted everywhere, which left me the perfect opportunity to take in her features. Almond eyes with fluttering long lashes swept against the bridge of her cheeks. A thin, slightly upturned nose rested above petal-soft lips tinted the slightest red. A narrow, elfin chin, brought the heart-shaped symmetry of her face to a beautiful point. She used minimal makeup, which only enhanced her natural beauty. A light spray of freckles feathered across her nose, and her strawberry-blonde hair framed her face, curving at her chin and cascading to drape across her shoulders where it continued its fall down her back.

I couldn't help myself and reached out to push back a strand of her hair and expose more of her face. "Strength and beauty are rare traits. Incredibly sexy when combined and even more powerful when offered in surrender."

Her gaze popped to mine, and I swore, a faint blush colored her cheeks, but it was difficult to tell beneath the colored light show flashing over our heads.

I placed my hands on her shoulders and turned her around to face the stage again, thrilled she hadn't shrugged off my touch.

Stooping down to speak directly in her ear, I brought her attention back to the couple. "He pushes until she gives and then challenges her again, pushing harder until he finds the point where she breaks. She meets his strength with her own. A submissive is strong, and a wise man uses that knowledge to conquer her while she captivates him. She becomes a part of him while he becomes her master."

Her breaths accelerated, and I took an opportunity to thread my fingers in the silkiness of her hair. I didn't pull or tug or yank her head back or sweep in for the kiss I craved, but I made her aware of my presence and waited to see if she would meet me with a strength of her own.

She didn't move but took in a shuddering breath as I wrapped my fingers in the hair at the base of her neck, mimicking what the male dancer did onstage. I placed the pads of my fingers on the bare expanse of her shoulder and walked them down to her wrist, paying close attention to her response. When I reached her hand and she still hadn't pulled away, I threaded my fingers with hers and lifted so that her palm rested against her belly. Taking a step, I closed the distance between us. I wasn't on her, like many of the couples grinding together, but I made my intent clear. A small gap remained between the swell of her ass and my rapidly hardening cock. We would get to that soon enough.

While the man and woman onstage deepened their sensual dance and wrapped flesh around flesh, I swayed to the pulsating deep beat, forcing her to move with me. To my surprise, she leaned against my chest and allowed me to lead.

"It's not real, you know," she breathed out. "None of it is."

"It's as real as you want it to be." Such words deserved to be whispered into a woman's ear, but I'd had to speak above the music.

My grip on her hair guided her head to the side, exposing her neck. Lowering down, I gently pressed my lips against her skin, getting my first taste of heaven. "How about a drink, and we can head upstairs and talk?"

She spun in my arms and rested her wrists on my shoulders. "Talk about what?"

"What we saw on that stage." I pulled her against me, this time giving her an idea of exactly what was on my mind. "How those dancers spoke to you."

Her gaze dropped and settled somewhere on my chest. She barely came up to my shoulders, and I could easily see over her head.

"Talking is fine. I like your accent, but I'm not sure about anything more." A deep sadness clung to her words, which made me determined to discover more about this unexpected find.

"That's a shame because I'd very much like to explore something more."

Her gaze cut to mine, and her lips parted with what I hoped was interest. Desperate to get her alone and continue our conversation, I shifted the focus of our current conversation. She looked ready to bolt.

"What would you like to drink?"

"Whiskey, please," she said, once again glancing up.

For a moment, I thought to lean down and taste the delicacy of her lips, but her arms fell from my shoulders, and she gripped my hand. Without another word, she tugged me toward the bar. I was more than happy to follow. My time to lead would come soon enough.

NINE

Whiskey Neat

ROWAN

WHAT THE HELL AM I THINKING, LEADING A STRANGE MAN TO THE bar? Now, that question deserved an answer, but I had no intention of considering a response. Until that call came from Infidelity, my days belonged to me, my nights as well.

No relationships? I was fine with that, but what about a meaningless one-night stand?

And, holy hotness, was this one a doozy. His words about strength and surrender had had my nerves fluttering and my blood heating. And that accent? It'd curled my toes and made my stomach dance. So yummy. I could do whatever I wanted and never have to see him again. That appealed to me.

The ability to control this one thing screamed at me because, for a year, the one word I wouldn't be able to say was *no*.

Karen had assured me Infidelity wasn't like that. They didn't sell sex, but who were we kidding? Someone rich enough to shell out twenty thousand a month for a companion certainly expected more than conversation. I needed this night, and then Infidelity and their client could have me.

Not that I was an expert in one-night stands. There'd been no time to date since coming to Pratt. I'd been too busy studying, ensuring I remained at the top of the class. Then, everything had happened with my father, and I'd been working my ass off simply to tread water and keep my life afloat. Never had the idea of giving up entered my thoughts. With all the chaos of the trial and what had happened later, my future hinged on success at Pratt.

One night at a bar wasn't going to lead to anything long-term, and it might prove one very important thing. I chose whether to tell this guy to take a hike. I chose whether I'd let him buy me a drink. I chose whether I'd allow something more.

Me.

Not my new employer.

Not their client.

No one but me owned this night.

I must have been insane to consider something as crazy as Infidelity. No reasonable explanation existed for why I'd traded my free will for cash. But there was a motivating factor that came in the rare smiles of my twin. Freddy had no idea how fragile his world was or how easily it could be lost.

Anger spurred me to grip this stranger's hand and tug him toward the bar. Alcohol was a great anesthetic, and I needed to become, as Pink Floyd would say, comfortably numb.

What a hand it was, too—strong, muscled, and sure.

He returned my grip with the confidence of a man who knew what he wanted. Although he kept a tight hold of me, he didn't hurt my delicate bones, showing he could temper that strength. There was just enough of a presence to remind me that he was bigger, stronger, and exactly what I craved. He seemed kinky, too—something I'd never tried but always wondered about.

What an odd conversation we'd shared. It was like he'd

sneaked a peek into my soul, uncovered my desires, and sifted through my mind until he found exactly what I craved. *How did he pull that from me?* I wasn't a submissive, not in public, private, or within any of my very few relationships.

My father had trained me to be strong and independent, perhaps knowing I would be the one to see to Freddy after he was gone. He'd raised me to act with deliberate intent and always have an eye on the future. When everything had fallen down around me, I had known success hinged on completing my studies. If I'd been weak, I might have taken Henry Porter up on the marriage offer brokered through mutual family contacts. I didn't want to think about Henry, the law firm of Hamilton & Porter, marriages of convenience, or anything else.

I needed to burn, and that began with a drink. Only the bar proved too much. I was too short. My voice too weak. The bartenders couldn't see me or hear me, and my drink order landed on deaf ears.

But I didn't have to worry.

My delicious stranger called out in a sure voice. "Two whiskeys, neat, and make them doubles." His British accent carried above the crowd, brought stares, and lowered the ambient noise.

I preferred my whiskey over ice, but I wasn't going to make a fuss.

Mr. Tall and Handsome traded cash for two tumblers of whiskey. Holding them in one hand high over his head, he reached for me and pulled me through the crowd. His large frame forged a path, and he headed to a staircase leading to the balcony overhead. At the top of the stairs, I expected him to head right, to an empty pair of seats facing one another. Instead, he continued around, turning up a second set of stairs, drawing me higher than I'd ever been at Club Infinity. He continued onward, passing the second balcony, and headed to the base of a third set of stairs where a bouncer perched on a stool, looking bored.

My stranger leaned down and said something I couldn't hear. The bouncer stood, removed the red velvet rope barring our way up the final set of stairs, and ushered us into what I assumed must be the VIP area.

Not once did my *date* release his grip, and he kept the tumblers from spilling throughout. We took the stairs, climbing into an even more subdued space.

He wandered to a leather couch tucked into a private alcove. I followed behind him, taking a moment to admire his ass and the broad expanse of his back. Trailing my finger along the brass banister, I shifted my attention below, amazed by the view. The performers looked small and different, less powerful but still fascinating.

I felt, more than saw, his approach. Much taller than me, he easily crested six feet. His accent made me wonder if he was a tourist or a transplant. That was the thing with New York. Like me, people from all over the world had turned this place into their home. People had said I spoke funny, too. I had the slightest hint of a Southern accent most found adorable.

"What are you thinking?" His eyes were hooded and his voice low, rumbly, and sexy as hell.

"We're so high," I said, blurting out the first thing that had come to mind.

"Are you afraid of heights?"

His eyes locked on mine and nearly stopped my heart. The intensity of his gaze swept over and through me. He looked like he wanted to devour me, and I might have wanted that, too. My pulse went ballistic as I simply thought about what trouble we could get to while hidden up here in the heights. Shrouded in darkness, we were invisible to anyone else and were the only people on this level. With adrenaline spiking in my veins, I feigned a casual attitude, as if his very presence didn't suck the air out of the room, leaving me gasping for breath.

"Not at all," I said, leaning far over the railing and lifting my arms out wide.

I wasn't at risk for tumbling over, but he yanked me back against six feet of unbending steel. The hardness of his body pressed against mine, protecting me from a nonexistent threat.

"Careful there," he said. "I'm not comfortable with you dangling over the edge like that."

"I wasn't dangling." I twisted around and wrapped my hands around his neck. "Kiss me," I said, feeling overly confident.

Without hesitation, firm lips pressed down on mine, and he lifted me against the hard planes of his body. Beneath his suit, I couldn't see the defined ridges of his body, but I could certainly feel them.

Heaven.

He tasted like the most delicious thing in the world. I breathed him in as his lips brushed against mine. The warm scent of his cologne flooded my senses—clean, crisp, and utterly delicious. My insides knotted, and goose bumps shivered across my skin as the kiss deepened. The world disappeared, leaving us in our private bubble. My heart thundered, and I gasped for air as his lips danced over mine, sparking tingles of electricity all through my body. I gripped his arms, holding on through that kiss, and explored the hard bulges of his biceps with my fingers. It made me want to explore a little bit more.

Feeling brave or perhaps a bit too bold, I allowed one hand to come between us. Pressing my palm between us, I traced the rippling terrace of muscles spanning his chest. A fever spread through me, a wildfire burning and firing up my pulse, but he pulled away, leaving me bereft. Canting his head to the side, his eyes locked on mine. He placed a finger over my lips.

"Now, that was an unexpected pleasure." His breath seared my skin.

The pads of his fingers teased me, making me want them everywhere at once. I pried my gaze from his lips and met the darkness of his eyes. There was a tingle in my chest and a hitch in my breath.

"Sorry, I'm not usually so…forward."

"Don't be sorry," he said.

"Well, I'm actually quite shy."

"Hmm," he said and then glanced down below. "Perhaps those dancers brought something out in you?"

"I don't think that's how a submissive is supposed to act."

"Is that what you are? A submissive?"

"Aren't you a dominant?" I asked, feeling self-conscious and unwilling to answer his question first. *Are we really having this discussion? Am I?*

Of course, I knew about that kind of thing. There was no way not to know with all the movies and flood of romance books on the market. I watched the movies. I read the books. I came to Club Infinity to watch the performers onstage. My fantasies included a lot of things, but those weren't real. This wasn't real.

I couldn't believe I'd asked him to kiss me. My nipples tightened beneath the thin fabric of my dress, shocked and a little turned on by my boldness. From the angle of his gaze, he noticed the sudden change. How could he not? I wore no bra. A wet throb pulsed between my legs, making me needy and a little scared. *Can he smell my arousal like the men do in those books? How far am I willing to go?* A one-night stand simply wasn't in my repertoire, yet I'd asked a stranger to kiss me, and here I was, wanting more.

"Titles can be misleading, don't you think? I'd rather say I'm learning more about myself every day, and I find my desires slant a particular way." The timbre of his voice flowed through me, hypnotic and drugging.

"What have you learned?"

"I enjoy control. I prefer taking the lead. I crave other things as well."

If he thought that comment would send me running, he had a thing or two to learn about me.

"What? No response?" he teased. "How about, I want a woman I can break in, nice and slow, without having to be gentle or ask permission for every little thing? That there are things I yearn to do privately that some might find objectionable. How it excites me to think you might want the same."

"To be broken?" This conversation should be sending me fleeing down the stairs; instead, my heart raced, and my pulse pounded.

"Cherished," he said, cupping the back of my neck. "To bend before me. To bow to my desires while seeking yours. To give me the power I crave and allow me to take what I need." As he whispered his desires against my flesh, his breath rustled my hair, and he dipped low to nuzzle my neck

His brick-hard body pushed me back. One step. Two steps. He walked me all the way to the wall, away from the railing and deeper into the shadows. He hooked an arm around my waist and pulled me to his body, even as he caged me in against the wall. Then, he stroked his thumb against my bottom lip.

His tone hardened, turning low and gravelly. "Now, tell me, is that what you want?"

My veins hummed with everything he'd said. My knees weakened, and I could barely stand. The fierceness of my will had brought me here. I had taken his hand and led him to the bar, determined to make a choice for the evening, but somehow, the tables had turned. I found myself in an unexpected position, and it excited the hell out of me.

A grin stretched across his face, devilish and arrogant, haughty even. He shifted closer and touched his forehead to mine. With his fingers gliding down my neck, he jutted his hips forward, letting me feel the swelling of his cock beneath his trousers. His breaths fanned my face, and his mouth hovered over mine.

"Tell me," he said, "do you like taking orders?"

I gripped the lapels of his jacket and followed his lead, pressing my tits against his chest. "I want this." My tongue darted out and licked the fullness of his lower lip.

He grabbed the hair at my nape, and we rocked together, and then his teeth gripped my lips. Mouth gliding against mine, he lashed at me with his tongue and demanded entrance to my mouth. He wrenched my head back, and I stabbed my hands in his scalp where I pulled at the strands of his hair. Shaky and more than a little off-balance, he drove me to a place I'd never been.

The man turned me on, lighting up all the nerves in my body like no one had done before. I ached for him. My nipples tightened into hard little buds because of him. Between my legs, the most delicious ache pulsed and made me squirm.

His powerful shoulders shook with a laugh. "Damn, but I want to devour you."

Would that be so bad?

My heart swooned and dipped as he seized my lips again. I parted them as his raw desire swept him away, taking me with him. With a bruising intensity, he fell on me. There was no tenderness, no coy nips or pecks. This man took what he wanted and claimed with an intensity that was both combative and primitive. Holy hell, it turned me on.

As his tongue chased mine, I ground my hips against the hardness of his erection, eliciting a groan from him. He palmed my ass and thrust against me, trying to rut. Punishing my swollen lips, he melted my insides, even while bringing a chill to my skin. I squirmed against him, my skin heating up. Hot and itchy, I'd never been so aroused. I ached for his fingers on my nipples, my inner thighs, and even diving deep inside my tender walls.

"Devour me." My voice croaked, and I cleared it.

His pupils dilated, and he traced a finger around the corners of my mouth and then pressed it deep inside. I wrapped my lips around his finger, licked the tip, and drew it deep into my mouth. My chest squeezed, realizing exactly where we were and what I was about to let him do. Thoughts of Infidelity ghosted through my mind.

I wasn't theirs. Not yet. For tonight, I belonged to this man.

TEN

Slipper

ROWAN

Between the realms of fantasy and reality, a line stretched in the sand. It was both tantalizing and terrorizing. As my tall stranger swept down for another kiss, several things came to mind.

We were about to have sex—and not just any sex. We were about to have the kind of sex I'd only read about. A dominant man like him expected certain things, and my body rose to meet his needs. My mind seemed to have turned itself off. Nobody was up here but us. I was alone. If I screamed, no one would hear. *If I say no, will he stop?* I hoped so, but he was much stronger than me, and I didn't think I'd be able to fight him off.

No.

Wait.

Is that what I wanted?

The ferociousness of his kiss transported me to a place hinted at by those dancers down below. Dominance and submission—

two things I had very limited knowledge about. I didn't have the first clue what it meant to be a submissive. Yet, here, I grappled with a stranger with needy and encouraging sounds emanating from my throat.

Do I want to obey? He'd asked that question.

His kisses made my mind draw a blank because I certainly didn't want this feeling to ever stop.

Then, his hand moved down, firing up my pulse until my heart felt like it would explode. Sparks of electricity zinged around my body, tightening my nipples to impossibly hard nubs. That power fired up a steady throbbing between my legs, driving me to want even more.

He cupped my breast, testing the weight of my unremarkable C-cup breasts. He seemed pleased because he took time to admire them, even ran his fingers across the peaks of my nipples, drawing a strangled cry from me in response. Then, his hand trailed down, gliding over the curve of my waist and sweeping across the flare of my hip.

Down.

Down.

Down.

His fingers feathered the hem of my skirt and then teased it up my outer thigh. My breaths turned to pants as those exploring fingers found their way around to my inner thigh. From there, they continued a relentless path toward the apex of my thighs, right to the edge of the thin lace of my thong.

I gasped and gripped his arms hard, trying to stop him. Wanting more but suddenly very much aware I didn't want any of this at all. That didn't make sense to me, not with the way I'd begged him to continue.

But I came face-to-face with a hard truth deep inside. I wasn't a one-night-stand kind of girl. My conscience whispered, growing louder and more insistent, as he trailed his finger over the outside of my thong, teasing between my folds. I lifted on my tiptoes, trying to escape, but he took my movement as a sign of encouragement because he lifted the thin fabric and dipped his fingers inside.

"No!" I screeched as I pushed him away. "Stop."

My cry resulted in him jerking away and stepping back, holding his hands up in front of his chest.

"Whoa, what's wrong?"

"I'm sorry. I thought…" I sniffed and rubbed my nose. "I just can't. I'm sorry. I didn't mean to…I thought…but I can't."

There was nothing to gather. I didn't have a purse. Tucked into a well-concealed pocket, I carried three things: my ID, a credit card, and my new, shiny MetroCard. Thankful for sensible but chic shoes, I dodged around him and headed for the stairs. Running down, I surprised the bouncer. His head snapped up, and his eyes grew wide as I barreled toward him. He barely had time to unsnap the red velvet rope blocking the way.

Using the banister to assist, I spun around the landing and headed down the second set of stairs. Behind me, Mr. Tall, Dark, and Dominant took up the chase.

"Wait," he called out.

The bouncer growled something, and the guy stopped in his tracks. A heated exchange transpired between them, but I couldn't hear what was said as I continued down the stairs. I had a pretty good idea though. There weren't too many scenarios where a woman ran from a man in a bar. Guilt speared through me to think of the accusations being placed on him right now. Because he'd acted exactly as he should and stopped when I said no.

Shit. I felt like crap now. My steps slowed as I swept around the landing. For a moment, I considered heading up again. If only to let the bouncer know that the guy had done nothing wrong.

My foot twisted on the stair, and my shoe fell off my foot. I stumbled down several stairs before I brought my downward momentum to a halt.

My gut said, *Keep running*, but this was New York. There was no way in hell I was walking the sidewalks without shoes on both feet.

When I turned around, Mr. Tall, Dark, and Dominant was at the landing. He knelt down and grabbed my shoe while my heart thundered, and my breath nearly stopped.

He stared at my shoe, a look of puzzlement on his face. With a slow shake of his head, he held it out to me. "You probably want this."

A deep breath fortified me, and I climbed the four steps to meet him. "I'm sorry," I said. "I'm—"

"Probably better you just put that on and go. I don't know what happened, but honestly, I don't care to know. It's not you; it's me—or however that goes. Either way, we obviously aren't meant to be." He took a step down, keeping far to the right, and put my shoe in my hand. Without another word, he disappeared around the next bend in the stairs.

From the second-floor balcony, I watched him breach the press of people on the dance floor. He walked right through them, taking his time but beating a very determined path to the door. When he reached the door leading outside, he paused and turned around. Over an impossible distance, his gaze latched on mine, and a tiny piece of my heart crumbled.

I didn't even know his name.

Putting on my shoe, I made my way out of the club. He was nowhere to be seen, not that I'd expected him to wait for some crazy chick from the club. In silence, I walked to the nearest metro stop and headed home.

ELEVEN

Client

RICHARD

THE ELEVATOR TO DAVID AND EVELYN'S FLAT OPENED, AND I stalked through the doors, brushing my shoulders on the smooth metal in my haste to get out. Marching to their bedroom, I banged on the door.

Yeah, it was a dick move, but I needed my buddy. Things had to change, and right now was as good a time as any.

Just past midnight, chances were pretty good Evelyn was asleep. The woman got up crazy early to get to the hospital, but David kept night-owl hours. A grumble of protest sounded from behind the door, and I stepped to the side, knowing he'd be out soon.

"What the ever-loving fuck?" David said from behind the door, spewing forth more curse words.

I pitched my voice to be heard. "I'll be at the bar."

While David pulled himself together, I returned to the front room and headed to the bar. I poured two tumblers of whiskey and set a glass down beside me. After swallowing the contents of mine, the smooth burn coated my throat. Alcohol headed straight to my stomach where it would absorb into my bloodstream and make me comfortably numb. I poured more whiskey and tossed it back as David strolled down the hall.

Without a word, he sat beside me and lifted his glass in a silent salute. I clinked my thick tumbler against his, and drank.

"Hit me up," he said.

Two more pours—one for him and a third for me. I was in a foul mood and intended to get drunk enough to sleep like the dead. We pounded those back, and I went to pour a fourth.

David's hand covered my glass. "How about you tell me exactly why we're getting drunk?"

"Because I'm tired; that's why."

"Very nonspecific." He took the bottle of whiskey and poured me half a shot. "Somehow, I have a feeling you need to slow down." He pushed my glass over and raised his to his lips.

I followed suit, and we swallowed the burning alcohol down together.

"Spill," he demanded, setting the whiskey bottle on his other side.

"There's not much to say," I admitted. "I went out. Found a girl."

"That sounds pretty good."

"She was perfect." I didn't want to get into exactly why she'd been so damn perfect because David didn't need to know about any of that. As good of a friend as he was, I'd been burned too many times by those I trusted most with my secrets.

"And then?"

"And then it wasn't."

"She wasn't? Or it wasn't?" His brows drew together,

confused. "You mean, the sex was bad? Or the girl was bad? I thought you were laying low. No scandals for the press. Please tell me you didn't hook up with some chick at a club." He poured more whiskey. "You know better than that."

I'd broken all my rules about the women I chose to bring into my bed. *Gah!* Images of that blonde bobbing up and down on my cock while that damn driver opened the car door flooded my mind. It had been nothing but one pulsating flash from hundreds of cameras. Thank God nobody had actually gotten a shot of my dick. Because, sure as shit, some tramp mag would've printed it or circulated it online. That poor girl had had her reputation ruined. Or maybe not. I'd been instructed to sever all contact. Correction, Her Majesty the Queen had made it a royal command.

Why the hell had I dragged the girl to the top of Club Infinity for a shag? Not any shag either. I'd brought her there to explore a fantasy.

Was I that blinded by her beauty?

Maybe.

She had been a looker and had the most adorable Southern accent. Her crystalline-blue eyes had entranced me, but I knew what had pushed me over the cliff. It had been that promise for something, a union of souls more pronounced than simple pleasures of the flesh. I'd sensed a longing in her, which stirred an answering response in me. We'd been fated to meet and then ripped apart, and I didn't know why.

David and Evelyn had mentioned Infidelity. According to them, that company had an uncanny knack for pairing kindred souls. Well, the fire of dominance burned inside me. There was no question if I would explore it, only when, and of course, I needed to do so without inciting yet another scandal. A woman who could meet my needs, be bound by an ironclad nondisclosure agreement, and come with no long-term strings was exactly what I needed.

Easy in and easy out.

"Tell me again about Infidelity."

David swirled his glass on the burnished wood countertop. "You've decided to give it a go?"

"I'm tired of the threat of scandals if something goes wrong on a date. Frankly, I'm tired of it all. Just set me up, and keep things quiet. Is that too much to ask?"

That bouncer had nearly ripped my head off, thinking I'd raped that girl. That kind of shit didn't belong in my life. Paying for a compliant partner seemed to be the safest bet. As long as she suited my needs, kept her mouth shut, and walked away at the end, I didn't care who the hell Infidelity paired me up with.

"I'll call in the morning and get you an appointment," David said. "You're going to be surprised with what Infidelity can do for you."

For twenty thousand a month, I'd bloody well better be one satisfied customer.

"Call them now," I demanded. Now that my mind had been made up, there was no room for further delay.

"You do realize, it's nearly one in the morning."

"So?"

"Don't you think this can wait until the morning?"

"You're paying them twenty thousand a month, David. I think that warrants an all-access pass."

He stared at me, eyes bugging, and then laughed and laughed and laughed.

"What's so funny?"

With his palm slapping the countertop, he poured another round. Bastard started wheezing, he was laughing so hard.

"Ah, Richard," he said, "now, this is funny. You thought I was the client?" He gripped his midsection and put his forehead on the top of the bar where he heaved with laughter. Wiping his eyes, he glanced up. "Oh, brother, I thought you knew."

"Knew what?"

"I'm an Infidelity employee. Evelyn is the client."

"What?"

TWELVE

Employee

Rowan

Five months later, and I'd heard nothing from Infidelity. My funds held an expiration date, leaving me precious little time to figure out the next step. There really was only one next step. Henry, bless his ever-lovin' heart, had my best interests in mind, but he didn't understand the cost to my soul if I accepted the proposal brokered through him. He'd asked again about Freddy's guardianship, but I wasn't ready to take that step.

Savannah, Georgia, wasn't anything if not an intricate web of familial connections. My family was one of the very few unofficial blue-blooded royalty of the South. My father had embezzled hundreds of millions, yet my family name still carried the weight of history. Henry had been approached by Brent Parker, a wealthy individual who was eager to capitalize on the connections my family's name might bring him as he explored new business ventures in Savannah.

Henry—by the grace of his Southern, Baptist heart—would

secure my future if I chose to accept Brent Parker's proposal. Henry knew the depths of my desperation.

He wanted nothing but the best for me and my brother, but I wanted nothing to do with brokered marriages and unions devoid of love. My best interests were on his mind, yet to me, those interests represented death. Whatever it took to keep Freddy in his happy cocoon was what I would do, but I hadn't yet reached the end of my rope. I was close though, seriously close.

One month.

That was all the time I had left. One month of freedom before I shackled myself to a man I didn't know. Henry had assured me I would be happy, but he didn't know my soul or the secret desires swirling in the corners of my mind. Those thoughts kept me up night after night. Images of my almost one-night stand flitted through my head, tantalizing me with the possibility of what might have been.

Nothing about my situation was fair, and I was angry. Angry with Infidelity for not calling. Angry with myself for my inability to find a different solution. There was even one moment, one night, when I'd felt my desperation the hardest, where my anger turned toward Freddy. It wasn't his fault life had dealt him a poor hand, but he was my responsibility. I hated my new apartment—a small studio with a twin bed, couch, and a counter with a hot plate for a kitchen—and that made me even angrier.

What did I do? Well, I didn't pay attention at school. Top of my class turned quickly to middle tier. My heart wasn't in my studies. My mind wasn't on my art. I went through the motions, but I wasn't invested in the future. Instead, I focused on my imminent doom.

Henry had a solution. All I had to do was pick up the phone and give my consent. I cursed Infidelity. I cursed their promises and the hope Patrick had given me. I cursed the yearning in my blood and the dark dreams that invaded my fantasies every night.

I wanted him, Mr. Dark and Delicious, but I had nothing but an empty bed and an even emptier bank account.

Did Infidelity lose my application? Did I fail their tests? Am I undesirable?

With a sour taste in my mouth, I pulled out my phone and dialed.

Henry answered on the first ring. "Rowan, sweetie, how are you doing?"

"Hi," I answered, "I've been better."

"How is school?"

"Challenging." No way would I tell him how far I'd fallen behind or how much my grades had slipped. A lump formed in my throat, making the next words nearly impossible to force out. I couldn't do it. I couldn't say those words.

"Honey," he asked, "are you okay?"

"I'm not," I admitted.

"Can I assume you've come to a decision?"

"I don't see any other choice, but if I do this, what happens next? Will I get to finish Pratt?"

Silence stretched on his end of the line. "Rowan…I've never lied to you, hon, but these things come with certain expectations, and you're not coming from a position of strength."

"Why does he want to marry the daughter of an embezzler?"

He cleared his throat. "You know the answer to that."

I did. I would make the perfect trophy wife, and I would give him Southern legitimacy.

"It's not ideal," Henry said, "but he's not a bad man. He's offered to ensure you and Freddy are taken care of. You know what this can do for you."

Not a bad man, but Henry hadn't said Brent Parker had a good heart.

"I know what it does for me. If I say yes, is there a chance of finishing school?"

"I doubt Mr. Parker wants his wife living in New York."

Especially since he was counting on me to break him into a very closed inner circle of Savannah business elite.

"You need to face reality, Rowan."

"I know," I said. "Will I have guarantees that Freddy can stay where he is?"

Everything hinged on keeping Freddy happy.

"I've explained your requirements, and Mr. Parker has made assurances that they'll be met. It will be easiest if you transfer guardianship to me, of course."

"Do you think less of me for considering such an arrangement?"

"Honey, you'd be surprised how common these things are. Don't worry; I have the papers drawn up, detailing exactly what is and is not expected of you as well as the financial obligations Mr. Parker must support. All you need to do is tell me this is what you want."

Brent Parker.

I needed to find out more about the man who would own my life. An entrepreneur, he had his hands in land development, pharmaceuticals, and energy companies. What he intended to start in Georgia remained unclear. Not that I expected a man like him to share the intimate business plans of his companies with a trophy wife, but I needed to know.

"And how soon would he expect the wedding?"

"Mr. Parker offers a six-month engagement. During that time, he will assume all your financial obligations. You would move back home."

"And is he expecting…" I swallowed against the thick lump in my throat.

"I know this is hard for you, but intimacy will be required, and there is the expectation for children. I'm certain he wouldn't be opposed to waiting until the wedding, but you need to understand, he intends you to be his wife in every way."

"I understand." And I hated every bit of it, but really, how was this any different from signing a contract with Infidelity?

Speaking of Infidelity, I would need to withdraw my application. Karen had been very clear about no dating. Announcing an engagement went far beyond dating. I made a note to call them in the morning.

"Can you send me the papers?"

"I'll e-mail the draft first thing in the morning. Take a look, and we can discuss any changes."

"I'm assuming there won't be much room to negotiate?"

"Not much, but the offer is fair. I made certain your interests were well represented."

"Thank you. I know you're looking out for me."

"It's going to be okay."

"I know." Except it felt like a life sentence.

My laptop lay on the couch. Not so long ago, I might have said I kept it in another room. My new apartment only had one room. I barely had space to take two steps from my bed before reaching the couch. Flipping open the lid, I drafted a message to Karen Flores at Infidelity.

Ms. Flores,

Thank you very much for your time, but I must withdraw my application from Infidelity. Please let me know if anything further is required.

Yours truly,

Rowan Cartwright

After hitting Send, it occurred to me that I might have to return the five thousand for my interview. Hopefully, that wouldn't be the case. I had no doubt, first thing in the morning, Henry would have the documents sent over for my approval. He'd likely call Brent Parker and share the wonderful news. My stomach twisted with that thought.

Saturday mornings brought no motivation to set an alarm, which gave me an excuse to sleep in. I had a flight to catch, my monthly trip to see Freddy, but it was later in the day. I needed the rest because my racing heart and incessant thoughts had kept me awake most of the night.

I awoke, restless and tired. When I flicked on my phone, my notifications flagged an e-mail from Ms. Flores. I'd thought my message would sit in her inbox until Monday, giving me the entire weekend to come to terms with shutting the door to the opportunity Infidelity represented. I should wait until Monday to open her message. If Infidelity demanded their five thousand back, I'd have no recourse but to scrape it together. My finger hovered over the notification, but I couldn't swipe to open the message.

Instead, I paced the small length of my room. It took exactly ten steps to move the distance from the door to the window. Ten steps for my anxiety to build. Ten steps where I pondered my life. Ten steps of defeat and resignation. Ten steps, and a profound clarity settled over my shoulders. I couldn't change the past, but I could choose my future. I opened the message, and took in a deep breath before reading.

Miss Cartwright,

Please call my office immediately upon receipt of this message.

Karen

That's it? No acknowledgment of my intent to terminate my contract? A fluttery feeling beat at my stomach, turning it light and unsettled. *They can't keep me in the contract, right? Not if they haven't matched me with a client. They probably wanted the five thousand back.* Couldn't she have said a little bit more instead of replying with such a terse message?

I didn't want to call her, but I didn't seem to have a choice.

Another notification flashed on my screen—an e-mail from Henry. While I wanted to respond to his email with even less enthusiasm than calling Ms. Flores, his held the bonds of my future. Setting the phone down, I pulled open my laptop to better read the conditions of the agreement with Brent Parker.

My phone buzzed, and I picked it up without checking the caller ID.

"Rowan?"

My gut seized. I recognized Ms. Flores's voice.

"Ms. Flores," I said, "good morning."

"Dear, please, call me Karen."

"Of course. Good morning, Karen."

"I received your e-mail last night."

"I'm sorry, but—"

"I need you to come in immediately."

"I can be there first thing Monday morning."

"You don't understand," she said. "I'm sending a car to pick you up."

"What?"

"This is important, Rowan. I'll be there within the hour."

"Why?" But there was only one of two reasons. One, I'd stirred up a shitstorm in withdrawing my application, and she was in damage-control mode. Or, two, which was a much more concerning option, Infidelity had paired me with a client.

THIRTEEN

Compliance

Rowan

Twenty minutes later, after a rushed shower and a quick dig through my clothes, I dressed in blue jeans and a cotton T-shirt. With damp hair and no makeup, I stood at the curb. I missed my doorman, Tom, with his easy smile. I missed our short conversations as he hailed a cab. I missed everything about my previous life.

Outside the dingy apartment complex, there was no doorman, only a sidewalk filled with trash and a decrepit tree clinging to a patch of bare ground—well watered not by rain, but the urine of countless dogs. Once the sun went down, I never stepped foot on the street. It wasn't safe.

A few minutes later, a dark town car pulled up at the curb.

The driver exited. "Miss Cartwright?"

"Yes," I said.

He opened the back door while my stomach took a nosedive south. I didn't know if I was in trouble with Infidelity, but it sure felt like I was meeting my doom. I didn't want to commit to getting inside that car.

"Miss?" He held out a hand, offering to assist me inside.

I took in a breath and let the driver help. Then, I gasped when Ms. Flores shifted to the far side of the backseat.

"Karen," I said, trying to conceal my shock, "about my message—"

"Miss Cartwright," she responded, her voice formal and cold, "it's nice to see you."

"My circumstances have changed."

I expected her to hear me out. Instead, she raised a finger, silencing me.

"My dear," she said, "we are unable to release you from the contract."

"But—"

"You've been matched, and the client is expecting you."

"You don't understand." My stomach tossed and churned. The inside of the town car spun about, making me dizzy. Gripping the armrest, I tried to find my balance. "I've—"

"Rowan"—she placed a hand on my arm—"we invest heavily in ensuring the perfect pairing of our employees to our clients. The client was notified yesterday and accepted immediately. It's not possible to back out now."

They can't force me to accept, can they?

"But I—"

"Breathe, Rowan," she said, alerting me to the fact that I'd been holding my breath.

The skin over the backs of my knuckles showed white. My focus went to my hand, and I forced myself to relax.

"You don't understand," I said. "I can't do this."

"It's natural to feel a little uncertainty when a match is made." Her voice was low and soothing. "I assure you, everything will be okay."

"It's not that," I said, except it was exactly that.

In the space of a day, I'd found myself tied to two men, both strangers, and neither option appealed to me. I had sold my soul and my body to men who would control my fate. Some sense of clarity should come as a result of that, but my entire world reeled while I sat in the back of a town car.

"I can't do it. I've agreed to a marriage—"

"Miss Cartwright," she said, turning formal again, "the terms of our agreement were clear regarding entering into other relationships."

"I've never even met him."

"Please elaborate."

"You know my situation." I twisted my fingers. "I hadn't heard anything from Infidelity, so I was forced to accept an alternate proposal. I have obligations…"

"Yes," she said, letting annoyance show in her speech, "you mentioned your brother."

I'd listed two hard limits, as Patrick had called them. The first weekend of each month—today as a matter of fact—I'd insisted on being allowed to visit Freddy. He only allowed visitors on the first Saturday of every month. If I didn't show up, it would set him into a tailspin. If I arrived any other day, it would upset him even more. Henry had graciously paid for a plane ticket the last two months, facilitating my visit. I had a ticket waiting, a later flight headed out, and a rental car arranged. My monthly sojourn to Savannah wasn't something I could miss.

"I'm really sorry," I said, "but I hope this won't take long. I have a flight to catch."

"You have more than that," she said. "You have a client to meet."

I shook my head. "This is Freddy's weekend, and I'm sorry, but—"

She crossed her arms. "I'm going to be exceptionally frank

with you, Miss Cartwright, and I hope you listen to what I have to say in the manner in which it is meant to be heard."

I didn't want to hear anything, but what choice did I have?

She continued, "You're broke and burdened with seeing to the long-term care of your brother. This brought you to Infidelity. Unfortunately, it takes time to find compatible matches. In your case, several months; however, we have found a match, one I think will be to your benefit."

"But—"

"Please, let me continue. You need a time-limited engagement that will meet your financial goals. One that guarantees two things..." She arched a brow and counted, using her fingers. "One, you have the freedom to see your brother as you've requested."

I would have that with Brent Parker.

"Two," she continued, "and I want you to really think about this because you do not have this with your arranged marriage."

"How do you know about the details of that agreement?"

My question was met with another arching of her brow. "We're paid very well to know details of our employees, especially when it places our network or clients at risk. It helps to mitigate disasters."

That was a fair response. The ability to protect their clients demanded a thorough intelligence network. This came as no surprise, but it did make me squirm, knowing someone had intimate knowledge of my life, and the agreement drawn up by Henry and Brent Parker.

"Your second request was to ensure your continued attendance and eventual graduation from Pratt. Infidelity will ensure this requirement is met. It's my understanding you'll lose this with the other arrangement."

That was true. I would lose everything. Brent Parker wasn't

going to pay twenty thousand a month, but he was going to buy my loyalty and steal my dreams.

"I don't know what to say," I said.

"Our client is waiting," she said. "He insisted on meeting you today, and if I understand correctly, he will be accompanying you on your visit to see your brother. As I mentioned, this is a relationship we're facilitating. What's important to you will be important to him. His desire is for your liaison to be viewed as a relationship despite how the two of you were brought together."

"He wants to come with me?"

"He will accompany you. There's one other thing you need to be aware of."

I hadn't yet agreed to meet with their client, but Karen continued on, as if it were a done deal. One thing repeated in my head. Whoever this man was, if I stayed with Infidelity, I could graduate from Pratt. One year and two hundred forty thousand dollars later, and I could walk away. Maybe even two years, if we liked each other. It worked for Patrick and Cyrus. Freddy would be set. I didn't have that with Brent, and Karen knew this.

"Rowan," Karen said, drawing me from my thoughts, "there is the matter of compensation and discretion to discuss before you meet."

"I'm aware of the compensation package." There were so many ways I could invest that money to pay for Freddy's care.

The car pulled away from the curb and headed into traffic. We headed toward LaGuardia, and my stomach did another flip.

"This is a high-profile, international client. While you've signed our standard nondisclosure clause, there will be another more stringent agreement you'll need to sign. He will provide that to you."

"Does he have a name?"

"His name is Richard," she said, "and your compensation

will be increased to meet his need for discretion and a certain amount of compliance."

"Compliance?"

"Yes," she said, "you'll be required to agree to abide by certain conditions."

"Why?"

"Because of who he is."

"And *who* is he?"

"First," she said, "your compensation will be double our standard package. You'll be required to obtain a passport, if you don't already have one. All living expenses and personal needs will be paid by him."

"Doubled?"

There was no need to do quick math. Double their standard package meant nearly half a million at the end of a year. With Henry's team, I could invest and fund everything Freddy would need for life. Two choices faced me. One year with a stranger, followed by freedom, or a lifetime with a stranger who intended to keep me in a gilded cage. Whore or not, my path was clear.

"The second piece is something you must agree to unconditionally," she said.

"And that is?"

"The terms of your agreement are that you submit to his authority. Our psychological tests reveal this is within the limits of what you would find acceptable."

"Excuse me?" *He wants what?* "I'm sorry, but there's no way I'm agreeing to that."

"You simply don't have a choice," she said.

"I can always say no."

There was much more I could do. Exposing Infidelity came to mind, but I'd read the contract. My father had taught me never to sign something I didn't understand. I'd sold my soul to Infidelity the moment I scrawled my signature on that bottom line. From the look on Karen's face, she understood the turmoil going on inside my head.

She reached out. "It sounds worse than it is, but once you understand who he is—"

"Who the hell is he? Because, if he's any sort of Dom, he'd never make that demand." There was little I knew about the lifestyle, but I understood the basics.

"That's not why the request was made," she said.

"Then, why? It makes no sense."

"His Royal Highness, Prince Richard of Wales is the man to whom you've been matched." She arched a brow, as if that name meant anything to me.

"And?"

She fluttered her lids and glanced up at the ceiling of the car. "You've been paired with His Royal Highness, Prince Richard of Wales, second in line to the throne of England."

"What the ever-loving hell?" I stared at her, mouth agape and heart racing a thousand beats a minute.

FOURTEEN

Meeting
―――――

RICHARD

I'D NEVER FLOWN COMMERCIAL. YET HERE I WAS, SITTING IN first-class, with an empty seat beside me. A seat that would soon be filled by the woman I was paying to call mine.

That messed with my mind.

Does it make me desperate to pay for companionship? Or a monster because I expect sex? Once I realized who Infidelity had paired me with, I added in the clause about submission. Did it make some twisted sense, or was I the twisted one? Infidelity assured me the match would be well received, but I wondered if I was playing too heavy of a hand.

Privilege allowed me to purchase whatever I wanted. In this case, I used privilege to buy companionship and demand submission. *Where are the lines of consent drawn in a situation such as this?* That question bothered me. What had happened in Club Infinity shaped us, but by the very fact that I was now paying for her time, how much consent could be freely given? This made my gut twist and had me considering canceling the entire agreement.

What thoughts tangled in her head? Did doubts fill her like they did me, or was she comfortable with selling herself for a year? More importantly, what would she think when she realized who I was? That we'd not only met before, but had also taken our first steps down a very definite path?

For hours, I agonized how our *first* meeting should go, especially considering this was anything but our first meeting. I'd had my fingers on her pussy and my tongue down her throat. She had willingly given me her submission and then ripped it away.

How cliché that night had turned out—a prince holding out a slipper as the girl ran away.

My mind dredged up any number of ways to introduce myself to Miss Rowan Cartwright. Such a lovely and unusual name, it spoke of a wildness of spirit. From the moment Ms. Flores had forwarded Rowan's picture, my heart hadn't stopped racing. I'd considered picking Rowan up in a limousine and laying down the tenets of our *relationship*. I'd imagined a dinner looking over the skyline of New York as the sun dipped below the horizon, passing her a list of rules. I'd even gone as far as booking a penthouse suite, determined to pursue an evening of decadent pleasure.

Infidelity had said she was mine, and I had every intention of staking that claim.

They'd also said there were conditions. I could've waited to meet her after her visit with her brother, or I could join her, not knowing how my presence might be received. Dick move or not, we would explore what had begun between us at Club Infinity. That meant, moving forward with strength and purpose.

Compassion ruled my heart, even as lust surged in my veins. Her dedication to family, an autistic brother who'd been institutionalized, intrigued me. Edmund and I had thin fraternal bonds.

We gathered when state events required it, but otherwise, we led separate lives. Rowan went out of her way to visit her brother. That spoke volumes to the values she held. It fascinated me because I desperately wanted to know what had brought her to Infidelity's doors.

Infidelity had assured me they'd completed a thorough investigation, but they wouldn't share her reasons for seeking employment. That would be something I had to discover myself. A simple Internet search revealed the fall of her family. It hadn't been difficult to connect the dots from there. Her insistence on completing her degree made sense, but it was the tie to her brother that held my interest.

Meeting her in such a public place ensured the beginning of our relationship would be circumspect. My fantasies revolved around placing her at my feet, forcing her to bow to my desires, filling my bed with her naked body, and listening to moans of desire as I ravished her without mercy, but the reality of our situation weighed heavily on my mind.

For one year, she would be mine. My intent was to explore the darker desires swirling in my blood. It would be the only time in my life where I could safely live out my fantasies and not have it leaked to the press. But I wasn't a dick.

I chose not to take advantage of the precious power entrusted to my hands. That decision had come after intense soul-searching because it wasn't what I craved at all. I wanted her on her knees, mouth open and welcoming, as I shoved myself between her crimson lips. I jacked off every night to images of Rowan on her knees, on her back, bent over the couch, and shoved against the wall. With those thoughts in my head, I met her gaze as she stepped onto the plane.

Instantly, I was hard for her, needing her and wanting to do a dozen inappropriate things to her. I sat in the aisle seat, a position that placed me where I could protect her from others. She immediately recognized me and placed a hand over her belly. I didn't know if that meant she was about to get sick or if my presence excited her, but I needed to put her at ease. Without a word, I stood, barely covering my hardness, and gestured for her to take her seat by the window.

She paused, eyes full of worry, wonder, and an intensity I found shocking.

"I don't know what to say," she said as the flight attendant observed our interaction.

I took Rowan's hands, giving the slightest squeeze. Most of what happened here would find its way back to my mother, back to the Crown, and splashed across front-page news.

I primly kissed her on her cheek. "It's nice to see you," I said. "I'm looking forward to this trip."

She opened her mouth, but I gave a quick shake of my head. To my relief, she followed my command and silenced whatever she'd been about to say. These first moments would set the tone for the year, and there was no way I would mess this up.

Rowan glided into the seat beside the window and lowered herself down. Her doe eyes stared up at me, wide, unblinking, and wet with tears.

My conversations with Infidelity had been frank and honest once I was assured confidentiality. They knew what I craved, and I had faith they'd delivered on their promises, but Rowan wasn't a thing to use as I chose. She was a beautiful and amazing woman, one trapped by circumstance and forced into an arrangement she likely hated. I respected that, more than she would ever know. I also craved what Infidelity could bring into my life. In short, I wanted it all. To my delight, she remained compliant and silent, obeying my unvoiced command.

A flight attendant approached. "May I get you something to drink?"

I glanced at Rowan and gave a nod. "Two glasses of champagne. We're celebrating our anniversary."

She glanced at Rowan. "Congratulations."

As the flight attendant departed, I whispered, "Breathe. Just breathe."

"But you're—"

I grabbed her hand and folded my fingers around her tiny bones. "I'm delighted to see you. Thrilled in fact, but you look terrified. I need you to relax."

Her eyes locked on mine, and my heart swelled with the trust she placed in me. The tremors in her hand eased. The pulse jumping in her neck slowed. Her breaths, which had been on the verge of hyperventilation, evened out. Impossible to say if I had that effect on her, but I took it as a sign that everything would be okay.

The flight attendant returned with our drinks.

"Thank you," I said, lifting them off her tray. Dismissing the woman, I turned to Rowan and handed her a glass. "To a year of possibilities, adventure, and mutual exploration."

Her eyes widened at this, perhaps understanding my resolve. I tipped the glass to my lips and paused until she mirrored my movement. Making a show of it, I took a sip and watched as she downed the entire glass.

"What happens now?" she asked.

"I think this is where the pilot says, *Sit back, relax, and enjoy the flight.*"

Her smile set off an explosion in my chest, a rattling of nerves I hadn't realized was there.

"What the hell have I gotten myself into?"

I whispered in her ear, "Whatever you want. However far you wish to go. It's just you and me and whatever we decide."

She drew back, but I refused to allow her retreat.

"We've much to discuss but plenty of time to sort things out.

I'm looking forward to finishing what we started." There, I'd set the tone. There was no way she could misunderstand my goals.

Her gaze cast around the empty cabin. I'd planned for this. Delving into the specifics of our relationship wasn't something I desired, not in such a public place, although I did have a surprise planned for later. I reached into my breast pocket and pulled out a folded sheet of paper. Our flight would last a little over two hours, plenty of time for her to ponder what I'd written down.

"Read this," I said, handing it over.

She took the paper with trembling fingers.

I'd poured out my deepest fantasies last night, spewing them onto that fragile sheet. According to Infidelity, she had no ability to refuse. I disagreed. The next step belonged firmly in her hands, and I would respect whatever decision she made.

For a year, we were a couple in every sense of the word. She would come willingly, exploring mutual fantasies, or not at all. Either way, I would honor my commitment.

FIFTEEN

Game

ROWAN

IS IT POSSIBLE TO DIE FROM A RACING HEART? THIS QUESTION burned at the forefront of my mind because there was no escape from Richard's penetrating gaze. My limbs trembled. My breaths pulsed in and out, moving much too fast to keep up with my need for oxygen. I couldn't string two thoughts together. *Out of all the men on the planet, why did Infidelity pair me with him?*

My current state?
Mortified.
Terrified.
Speechless.
Minimally aroused?
Okay, slightly aroused.
Hell, my entire body lit up like a firecracker.
It was him!
I pinched myself, hoping this was a dream. The man was a

prince who had bought my discretion, my companionship, and maybe something more for the entirety of a year.

Dear Lord, save me because I could barely look at him. He knew my deepest, darkest fantasies and shared them. That gave him an unfair advantage because there was no way to hide the things I'd said, what I'd let him do, or ignore what we craved.

The problem? I'd only pretended...*I think*. With my nose buried in books, submissive desires had taken root in my heart, but I never acted on them—until that night at Club Infinity. To him, I'd exposed everything.

Sure as hell, I knew nothing about being submissive, and this was a man who exuded dominance. Those had been the words tossed between us during that indescribable night, words I wished to take back and secrets I wished he knew nothing about. In the heat of the moment, I'd been protected by the assurance that whatever I did would only be for the span of one night. But to spend a year with a man who knew my darkest cravings? There would be no way to hide from it. *What am I going to do?*

Maybe I should start with the paper he'd given me, but reading it would open doors I might not want to enter.

I kept the paper gripped tightly in my hand. "You mentioned an anniversary. We don't have an anniversary. It's more of a countdown—three hundred sixty-five days and done."

His smile caught me unaware and had a soothing effect I had not expected. He'd bought the rights to me, yet he had barely touched me. It wasn't anything I'd expected from a man who'd had his tongue down my throat in the VIP area of a club and fingers pressed against my most private parts. Thinking about that kiss and all the rest had me pressing my thighs together. I was surprised by the pulsating ache between my legs. I definitely wanted more of that.

He leaned close. "Infidelity no doubt has informed you as to who I am."

"They have."

"There will at some point be a media frenzy. You and I met in a club, and we've secretly been seeing each other ever since. Today is the first time we're allowing others to see us in public. From here on out, as far as anyone is concerned, we're officially a couple. It's our five-month anniversary."

"I see," I said, shifting in my seat and leaning back. "I suppose there needs to be some backstory."

"I prefer to keep things as close to the truth as possible."

I lifted the glass, and the fizz of bubbles tickled my lips. My body vibrated with the remembrance of his touch and the way my insides had combusted beneath the magic of his fingers. Within moments, he'd had me unglued. I both yearned for more of that and feared it, too.

He watched my every move, and his gaze lingered on my lips longer than it should have. I took a small sip and let the flavor of the champagne coat my tongue before swallowing it down.

"I don't know what to say."

He squeezed my hand. "We'll have time to discuss things later. For now, sit back, relax, and enjoy the flight. I have a car arranged to take us to your brother. How long do your visits generally last?"

"It depends," I admitted. "Freddy can be wildly unpredictable. He's not going to take well to meeting a stranger."

"It's not my intention to insert myself on your visit with your brother," he explained. "I'm here because you and I are seeing each other, which means I support the things that are important to you. In this case, your visit." He lifted a finger. "I only asked how long because I didn't know if I should wait or otherwise occupy myself for most of the day. This is important to you, but I'm eager to begin."

To begin…

My chest seized. *What is he expecting? Do I have that little say in how our relationship progresses?*

"About that," I said, my voice wavering with my fear.

He pointed to the paper. "Perhaps you should read that first."

I unfolded the paper.

My sweet Rowan,

Breathe…and relax. I intend to respect your boundaries and take this slow. You know my desires, and I know a hint of yours, but this weekend is not the time to pursue them.

This is my pledge. Until we discuss what happened in that club, what brought us together and what pulled you away, you may expect me to conduct myself as a gentleman. All I ask is to discuss the fears you have, so we might navigate through them. Be open to the possibility between us, but be honest in everything you do. When you give your submission, know I will treasure it as the priceless gift it is.

Yours truly,

Richard

The note was nothing like what I'd thought it would be. My expectations had been much harsher, more demanding, more authoritative, more domineering. He spoke as if we'd entered a partnership instead of a contracted relationship where he held all the cards. I'd thought he'd sweep in, impose his rules, and force me to comply to his authority. In a few words, he'd laid my worries to rest while emphasizing his expectations. I folded the paper back into its small square and tightly held it to my chest.

Tipping my chin down, I said, "Thank you. I appreciate this more than you know."

The kettledrum that had become my heart settled into an easier rhythm. Richard intended to work with me. Truthfully, his words touched my heart in more ways than one. They endeared me to him. They helped me trust his motives. Most of all, he'd earned my respect.

Not knowing what the rules were regarding Infidelity pairings, I'd thought I'd given up all my rights. Richard had shown me this was not the case at all. We were in this together, and that gave me all the breathing room I needed to relax.

"I mean every word," he said. "Now, our flight is just a couple of hours, so how about we get to know each other a little bit better?"

With a shrug, I settled into my seat, making myself comfortable. There was literally nowhere to run this time, but I had no intention of going anywhere. "What do you have in mind?"

"How about a game? I call it Truth and a Lie. I tell you two things—one true, the other a lie. You do the same. We guess which is true."

"Okay." *Easy enough.*

His large hand encapsulated mine. "There is only one rule."

"Yes?"

"These will be the last lies we tell each other. When the game ends, there will be no more lies, no half-truths, and no omissions of the truth. We pledge to be open and honest in every way, man to woman, and Dom to sub."

My heart skipped a beat, and in that pause, a hollowness filled my chest. This wasn't about a silly game. It was my first test. Swallowing against the lump in my throat, I gave a slow nod.

"I promise to try very hard to always tell you the truth," I said.

"That's not exactly what I meant," he replied with a quirk of his brow.

"Well, it's impossible to always tell the truth," I asserted. "So, I can't promise because that would be a lie. But I'll try very hard not to lie."

"Now, that is probably the most honest thing anyone has ever said. I accept with one condition."

"What condition?"

"If you lie after our game, you accept the consequence and submit to my authority."

I shifted in my seat because he could only mean one thing by that comment.

"I intend to explore what began between us," he said.

My throat closed in because this was anything but a game. "And if you lie to me?"

"I will never lie to you, and that is my word not only as a prince, but also as your Dom. Now, do you want to go first, or shall I?"

My lips twisted, but there was no way I would begin his game of questions and answers. "You go first."

He kicked his ankle over his knee, affecting the perfect posture of ease. In contrast, I leaned forward and pressed my hands between my knees where I could wring my fingers together.

"Okay, two statements. One is the truth, and one is a lie."

"And if I guess the truth?"

His lips twisted and bowed into a smile. I loved the way his eyes twinkled, like he was getting away with something.

"If you guess correctly, you get to kiss the back of my hand. I get to do the same. Guess wrong, and no kiss."

"That's it? A kiss to the back of your hand?"

He glanced down the aisle. "I thought that would be more appropriate for such a public place. If you'd rather, we can tally up the numbers and change the location of the kisses?" His left brow arched, but his gaze narrowed to my lap.

That sounded dangerous.

"Um, back of the hand, it is." I waved for him to begin. "Lay it on me."

"I was born a prince, and someday, I'll be king." He brushed off a speck of lint from his trousers and crossed his arms. The bulge of his biceps filled out the fabric of his oxford, and the shirt stretched across a powerful chest. He glanced down, letting me know he'd caught my stare and then flicked his gaze to my heated cheeks.

"Well, I already know you're a prince and second in line, which means the other one is a lie."

"My brother, Edmund, is eight years older and will be king. Your turn," he said.

"Okay…"

"Wait." He offered his hand, turning it palm down.

I leaned down and brushed my lips against his skin. That fractional contact brought the taste of him flooding back to my senses. Dark, powerful, a little salty, he tasted decadent. I drew back with a sharp inhale, surprised by my reaction. He glanced at his knuckle and pressed it to his mouth.

"I have a metro card," I said, "and I love riding the subway."

He laughed at this and grabbed my hand. Holding a light grip, he pressed his lips to my knuckles. Unlike me, he lingered, eyes closed, while he took a deep inhale. The heat of his lips had my pulse pounding and heat building at my neck.

"There's no way you enjoy riding the subway," he said.

"Fair enough," I said as he pulled away. Rubbing where his lips had touched, I was no longer certain this little game was such a good idea.

"My turn," he said. "I remember the taste of you on my lips, and I want to taste you again."

My brows pulled together with this one because I hadn't been able to get the memory of his taste out of my head since that night at Club Infinity.

He arched a brow. "That one shouldn't be so difficult."

"I remember exactly how you taste. I can't believe you don't remember how I—"

He leaned over, turning my chin, and swept in for a kiss. The warmth of his lips brushed against mine, and his tongue pressed forward. "Mmm," he said.

Soft and gentle, that kiss had been nothing like the rough and punishing kiss from the club, but the tenderness of his touch couldn't have been more damaging. I leaned into him and parted my lips, letting our kiss deepen. It was with some surprise when he pulled away.

Glancing up and down the aisle, he gave a slight shake of his head. "Sadly, more of that must wait for a private place, but now, I remember what heaven tastes like."

I ran my fingers over my lips, tracing the path of his tongue, needing more and terrified by the depth of that desire.

"Your turn," he said.

"But I never answered…"

"Your turn," he insisted.

"Okay." I struggled to find something easy. "I'm the second born as well, and I have an intense fear of snakes."

He pulled a face. "That's random."

"I felt you needed a challenge."

"Well, I know you're a twin, but that's the extent of it. I have a fifty-fifty shot with that one. I'm going with an intense fear of snakes as the truth."

He reached out to take my hand, but I pulled back from him.

"Freddy was born first."

"So, snakes?"

"I wouldn't say I loved them, but Freddy is fascinated by them. We shared a room together until he moved out, which means I had snakes for roommates."

"I find that surprising. It's kind of cool to be dating a girl who likes snakes."

"I tolerate them, but I am an expert snake-handler."

"This isn't such a bad game, is it?" he said. "Think of all the things we can learn."

"Well, it's your turn."

"I prefer cats to dogs, and when I was young, I had a pet bunny who was my best friend."

"Hmm…now, I'm thinking, if I were British, I should know all the intimate details of your life. I prefer cats to dogs, but I'm thinking a little prince and his bunny is rather funny, so I'm going with the bunny as being true. Please tell me you like cats because I've been wanting one for years, and New York isn't the best place for dogs."

"I'm allergic to cats," he said with an apologetic face. "I'm sorry, but we won't be getting a cat."

My heart did another of those thudding things because he spoke of our cohabitation as if it were a done deal. Yet again, I was reminded of exactly what I'd agreed to when signing with Infidelity.

He didn't seem to notice my little hiccup because he continued on, "I'm definitely a dog lover. I grew up with wolfhounds as a kid, which was kind of funny, considering I carried a bunny with me almost everywhere when I was little."

"The dogs never tried to eat the bunny?"

"No, they were actually really good friends," he said with a chuckle.

"I take it, there's no bunny in your life now?"

I loved the richness of his laughter. The warmth of it wrapped around my insecurities and soothed the rough edges. He put his entire being into his smile, and that made it easy to relax. Relax but not let down my guard. Richard intended to devour me—of that, I had no doubt. I hadn't decided if I would allow it, but I felt he might take that choice from me. Odd, how that excited me even more.

"No bunny. No pets at all. My dogs are back home."

Ah, right. Him living in England was going to be a problem.

"Maybe this was a mistake. I was pretty clear about needing to finish my degree. If you're in England—"

He reached for my hand and rubbed the skin over my knuckles. "I have every intention for you to succeed in all your goals."

"But—"

"I might be a Prince of England, but my presence in England is not required. That is for my mother, the Queen, and my brother, the Prince of Wales. I'm afforded great freedom in my comings and goings. I have a place in New York."

"They mentioned a passport."

"There will be times when I need you to travel with me but never at the expense of your studies. Trust me, I'm enjoying New York very much and even more now that you'll be by my side."

"Is that where I'll be?"

"For now."

"And later?"

"We'll discuss what comes next."

SIXTEEN

Push

RICHARD

What came next were fantasies of Rowan on her knees, my cock sliding between her lips, and other more decadent things. Things that a Prince of England would never engage in because, if ever brought to light, those actions would generate a scandal, making that blow-job incident a tiny blip of indiscretion.

One day, I hoped she would choose to take to her knees. Her submission wasn't something I would force, but I aspired to entering a realm where we willingly chose our roles.

"As I said, there's much to discuss." I shifted the topic of our conversation. "Before we begin, there's a matter of nondisclosure."

There was little we could discuss within the confines of the plane. The first-class cabin remained empty, except for us. This had much to do with my request and Infidelity's help in orchestrating this first meeting.

I pulled my briefcase out and flicked open the latches. Infidelity had their contracts and nondisclosure agreements, but my lawyers had even tighter restrictions for Miss Rowan Cartwright.

"You've signed the NDA from Infidelity, but I require even more discretion. You must understand the delicate situation this places upon the Crown."

She took the manila envelope and cradled it in her lap. "I'm not a stranger to such things, but I have a question."

I gave an imperious sweep of my hand. "Of course."

"What exactly do you expect this relationship to be?"

"In terms of…"

Her gaze flicked through the cabin. The flight attendant was absent, passing out refreshments in coach. Rowan and I were blissfully alone. This presented many opportunities. She looked uncertain.

I gripped her hand. "Are you asking about defining roles?"

Her nod informed me I was on track.

"I see us as a dominant man and a submissive woman interested in seeing where those character traits might take us." I kissed the backs of her knuckles, needing her to know I valued her as a person. "You're a smart woman with aspirations and desires for a better future. I respect and support your dreams. It's my intent for us to become something uniquely us, but at the end of our time, we'll head separate ways. I'll return to my duties, and you'll pursue your career. This is a unique opportunity to explore our innermost desires. We do that with trust and with the utmost discretion." I gestured to the papers in her lap. "It's why we sign legal agreements. Because, no matter what our hearts want, the realities of life rule our actions. I need the protections granted by your signature, just as you need mine."

"It's one big game of pretend?" She gave a sigh.

I cupped her cheek and turned her to face me. "If that's what you think, you've misread my intent."

"How is that?"

"Expiration date or not, what develops between us will be real to me."

"I don't even know what this is."

"It's nothing more or less than you agreeing to be mine."

Her glance down at the envelope told me she still wasn't convinced. I looked down the aisle again. Our flight attendant's attention was occupied with handing out drinks along with packets of nuts and salty pretzels.

"Maybe we should begin with why you ran off the night we met."

Thoughts of exactly what we'd been about to do at Club Infinity filled my mind and hardened my cock. Rowan had an otherworldly ability, it seemed, to keep me in a constant state of arousal. If I didn't seek some relief, I was going to climb the walls.

Her soft laugh caught me off guard. "It was this actually."

"This?"

"I met you the day I signed with Infidelity. That contract felt like a death sentence, and I needed one night all to myself."

"A death sentence?"

She flicked her hair over her shoulder and looked at me with those amazing, soul-sundering eyes. "Like the death of my soul. You said to be truthful. Desperation drove me to Infidelity. It came at a cost, and I regretted it the moment I signed, but there was no other option."

"The cost of your soul?"

She squeezed her knees together and wrung her fingers, a tell of her nervousness. "At the time, that's how it felt. Club Infinity was my way of blowing off steam. I wanted to forget what I'd done, if only for a night."

"That doesn't explain why you ran off."

The heat skating through my body cooled with the realization that she hated what she'd done. There was no way I could hold her to this contract, not if she wasn't willing. *Had Infidelity been that wrong?* David had said they were impeccable matchmakers, and I couldn't have been clearer about the kind of relationship I desired.

We'd been together less than an hour. Already, I was considering terminating our arrangement. That might not be an option. Would they force us to stay together for the entire year if Rowan and I mutually agreed to end this? There wasn't time to wait a year for a second match, not with the obligations of the crown weighing down on me. It would be necessary to have another look at the contract.

With that thought in my head, another more important one pushed to the surface. That night in the club, she'd had no idea who I was. Compliant and very willing, we'd hit it off until something changed.

I cleared my throat. "Explain why you ran." Images of holding out her shoe had me shaking my head.

She refused to look at me and focused on her hands in her lap. "I don't know about the contract you signed, but a clause in mine stated I couldn't seek out any relationships while waiting for Infidelity's match."

We'd been far from developing a relationship. I'd intended on nothing more than a one-night stand, one full of dominate sex that wouldn't get me in trouble when she found out who she'd spent the night with. Women always seemed to figure that out, and those kinds of stories paid well to paparazzi hungry for a million-dollar story.

"I still don't understand."

I didn't want her hiding anything. For this, we would have a face-to-face conversation. She tried to tug her hands out of my grip, but I held firm and asserted my authority.

"I asked a question."

She bit her lower lip, and her eyes cast to the floor. "I'm not sure I understand myself."

"That's not good enough, and perhaps I haven't explained myself, but when I ask a question, I expect an answer."

This could very well blow up in my face, but for good, bad, or plain disastrous, I'd jumped into bed with Infidelity. This was something I needed on a gut level, and I wasn't about to let my fantasies go without a fight. I'd asked for a submissive, and I was pretty damn sure Rowan fit that bill. Forcing the issues wasn't an option, but that didn't mean I would give up without a fight.

Her eyes widened with my command.

"Why did you run?"

Tears shimmered in her eyes, but she held my gaze. "I'm not a submissive."

"Are you certain?"

She nodded. "I've never done that before. It was a fantasy."

"A fantasy?" I needed to get to the root of her fears before I could begin to untangle them.

"Yes."

"Go on."

"I pretended…"

"Are you certain it was pretend?"

Her need had risen and met mine.

"I remember a woman desperate for me to take control."

She gulped. "I didn't think I'd ever see you again. I felt safe, pretending and talking like I knew what I was doing."

"Did you?"

"No."

"Well, let me remind you what you said."

Her cheeks flushed bright pink. "You don't have to remind me. I remember every word."

"Everything?"

"Yes."

"Then, I'm even more confused." It would be easiest to show

her the truth of what we could be. "Come," I said, standing. I waited for her to join me.

"What?" Her eyes widened, and she glanced back down the aisle.

No one paid us any mind.

"Unbuckle, and come."

"But—"

"Stop," I said, lacing my voice with steel. "Obey, and follow."

Her eyes rounded, but to my delight, she unbuckled and stood. I expected more of an argument, but Rowan kept her mouth shut and tightened her grip as I led her to the lavatories at the front of the plane, reserved exclusively for first-class passengers.

"What are you doing?"

"Shh," I said. "Silence."

Her protests quieted as I opened the lavatory door. Before one of the flight attendants turned around, I urged Rowan inside. A man sitting on the aisle of the bulkhead row in coach saw us and gave a thumbs-up. Not that I needed the encouragement, but I appreciated his enthusiasm.

The thing about airplane lavatories and the Mile-High Club were that both were severely overrated. Closing myself in with Rowan put us in a position where we could barely move. With no idea of how this was going to work, I found myself catching strands of her hair in my mouth as I breathed. I pulled her hair from my mouth and managed to spin her around. Our proximity forced us into a kissable embrace, but I had other aspirations in mind. She said nothing, relying upon me to lead. This, I took to be a positive sign, but I still wrestled with one question.

"Red and green are your safe words."

Her eyes rounded, and her breath hitched.

"When I ask how you are doing, you'll reply with either *red* or *green.* Red tells me to stop, and green means you give your permission for me to continue. Do you understand?"

She gave a slow nod.

"Let's try something," I said.

Her gaze lifted to my eyes. Her pert red lips begged for a kiss, but we had some work to do first.

"I suppose," she said.

Her words sounded like defeat, exactly the opposite of what I wanted, but an eagerness in her eyes spoke volumes. Reservations filled her mind, I could see these—or at least, I'd anticipated them—but it was time to place those firmly behind us.

I brushed a lock of hair away from her face. "We're going to play a game."

"Another game?" Her brows drew together. Even as her face contorted in confusion, she was still stunning and sexy as hell. But there was a purpose to what I had in mind.

"Truth and a Lie—only, this time, I ask all the questions. You respond by telling me if it's a truth or lie."

Her mouth parted into an O of surprise.

"If what I ask is the truth, I'm going to kiss you wherever I want."

With my finger pressed to the soft tissues of her chin, I tilted her head back, and swept down for a kiss. Nothing soft and gentle like before. This kiss reflected the desires she'd stirred within me at the club.

"You decide when we stop. Are you willing to play?"

I swept my fingers over her lips and pressed one inside. The roughness of her tongue curled around the tip of my finger, teasing me. Removing my finger, I brushed my lips against hers, savoring the contact. My dick throbbed with each beat of my heart, becoming long and hard, ready to plunge into the heat of her mouth. Whatever she chose, I would oblige, but it would be a very uncomfortable flight if I didn't get some relief.

"I don't get to ask any questions?"

"No," I said, keeping my voice firm.

"Why did you bring me in here? We could have done this outside."

"You already know the answer to that."

Her cheeks flushed pink. I very much enjoyed that color on her face.

"Ready to begin?"

SEVENTEEN

Mile-High

ROWAN

I couldn't move. The lavatory barely fit one person, let alone two, and Richard was a very large man. He had me trapped, unable to exit, not without going through him, and there would be no moving him. Not with the intensity of his entire being latched on to me. For the moment, I was at his mercy.

I didn't know how I felt about that, except my entire body thrummed with nervous energy.

Another game of Truth or Lie? My lips tingled from that kiss. I wanted more, but this round of Truth or Lie found my knees knocking and my stomach doing flips.

"How are you doing?"

I simply stared until he pinched my chin and forced me to look at him. He seemed to like doing that—controlling where I looked. My preference would have been to focus on the floor. It was easier to hide from his penetrating stare than meet it.

"Red or green? How are you doing? You must answer either red or green."

He'd been serious about that?

"Um, green."

"Good. That makes me very happy. Now, first question."

My voice shook. "Y-yes?"

"Truth or lie? You've never engaged in a D/s relationship before."

"I already told you that."

He shook his head. "Answer only with truth or lie. Those are the rules."

"Truth," I said, not understanding why he'd asked the obvious, but when his lips pressed against mine, all thought fled.

Warm, firm, and demanding, he stole my breath as he breached my defenses. He nipped at my lips and pushed his tongue inside my mouth where he probed and lay claim to what would eventually be his. *Who am I kidding?* He already had me.

This man heated me from the inside out, keeping me in a perpetual state of simmering need. I gripped his arms, feeling the power bunched in his muscles beneath his starched oxford. I ran my hands up to his shoulders and wrapped them around his neck.

Strong hands gripped my waist, and he yanked me against him. Like that night in the club, he wasn't shy about letting me know how I affected him. The hard length of his erection pressed between us, making my mind spin with the need for more.

His eyes glinted with a sharp hunger. "You taste like sin."

I lifted on my tiptoes, needing another taste, but he touched a finger to my lips.

"No," he said.

I nearly whimpered with my distress.

"You don't get to kiss me. Another question."

"Okay," I said, frowning. *Why don't I get to kiss him?*

"Truth or lie? You make a habit of kissing men at clubs and running off."

"No, I don't do that."

His hand came down on my ass, a light swat but attention-getting. "You have only two answers—truth or lie."

"Lie," I said and then shifted on my feet.

The slap of his hand hadn't hurt. It had done something else entirely, bringing a steady throb pulsing between my legs.

"Truth or lie?" A mischievous look glinted in his eyes. "You enjoyed that."

"The kiss?"

He swatted my ass, another tap, this one harder than before. It brought me up on my toes.

"Not the kiss."

Averting my eyes, I tried to push away, but the lavatory seat pressed against my legs, and his arm wrapped tightly around my waist. I wasn't moving. Neither was he.

"New rule." The low growl to his voice turned my insides to mush. "When I ask a question, you look me in the eye. Now, did you enjoy me swatting your ass?"

I didn't like this game anymore. Remembering the rules, I gave my answer because it would bring another of his amazing kisses. "Truth."

"Good, because I enjoyed it, too."

I thought he would kiss me on the lips. He did not. A chaste peck on my forehead was all I received for that truth.

"So," he said, "if you don't make a habit of kissing strange men at clubs and running off, that leads me down an interesting path. Are you ready?"

"Yes," I said, breathless for his next question. I hoped it would be a truth. My skin burned for more.

"You didn't enjoy my kiss."

"Lie," I said, breathing out with frustration.

"Good, because I enjoy kissing you. Truth or lie? That night in the club, you didn't want to have sex with me."

"No…yes," I stammered, confused with the negative.

His hand came down hard this time, eliciting a yelp from me. "Truth or lie?"

I blinked a tear from my eye and reached around to rub at the sting of my skin.

He gripped my wrist and pinned it to the wall. "Truth or lie?"

Deep and powerful, his words fogged my mind and made it difficult to think.

"You don't want to keep me waiting," he warned.

Remembering his command to look him in the eye didn't make it any easier to drag my gaze up the expanse of his chest, trail up his kissable neck, and meet the fire in his eyes.

I answered as truthfully as I could, "I don't know."

"You don't know if you wanted to have sex with me?"

"I mean…I did, but then I didn't."

He frowned. "I'm not sure I understand."

"I signed over my life to Infidelity, and I wanted one night that was mine. I've never had a one-night stand. I thought I could, but then I met you, and you had me feeling all these things. I-I wanted to know what it might be like to let go for a night."

"To submit?"

"Yes. That's the only reason I let you take me upstairs."

"Then, what happened?"

"I realized it was no different from what I'd done with Infidelity. It was cheap—"

"Cheap? Cheap what?"

"I don't know." I barely understood what had been going on in my head. None of the previous months of lonely nights had brought any clarity either. Trying to sort out why I'd freaked out had kept me up more nights than not.

I had run. From him, the situation, the pretend submission, or my concerns over safety was anyone's guess. It was probably a mixture of all those reasons, but how did I explain that to a prince? The chances of any woman turning him down had to be next to zero, and I was pretty certain he expected complete compliance from his dates.

I had been bought and paid for and placed in a position where the word *no* didn't exist anymore. It terrified me, even as he excited the hell out of me.

"Did you think I forced you?" He backed against the door to the lavatory, a look of mortification etched in his face. "Because I remember very clearly stopping. I've never, nor would I ever, force myself on a woman."

"No!" I said, realizing how that sounded. "That's not what I meant. I'm sorry, I suck at this. I didn't mean you—" I never finished my thought.

Tears poured down my cheeks, and deep sobs racked my body as he pulled me against his chest.

He tucked my head beneath his chin. "When the flight ends, I'll take you to your brother. I'll call Infidelity and explain this probably wasn't the best match. There's no way they could have known we'd met before."

Tight spaces and all, there was no way to ignore the slackening of his erection. Could I be any better at killing the mood? How stupid could I be? I couldn't afford to have this fall apart. I needed the money, and when choosing between the lesser of two evils, a year with Richard scared me a whole hell of a lot less than a lifetime with Brent Parker.

My tears wet his shirt, staining the crisp white fabric with my makeup.

"I'm sorry." I should have said something else, something that would have prevented what came next.

He took my hand and tugged on the lavatory door. He twisted us as a unit, allowing the door to open. Without another word, I found myself back in my seat, buckled in, while the muscles of his jaw bunched.

EIGHTEEN

Nothing

Richard

What the hell just happened? For the second time, we'd gone from hot as hell to a cold, withering nothingness in the blink of an eye.

Bought and paid for and forced into sex—not exactly her words, but that was what they amounted to.

I thought back to that night, worried that, in my eagerness to dominate, I'd unintentionally forced myself instead. It didn't fit with my memory, but I'd done something wrong.

Something horrible.

Now, I found myself matched with a woman who couldn't stand the idea of selling herself to a stranger and who'd already run from me once.

Rowan's body told a different story from the words spilling out of her mouth, confusing me to no end, but that night, she had definitely said no. The moment she'd spoken that word, I'd removed my hands and stepped back. *What do I do now?*

Many women passed through my bed. With most, the sex was good. For some, it had been great. It had never been nuclear explosive like with Rowan, and we hadn't even had sex yet. I couldn't explain how I felt, except that sitting beside her and not being able to have her was the worst torture imaginable.

She belonged to me, was a part of me—if that made any sense. Not because I was paying for her companionship, but because not having her left a gaping hole in my sense of who I was. There should be no hole. I shouldn't feel this way about any woman, but that ache pulsed within me.

Lost a part of her soul? That wasn't a statement anyone tossed about without serious thought.

"Richard..."

I silenced her with a shake of my head.

The flight attendant returned, and the last thing I needed was any part of this conversation reaching the wrong ears.

"Later," I said, perhaps a bit harsher than necessary.

Rowan flinched and then stared out the window. Not engaging seemed to be a reflex, one I intended to change.

For the rest of the flight, the words exchanged between us were polite but strained. I inquired about her brother, wanting to know about his situation and their relationship. Speaking about Frederick—or Freddy, as she referred to him—brightened her entire being, but it did nothing to ease the tension swirling between us. Her love for her brother wasn't something I shared with Edmund.

He and I tolerated each other. Some of that might have to do with the differences in our ages. I'd always been the annoying little brother. She and Freddy were twins. They had grown up in the same room, and according to her, they had been inseparable until he turned fifteen. Edmund and I'd lived in different wings of the family estate, and he'd moved out to attend boarding school when I was barely seven. We led separate lives while Rowan and her brother shared everything.

"Why did your brother leave?" I asked, curious as to what had finally separated them.

"Freddy can be wild when he goes into a fit. One time, he came close to hurting me. My father decided it was no longer safe for Freddy to stay."

She had yet to mention a mother, and I sensed some pain in her past. I was curious whether her mother had agreed with the move. Rowan came from the South, and patriarchy persisted there, especially in the older, more established families.

"Did he ever hurt you?" *What concerns do I need to have with this visit?*

"Some bruises but nothing serious. I'm the only one who can calm him down when he gets out of control."

"What calms him?"

"Oddly enough, a hug—the tighter, the better. Any other time, he doesn't like physical contact, but when he gets out of sorts, I hug it out of him."

"I'm not that familiar with autism. As I understand, they have difficulty with processing sensory input. I thought touch set them off."

"I don't think anyone knows for certain, but Freddy is harmless. My father did the best he could, and Freddy is happy. He loves his home, and I'll do anything to make certain he stays that way."

Like sign away her soul? My respect for her deepened, as I knew how willing she was to sacrifice for her brother's happiness. I didn't have that and never would.

"He's the reason you signed with Infidelity."

The depths of desperation that drove her to make such a choice made sense now. It hadn't been about a destitute socialite looking to maintain a certain standard of living. Rowan made her choice for her brother, and I profited from that love. While she visited with her brother, I would be having a discussion with the people at Infidelity.

There was one other thing I needed to arrange.

NINETEEN

Consequences

ROWAN

I'D RUINED EVERYTHING. CHEMISTRY BETWEEN TWO PEOPLE WAS something I'd only read about. Like Moby Dick, the great white whale, people sought it but rarely ever found their soul mate. What about the attraction sizzling between us? *Do I take advantage and sink into the fantasies swirling in my head?* I should, but I was a coward.

Who cared if I signed a contract? I was the one who'd agreed to meet with Infidelity after Patrick mentioned how they could help. It wasn't like I'd been forced against my will. Nobody had kidnapped me and enslaved me. And, while I was peripherally aware that sort of thing happened in the world, my current situation belonged solely to the choices I'd made.

I'd chosen Infidelity.

I'd signed the contract.

I had known the consequences of my actions.

So, why am I acting like a victim?

What am I so damn afraid of?

Richard probably thought I was insane. Even worse, he probably regretted the match Infidelity had made. I had to fix this. But how? How could I circle back to our initial meeting and begin with more enthusiasm rather than all the shit I'd dumped in his lap?

His patience astounded me. On every level, he remained the consummate gentleman. Even after the disastrous end to what should've been a hot introduction to the Mile-High Club, he'd treated me gently, asking questions about my family. Only now, a great distance separated us. I had done that.

I didn't ask about him, but then what was there to ask a prince? From the multiple nondisclosure agreements I had signed, he clearly meant to keep me separate from that part of his life. I had a feeling it was best not to ask too many questions and I decided I wouldn't grow too close.

I was being paid to be his companion and nothing more. He was paying a premium for a compliant submissive to meet his dominant needs. My response had been to insert my insecurities and destroy his hopes.

It wasn't necessary for him to hate me. I held the corner on that market and detested what I'd done.

Holy hell, what have I done? I need this money. And Freddy…holy hell!

His hand pressed down on my arm. "Breathe, Rowan. You're hyperventilating."

I gulped for air. Turning wide eyes on him, I clawed at my throat. The cabin dipped down, and I gripped the armrest, terrified, until I realized the pilots must have begun our descent. That knowledge did nothing to help. *Why can't I catch my breath?*

I'd ruined everything. Freddy would suffer. I would be on the streets. My entire future was destroyed because my pride couldn't accept the truth. Darkness gathered at the edge of my vision, and I swayed in my seat. Richard pried my fingers from the death grip I had on the armrest and threaded his fingers through mine. I barely registered his presence. Breath pulsed in and out of my mouth, but my inhalations were too shallow to fill my lungs.

"Rowan!" The shout barely registered through the fog of my thoughts.

Something scratchy covered my mouth. It smelled dry and stale, like paper, and I batted it away. Then, warmth pressed against my lips. The entire world stilled as the rich flavor of Richard invaded my world. I breathed him in. One intoxicating pull sent his aroma flooding my senses. Gripping his neck, I pulled him closer, my lips parting as my lungs took a long drag of air. Another breath drew in more of his warm, dark essence until I was awash in everything Richard. A whimper escaped me as I hung on to his neck, needing more of his taste, his scent, needing more of the strength he supplied.

His kiss continued, slow and determined. I wanted more but found him pulling away. I chased him, nipping at his lower lip until his entire body crushed me against the seat. I floated then, drowned in sensation and devoured by his lips. My breaths came easily now, as if the contact had short-circuited the panic of my mind. I held on to him, my hands dropping to his shoulders where they then skated down the muscles of his arms. The kiss softened, turning into more nips and licks, and then he pulled back.

"Better?"

I blinked and blindly sought his hand. Threading my fingers with his, I brought his knuckles to my lips.

"Truth or lie?" I said. "You think I'm crazy."

He brushed back a strand of hair from my face. "I think you're overwhelmed. You've found yourself trapped in a situation you're not prepared to handle."

The bottom of my world dropped out as the wheels of the plane hit the runway.

"What are you going to say to Infidelity?"

He brought the back of my hand to his lips and pressed gently. "A whole hell of a lot actually," he said, "at least until a moment ago."

My eyes widened, and my heart fluttered with hope. "And now?"

"Do you trust me?"

"I do."

"How are you doing?" He gave me a significant look, alerting me that this question demanded only one of two answers.

"Green."

Placing my hand in his lap, he gave a squeeze. "Good. Now, stop overthinking. Let me lead."

TWENTY

Freddy

ROWAN

GOOD? WHAT THE HELL DID GOOD MEAN? IS THIS HIS WAY OF GIVING me a reprieve? And what is he going to say to Infidelity?

My thoughts were in such a tailspin, I barely remembered him leading me off the plane.

My answer to, "What suitcase is yours?" was monosyllabic at best. I might have even grunted. I didn't know.

It passed in a fog. One moment, I had been on the plane, answering his red or green question, and the next, he was opening the door outside Freddy's group home. I might have gaped until he swatted me on the ass and propelled me inside. He stayed with the car, and by the time I had my wits about me, he'd already driven down the long, sweeping drive.

Next I knew, Freddy shuffled up to me and tugged my sleeve.

"Hey, sis," he said. "Nice to see you."

I swallowed down the lump in my throat and batted away the tears in my eyes. "Oh, Freddy, I'm so happy to see you." It would be great to give him a big hug, but this was Freddy. I mirrored his greeting, barely touching his sleeve, grateful not to see him flinch. "I missed you. Did you miss me?"

"Always," he said, smiling down on me.

Freddy had grown into a handsome man. I hated he would never know anything more than the love of his sister. Autism profoundly affected him, and it was impossible for him to develop relationships with anyone outside of his very narrow world.

"What are we going to do today?" I asked. "How are your snakes?"

"Rex is full," he said. "Ate two mice."

"Two! And Sally?"

He grinned. "She's sleeping."

"Oh."

He didn't like bothering the snakes if they weren't active.

Pointing down the lane, he took a step outside. "Who was that?"

"Who?"

"The man who dropped you off. He looks familiar."

"A lot of people can look familiar."

Odd for Freddy to show interest in anyone outside of me or his caretakers.

"Is he a friend?"

Glancing at the ceiling, I took in a deep breath. This was not a conversation I wanted to have with my brother. "He is."

"I know him."

"I don't think you know him."

"He's Prince Richard of Wales. You should know that."

"Freddy! How do you know that?"

"I know a lot of things," he said. "Come, I wanna show you what I've been learning this week."

Freddy wasn't a savant, like some severely autistic individuals, but he did tend to focus in on different things. I never knew if he'd be teaching me how to play bridge or if he'd educate me about the migrational and breeding habits of swans or any number of obscure subjects. Once something caught his interest, he tended to run with it, scouring the Internet for every possible detail until he was an encyclopedic expert.

What I'd learned was, I sucked at playing bridge. Swans mated for life and mourned the loss of their mate when it died, and there were tens of thousands of orchids in existence. I was also an expert on how to take care of snakes. I hadn't lied to Richard about that. Rex and Sally were relatively new acquisitions, less than a year old. I'd given them to Freddy as a Christmas gift when his last snake died.

"I want to meet him."

"Who?" Although there could only be one person my brother meant.

"Prince Richard," he said, rolling his eyes like I was an idiot. "Your friend."

"Are you sure?"

"Yes, I have questions."

"What kind of questions?"

He brushed his pants. "You wouldn't be interested."

We spent our day chatting about my studies at Pratt. He enjoyed looking at the projects I had been working on. We visited Rex and Sally, careful not to disturb them. Freddy even took me to his garden to show the progress of his carrots and snap peas. Then, like always, Freddy decided our visit was over.

"It's dinnertime. Time for you to go," he said.

Freddy's good-byes came abruptly. He meant nothing by it, but I was dismissed. Not for the first time, I wished things had been different for my brother. My recent troubles would've been easier to handle with a normal bother. I hated when those thoughts crept into my mind. I loved Freddy, adored the hell out of him, and wouldn't change a thing about him, but I was human. Sometimes, I wished I had an older brother who would take care of me and not one who depended on me for everything.

With a sigh, I made my way to the lobby and hit the guest registration desk.

"Hi, Miss Cartwright," Benny Hart said. "How is your visit going?"

"Good," I said. "Freddy went to get a bite to eat. I need to speak with the business office about my payment."

It would be late, but I intended to pay it. Ms. Flores hadn't mentioned when the first deposit would make it into my bank account, but I hoped it would be soon.

"I'll call Ms. Angelo," he said.

"Thank you." I stepped away and took a seat.

"Oh, Miss Cartwright?" Benny said.

"Yes?"

"Ms. Sara Donaldson from your law firm left this." He pulled out a thick manila envelope. "She said Freddy needed to sign the documents inside."

Odd, they hadn't mentioned anything to me.

"Thanks, Benny. I'll have Freddy sign as soon as possible." As I tucked it under my arm, Ms. Angelo walked out.

"Miss Cartwright," she said, beaming. "What a pleasure to see you."

"Nice to see you, too," I said, surprised by her smile. Over the past few months, we'd had difficult conversations, especially when my payments had started coming late. "I wanted to talk about Freddy's account."

The smile on her face spread even wider. She came to me, clasped my hands, and gave me a hug. "Oh, yes! We're so very excited about the endowment."

"The what?"

"The endowment in Freddy's name! Your friend"—she

lowered her voice—"*the prince*, said it was a gift. Very hush, hush. It's going to do so much for the institute. Of course, it covers Freddy's costs, but there's so much more potential. So much good it can do for all our residents. Thank you! There simply aren't enough words."

I didn't know whether to be relieved, happy, or angry. In the end, I went with relieved. I had intended to do the same with whatever residual was left at the remainder of our contract, but Richard's donation floored me.

We talked about her plans for the facility, but eventually, her duties called her back to her desk. I took a seat in one of the chairs facing the bay window and waited for Richard's return. I decided one thing while I waited. I didn't want Freddy anywhere near Richard, especially if Freddy found out we were dating—or at least pretending to be a couple. When the time came for Richard and I to separate, it would devastate my brother.

TWENTY-ONE

Termination

Rowan

With Richard's arrival, I made my way to the circular drive. A chill set in the air as the sun crept to the horizon. There'd been no discussion about where we would spend the night, although I assumed we would not be getting two rooms.

What do I say about the endowment?

Tires crunched over the crushed stone, and dust drifted behind the car. A light breeze gusted away from me, sparing me from the airborne grit. I resisted the urge to open the passenger door. Knowing the kind of upbringing he must have had, I waited for him to open my door. The moment our hands touched, an electric shock coursed up my arm, eliciting a tiny gasp. He gave a peck on the cheek, short, sweet, and completely devoid of our previous heat. *Maybe I imagined that electrical charge?*

"How was your visit?" he asked.

"It was nice."

"I'm happy to hear that."

"He wants to meet you."

"Me?"

"Evidently, Freddy has questions."

"I'm happy to answer any of his questions." Richard arched a brow. "How do you feel about me meeting your brother?"

"Honestly," I said, remembering Richard's comments about truth, lies, and omissions, "I'd prefer you didn't."

"May I ask why?"

"Freddy's autistic, but he's not stupid. Once he realizes we're together, he'll want to get to know you."

"Why is that bad?"

"Because I don't want to deal with what happens when we're no longer together." I bit my lip, hoping he understood. "I don't mean to sound rude, but in the off chance he likes you…"

"I understand." Richard tossed the keys high and snatched them out of the air.

I couldn't tell if he had done it from anger, irritation, or frustration or if it was simply a habit of his.

When he climbed in the driver's seat, I explained my reasoning, "There are only two kinds of people in his life: family and others."

"Others?"

"Autistic individuals have difficulty differentiating people from things. Other people are things—props, if you would. They're no more or less important than any object. But family? He holds family very close. The people who take care of him are family, and the staff have very strict protocols for introducing any new personnel into his routine. The same goes for the rare times someone leaves. If Freddy thinks we're together, you'll become family. When you leave, that will cause chaos."

"I respect your wishes even if I don't understand."

"It's better if you never meet him, and trust me, you don't want him grilling you with questions."

"I don't see why not. I'm very well versed in my heritage."

"While I don't doubt that, I would bet on Freddy over you any day. Once he decides to learn something, he learns everything about it. He's encyclopedic in his knowledge."

"I see." He turned on the engine and gripped the steering wheel. The tendons on the backs of his arms stood out as he tightened his grip. "Don't worry, Rowan," he said with a sigh. "I respect your boundaries. In your shoes, I'd probably feel the same."

"Thanks for understanding. And thank you for the endowment." My thanks sounded pathetic, but I had to say something.

He grinned. "You're welcome."

"You didn't have to do that."

"I wanted to. Besides"—his lips quirked up—"it looks good for my philanthropy."

"Is that all it was?"

"You know better than that. I take care of what's mine."

My throat closed up with that one word. We were officially alone, together, and for the next year, I belonged to him.

"Um…"

He laughed. "Relax. I have a surprise and dinner planned. We still have much to discuss, but until then, how about we try to enjoy the evening?"

"More of a surprise than the endowment? What's the surprise?"

He grinned. "Now, what kind of surprise would it be if I told you?"

The drive back to town took less than an hour. Rather than talk about the big elephant sitting between us, we played a game of favorite songs. He gave me his phone and access to his music. Behind us, the sun dipped beneath the hills, and the blanket of night crept across the sky.

In the darkness, I relaxed, not realizing how tense I'd been.

Richard did that to me. His presence set me on high alert, but then he started talking about the things he liked—in this case, music—and I forgot about the circumstances that had brought us together.

"How did you compile such a massive list of music?"

A smirk lifted the corner of his mouth, turning his smile mischievous and crooked. "There are perks to being a prince."

"I see," I said. "Speaking of, how is it that you travel around without a security escort? Aren't you kind of important? Second in line to the throne and all."

"I have a security detail."

"I don't see them."

"You're not supposed to, but they're all around us." He pointed to two cars ahead of us and to two behind. "They're paid for discretion."

"I thought they'd be with you all the time."

"When I attend public events, they are, but I like to pretend I can live a normal life. It wasn't much of an issue when I was in school, but when I went to Oxford, Mum and I had a conversation."

"Is it different for you?"

"What?"

"With your mother? When you're with her, do you see a mother or the Queen of England?"

"It's a little bit of both, to be honest. Being a royal comes with many privileges, but I sacrifice my personal freedom as well. Mum and I carved out an agreement between us as to how long of a leash she would allow." He pointed to the cars shadowing us. "My freedom is nothing more than a well-crafted illusion."

"I'm sorry. I never considered what that must be like. Is that why you chose Infidelity?"

I'd been so incredibly mired in my own circumstances that I hadn't stopped to consider his motivations. I'd assumed he took advantage of his wealth to buy what he wanted, which he had, except the reasons behind it became clearer as I reflected on what he wasn't saying.

The muscles of his jaw clenched. "Have you Googled me at all?"

I shook my head. "I haven't had a chance. Ms. Flores informed me this morning that we'd been matched, and next I knew, you met me on that plane. Should I?"

"It's up to you, but let's just say, I'm not the picture-perfect prince, and there is a very good reason I'm taking a year abroad."

"Oh?" My ears perked up. "Some royal scandal?" I teased, relaxing into our easy banter.

"Truth?" He placed his hand on my thigh and gave a light squeeze. "I'm known to be a bit of a playboy. I suppose it's as much a badge of honor for me as it is for the women who wind up in my bed."

"Oh," I said, placing a hand to my belly.

The terms of my contract with Infidelity had been crystal clear on the issue of monogamy, but I didn't think the same went for him. In fact, Ms. Flores had mentioned married men used their services.

News would spread about our relationship, and I would have to live with that for the rest of my life. I'd be the American fling. Just one of many women he dated through the year.

"I know what's going through your head right now," he said.

"You do?"

"Hear me out."

"Okay."

"When you Google me—and please don't do it while I'm sitting beside you because it's embarrassing."

"Must have been bad."

"Well, I was headed to a charity event, and I had a new date.

She was eager to show me what she could do, and I was arrogant enough not to stop her aspirations to make an impression on a prince. It wasn't the first time I'd had sex in the back of a car, but I never expected what came next."

"And what was that?"

He shrugged. "She went down on me, and I thought we'd have plenty of time. All my regular drivers are well schooled in my habits."

"I sense a *but* coming."

"Right. This was a new driver. He was supposed to wait for me to tell him he could pull up to the event."

"Oh no!" I squealed, loving where this was going because I had a good idea.

"But," he said, dragging out the word, "this driver only knew to take us to the event. My date was going down, and my driver pulled up to the venue. Now, if you've never seen these things, there's a red carpet and tons of photographers, and the drivers don't get out of the cars. They have people standing by the curb for that. So, this girl was bobbing up and down…"

"Oh my God…" I said, laughing hard. "They didn't open the door, did they?"

"That's exactly what happened, and there were hundreds of photographers. Needless to say, Mum was not pleased. That conversation was one held between me and the Queen of England."

"I'm sure it was."

"We decided it would be best if I took a year off, so I came to stay with a good friend of mine in New York."

"Wouldn't the paparazzi follow? I know we're not as into the royal family as England, but there is still a lot of interest."

"You didn't recognize me at the club."

"It was dark, and I was more interested in your accent and the things you were saying."

"You wanted my body," he said, teasing me.

"I did." I'd wanted a lot more than that, but I'd chickened out at the last minute. Those desires lay inside me, dormant until he'd arrived, but I didn't have the strength to follow through.

"Well, Mum thought America would be a good place for me to kind of disappear while the scandal died down. I'm under strict instructions to *behave*. Instead of a new girl in my bed each night, I've hung out in different clubs, ones which cater to certain tastes but aren't too risqué that they'd draw attention. They are places I can be seen in while tasting a bit of the lifestyle and not inciting a paparazzi event."

"Like Club Infinity?"

Club Infinity created a gray zone for the lifestyle-curious to mingle with those much more adventurous. It was what had drawn me to the club and ultimately brought us together.

"If it ever got out that I was involved in anything other than a normal relationship, it would be another scandal, one I don't think I'd survive. Mum is not against yanking me home and seeing me settled down."

"An arranged marriage?"

"It's not called that, but that's essentially what it would be."

"And you have no say?"

"In who I marry?"

"Right."

"I can date whomever I choose. I can even propose to whomever I want, but an odd bit of royal prerogative remains. The Queen must approve who I marry."

"Sounds outdated."

"Those rules govern my life. It's a law actually. My mother would never force me to do anything I truly abhorred, but her intent couldn't be clearer. I'm on a reprieve after that last scandal. I can't afford another."

"Which is where Infidelity comes in?"

"Correct."

"Do your bodyguards know about it?"

He shook his head. "I'm bound by the same nondisclosure agreements as you. The only people who know I'm a client are the employees at Infidelity, my sponsor, and you."

"Did you have a chance to speak with Infidelity?"

"I did."

My shoulders slumped. I couldn't afford for this to fall apart even if I had a backup plan.

"So, what happens next?" I asked.

"What do you mean?"

"Will they terminate our agreement?"

He wanted a fully compliant submissive, and I'd demonstrated more than once that I was not that person.

He gave me a long, hard look. "I have no intention of terminating our agreement."

"You don't?"

"Not in the slightest."

"But—"

"But nothing. I spent a lot of time thinking while you were with your brother."

"And?"

"Do you want to end this?"

"I…" I had no idea what I wanted.

The honesty we shared with his silly game, while scary, had also been exhilarating. I'd never connected with anyone on that level before. It's like we'd shared hidden pieces of ourselves with each other. Only each other. I wanted to explore that more, because despite what brought me here, I couldn't ignore my growing fascination with Richard, or the butterflies dancing in my belly every time he looked at me.

The terms scared me. Despite barely knowing him, I'd been more truthful in the past twelve hours with Richard than I had ever been with anyone. That included Freddy. Richard and I talked about things. Scary things. But we discussed our fears, and there was no way to deny the chemistry sizzling between us.

"How are you feeling?"

There was that question again. There were only two answers I was permitted to give, but I chose an alternative. "Terrified."

"Now, that is an answer I respect."

TWENTY-TWO

Tower

RICHARD

THERE HADN'T BEEN A LITTLE BIT OF THOUGHT ON MY PART; there'd been a whole hell of a lot of soul-searching. While Rowan had visited, I'd called David. I'd told him very little, not certain how comfortable I felt about sharing the difficulties Rowan and I faced. Instead, I'd asked about his arrangement with Evelyn.

"Up and down," he'd said. "We fight and make up like any other couple."

Their relationship was real, he'd said, and he'd urged caution with the beginnings of mine. Maybe he'd sensed my frustration, but he hadn't pressed for details.

Our conversation had left me to think about exactly what I wanted from Rowan. That, more than anything, had been my takeaway.

Rowan and I would be together for a year. Not all of that would revolve around sex—very little in fact. My expectations were not aligned with reality, and I had taken a long, hard look at what had brought me to Infidelity. I wanted something uniquely mine. Not something that would find its way into the press. Not something I had to share with the world.

Not once had I been able to date without the media speculation that followed. With the high visibility my romantic entanglements brought, it felt as if I dated the world rather than a woman. News of Rowan would get out, but Infidelity had given me something no one could take away. The bond I planned to forge would be something known only to the two of us, a connection I'd been craving for far too long.

"Caution," David had said. "Approach the first few weeks with caution, and expect a few bumps along the way."

When it came down to it, other than limited online research on my part, I knew next to nothing about being a Dom. Given Rowan's complete lack of experience, everything pointed to disaster if we continued. That alone was reason for caution.

When I'd contacted Infidelity, it had been with the intent to call the arrangement off, but Ms. Flores had expressed the same message as David. Infidelity fostered a relationship and wasn't an escort service. There would be highs, lows, and long stretches of daily living to break up the other more exciting parts. She'd encouraged me to take a step back and get to know Rowan before placing too many demands. Great advice even if it wasn't what I'd wanted to hear.

Contractually, I was bound to complete the year with Rowan. I didn't have to spend it with her, but the payments would be made.

Why walk away? Even if we never explored our darker desires, there was no way to deny our mutual attraction.

After we traded our favorite songs, I parked outside a luxury boutique. Earlier, I'd noticed the upscale shop and spoken with the owner.

Rowan leaned forward, peering at the glowing sign as I cut the ignition.

"Clara's Boutique?" She turned to me, her eyes widening. "What are we doing here?"

The front windows of Clara's Boutique displayed fashionable women's wear—dresses and pantsuits suitable for a wide range of social venues. Tucked into the back of the store, Clara sold an impressive array of lingerie. Anticipating the types of appearances we would make, this would be a perfect way to spend our evening. With one significant twist.

"Shopping," I pronounced without elaborating further.

"You're taking me shopping?"

"No. I'm shopping."

"At a woman's boutique?"

"Yes, at a woman's boutique."

"I don't get it."

"What's not to get? I want to buy you something to wear to dinner tonight and a few outfits for later."

"Sooo," she said, drawing out the word, "you're taking me shopping." She asserted her original statement.

I couldn't help but snicker. Reaching over, I took her hand in mine. Her hand was so tiny, it barely filled half of my palm.

"No. I am shopping. You're accompanying me. Ready for the rules?"

There was a slight catch in her breath. David had mentioned being cautious and feeling our way through these first days. He knew nothing about my desires but had a lot to say about the first week he and Evelyn had been together.

"Things," he'd said, "were awkward."

Thoughts of being bought and paid for had nearly destroyed them. After a week, he'd said, that had receded into the background, and they'd found their rhythm. I wanted to do that with Rowan, but I wasn't willing to forgo my desires. What I'd learned in the last few hours was, there was more to dominance than taking control in the bedroom.

"Rules?" Her left eyebrow arched.

I sensed uncertainty layered with excitement and took that as a good thing.

"There really is only one rule. I picked out several outfits. You tell the hostess inside your size, and you'll model them for me."

"That's the rule?" She looked confused.

"No. That's the explanation. The rule is, you have no say in what I purchase, and you'll wear what I buy to the events I choose."

"And if I don't like what you buy?"

"Whether you love or hate them doesn't matter. I'm going to buy what I like, and you're going to let me."

"Even if I hate it?"

"How could you hate something I think is beautiful?"

Her cheeks flushed. "Well, when you put it that way…"

"Are you game?"

"Do I have a choice?" She sounded hesitant.

"You always have a choice."

"And if I say no?"

I shrugged. "I'll be disappointed, but we'll continue with our evening. Reservations are at eight."

She bit her lower lip and glanced at the window displays, looking uncertain.

I would give a million dollars to know what was going on inside her head. Would she say yes because it sounded like fun? Would she refuse because she didn't trust my taste? Or would she agree because it pleased me, and if she did, would it lead to more?

"Do I get to at least tell you if I like it?"

I shook my head. This needed to be absolute. I decided. She did not.

"No, you have to trust me not to dress you in a sack."

"You wouldn't!"

"If all I had was a sack, I'd keep you locked away."

She giggled. Then, she wrapped her arms around her midsection and bent over.

"What's so funny?"

"Images of you locking me in a tower. All I can think of is, *Rapunzel, Rapunzel, let down your hair.*"

"Oh," I said, getting the gist. "I guess it's almost as funny as leaving behind a slipper while running down the stairs."

Her hand flew to her mouth. "Oh my God, that actually happened!"

"It did."

"Wow, how many times has that happened to you?"

"Only the one."

"Well, if you promise not to lock me in a tower, I promise not to run off again."

I pulled her to me. "Be careful, my sweet Rowan, because I certainly won't be pleased if you do."

Her eyes widened, and her mouth parted as the undercurrent of my words sank in. We were doing this. Perhaps not in the way I'd imagined, but we were definitely forging our path.

I swept in for a kiss. Nothing slow and gentle, I meant to devastate.

She would be mine.

TWENTY-THREE

Dais

Rowan

There was no one inside, except a sweet woman in her mid- to late-fifties named Clara. She greeted Richard with a smile and a flushing of her cheeks when he kissed the back of her hand. For me, she didn't offer anything more than a pinching of her brows, a twisting of her lips, and a head-to-toe assessment as she sized me up.

Richard crossed his arms and took a few steps back. Chin to chest, he mirrored Clara's pose.

"She's beautiful," the woman spoke with a light Georgian accent.

"Yes, she is." The words came out in a possessive growl.

"Sweetie," she said, finally acknowledging me, "what size are you?"

My gaze flicked to Richard, and I swallowed to calm the nervous flutter in my belly. "Size six."

Her lips pressed together. "Hmm, you look more like a four."

She pinched at my shirt and tugged on the waistband of my jeans. "You prefer looser-fitting clothes, but I bet you can go down a size."

"Okay." I shifted my gaze back to Richard.

Too many questions flicked in my mind, and I resisted the urge to let them loose. I held my tongue because the stern look on Richard's face gave me pause. This was either a test or his way of setting the tone—or perhaps it was both. I had a choice to make. *Would I follow where he led?*

Submission wasn't something I thought about—at least, not until that night at Club Infinity. Maybe it had been the music, the dancers, or Richard's overwhelming presence, but something dark and delicious spoke to me. I could choose to follow my desires or run from them. *What do I want?*

I came to a decision as the saleswoman disappeared.

Closing the distance between us, I peeled apart his arms and snuggled against the warmth of his chest. "I trust you not to put me in a sack."

His hand cupped the back of my head, and his fingers trailed in my hair, combing through my gentle curls. He gave a soft laugh, a low rumble vibrating in his chest.

"You might want to reserve judgment on that. How far does your trust extend, my sweet Rowan?"

My chest pinched.

Long and narrow, the shop held many styles of clothing but clearly catered to a wealthy clientele. There wasn't anything that wouldn't look good on me. I had no worries about any dresses, skirts, or blouses he'd chosen to put me in. What had me concerned was at the back of the store, placed far from view of the front windows. An impressive array of lingerie hung on racks, and I had a sinking suspicion Richard had explored every square inch of this place during my visit with Freddy.

While I would like to believe Richard had kept his choices to the clothes up front, the tone of his voice had said he expected to keep me on my toes.

Time to back out, if that was what I wanted, but what if I gave him control? For just this little bit? What harm would come from trying on a few outfits?

As I stood this close to him with his arms wrapped around me, his essence flooded my senses. Submit or not, there was no way the heat between us wouldn't combust.

I gave my answer, "Those are the rules, right?" I sounded much braver than I felt.

"That's true."

"Got them," Clara called out, interrupting our moment. "I grabbed a few other outfits I thought might strike your fancy." She grabbed my hand and tugged me away. "Come, sweetie, the changing rooms are back here. And you," she said, giving Richard an exaggerated wink, "let me show you where you may wait."

I half-expected him to insist on coming back to the dressing rooms, but Richard let Clara lead him to the back of the store. We threaded past the lingerie section, and Richard slowed his steps near several barely there outfits. Clara glanced over her shoulder, noticing his pause, but managed to keep me going.

"I have the first outfit hanging for you," she said, pushing me toward the dressing room.

Right outside, a three-panel mirror stretched from floor to ceiling. In front of it, was a low-raised dais. Two overstuffed chairs faced the mirrors—places for mothers, daughters, friends, and reluctant male companions to admire potential outfits.

As I headed into the changing room, Clara returned to Richard.

I paused for a second while Clara lifted a white lacy thing off the rack. My heart rate spiked. Did he expect me to model that in front of her?

I'd grown up shopping in stores similar to this one. Trying on clothes was usually accompanied by flutes of champagne, light classical music, and socialites networking over their husbands' careers.

White linen wallpaper lined the walls with the faintest scroll-work providing a hint of texture. Diaphanous curtains hung at the corners, purely there for the impact of their design.

The room was an octagon, and a mirror filled every other wall. A watercolor of flowers hung on one of the empty walls. A low bench sat next to the back wall. Not a place for sitting, it was meant to hold a client's street clothes. Small shelves and ledges on the third wall held bouquets of baby's breath and roses, and scented candles imbued the entire room with the lightest fragrance of lilac and rose. There, on a hanger, a red dress waited.

I stripped down to my bra and panties and glanced at the deep crimson dress. Made from a knit fabric, it would hug my figure. With mid-length sleeves and a hem that would come to the tops of my knees, it was demure with a scooped neckline and high back, conservative with a hint of sexy. Smooth to the touch, the knit fabric had a slight give as I pulled it over my head. With a shimmy, I settled the dress over my body.

"Oh, that looks amazing," Clara said, entering the dressing room. "Here, sweetie, let me get that zipper."

Richard had said to trust him, and this was his shopping adventure, not mine, but I really hoped he loved this dress. Turning around, I viewed myself in the mirrors. The fabric clung to my body, revealing nothing yet hinting at everything. The design was demure, but I felt naked and exposed. No doubt it would knock Richard's socks off.

"How many outfits will I be trying on?"

"Oh, he has picked several."

"Any ugly sacks in the bunch?"

Her laughter came out as a light twitter. "Sweetie, trust me, he has very good taste. Now, go out there and show him while I gather the rest."

"You're not coming with me?"

She shook her head. "No. That's not what he wanted."

"Oh."

My knees knocked with each step, and the butterflies in my stomach took up a wild dance. I was fully clothed. Why did I feel so nervous?

When I exited the dressing room, it was to find Richard lounging in a chair. A tumbler of amber liquid sloshed in his hand. When he saw me, his entire body stilled. I headed to the raised dais, intending to model the dress to the best of my ability.

"No," he said, his voice coarse and rough. "Come here."

I obeyed the command, skirting the round dais, and closed the distance. He placed the tumbler on the table beside the chair and leaned forward, placing elbows to knees.

"Closer," he said.

I took a step closer.

"Closer," he demanded.

I fiddled with the fabric as I took the next step. Any closer, and I'd be in his lap.

"Closer." He spread his knees wide.

The deep timbre of his voice sent shivers down my spine. I stepped into the space between his knees. He leaned forward, which put his face at the level of my belly. It took every ounce of self-control not to step away, but I was determined to follow his every command.

He placed his hands against my knees, below the hem of the red dress. The heat radiating from his skin sent shivers racing up and down my body. My breaths deepened. Slowly, his hands inched up, moving from my knees to my outer thighs. He dipped his fingers beneath the dress and gripped my thighs, tugging me close.

"Amazing," he said, breathing deep. "Truly amazing."

"You like the dress?"

"Shh," he said.

I could follow that command because the shakiness in my voice had betrayed the nervous energy swirling in my body. What I couldn't do was suppress a gasp as his fingers climbed up my legs and dug into the flesh of my ass. He didn't stop the upward movement of his fingers. At least, not until he reached my thong.

He hooked his fingers on the elastic and pulled the lacy fabric down over my ass, tugging them all the way below my knees. With a wink, he lowered them to the floor and helped me to step out of them.

"You won't be needing these," he said and balled my panties before tucking them into the pocket of his suit jacket. He spun me and slapped me on the ass. "Now, go try on the next outfit."

I wobbled back to the dressing room, stunned by what had happened and incredibly turned on by it as well. Clara waited, fiddling with another dress.

The next dress was a melt-the-eyelids-off-a-man wonder. Dark teal lace with a halter top and three peekaboo openings up front. Clara helped me adjust the straps and zipped me into the dress with its flirty skirt. She said nothing about my lack of panties.

I took two steps out of the dressing room before Richard spun his finger in the air, ordering me back inside. Blowing out my breath, I returned with reluctance. I loved this dress. Not to worry. Clara had another waiting, an evening gown.

Runway ready, the blush-pink lace dress indulged my dreams of being a celebrity, maybe even a princess. Wearing it invoked images of walking down the red carpet. With a lace overlay, the dress featured a double-V neckline, one that plunged deep. Side slits for the legs revealed glimpses of my bare skin. It was the perfect sexy tease.

Richard allowed me to make it all the way to the raised dais and even had me do a twirl before dismissing me without a word. Back to Clara, I went, wondering what would come next.

She helped me into a sleeveless black sequined dress with black-and-gold detailing. It hugged my curves and had a short, tight skirt that came mid-thigh. Richard seemed to have more interest in this, demanding two spins on the raised dais and one visit to the chair. Instead of leaning forward, he reclined and took his time eyeing the dress.

Several other dresses waited, and I lost count as the evening progressed. My favorites included an all-white satin dress with a high neckline, long sleeves, and a pleated skirt. Clara put me in a baby-blue coatdress, cinched at the waist and finished with an A-line skirt. A crimson honeycomb dress with its long, flared mid-calf skirt had me imagining an evening ball of Cinderella proportions. With all the dresses, I was surprised when she had me try on a ruffled white blouse and black pants. Richard's jaw twitched, seeing me in the form-fitting pants.

It killed me, not knowing what he liked, loved, or hated because he gave me no indication what interested him.

"Next," he said, giving an imperious wave of his hand.

I retreated to the dressing room, wondering what dress Clara would have next. Only there were no more dresses. Instead, she had four lingerie ensembles lined up. On the shelf beside the fountain, she left a note.

He's quite the catch. Good luck, sweetie.
Enjoy your evening,
Clara

She'd labeled the pieces with the numbers one through four, leaving me little doubt as to which outfit to model first, second, next, and last. As I gazed upon the pieces, my mouth turned dry with anticipation, and my nerves fired up, sending tingles shooting through my body.

The first piece continued with the lace theme for the evening. A cute ensemble of a triangle bralette and panties, it was more cute than sexy. The same could not be said for the red satin Teddy with the push-up cups, G-string, and barely there scraps of fabric. The third piece was a simple black corset with matching thong. I had the figure to pull it off, and it would look good, but that wasn't what caught my breath.

The fourth outfit broke all the rules. No lace. No satin. I dared to say there wasn't a scrap of fabric on the contraption one could barely call a thong or even a G-string. Leather and chain formed its base—leather straps beneath my breasts and another resting at my waist. Between those, a crisscross filigree accentuated my breasts, dipped between my legs, and skated down my belly. A triangle of the silver chain angled up to attach to a choker around my neck.

Clara might have labeled the order in which I wore these outfits, but she didn't control me. This outfit embodied everything Richard desired—or what I thought he desired. And, even if my belly fluttered as I sorted through how the leather and chain lay on my body, it was time to give him something and stop fooling around.

Damn if it didn't look positively sinful.

For many long minutes, all I could do was stare at my reflection, tracing the curves of my body and imagining more sinful things to come.

A low cough caught my attention, and I nearly tripped as I spun around.

"Rowan…"

I knew exactly what he saw.

"Richard," I said with a trembling in my voice. "I—"

Whatever I'd been about to say disappeared beneath his reckless hunger. He yanked me against him, and that contact ignited my flesh. As I squirmed, my nerves rioted.

He cupped my face, and his voice poured out thick with arousal. "How do you feel?"

"Green," I said, breathless with what we were about to do. I wasn't going to run because I'd made a promise to let this happen.

His tongue demanded entrance to my mouth. With his head slanted, his fingers pulled at my hair, digging and twisting until he had a handful in his grip. He wrenched my head back and forced me up against a mirror. The cold glass had me gasping, which merely invited him to take even more.

His mouth floated over mine. "You look positively sinful." Filled with his arousal, his words sank in, slower than they should have, especially considering the racing of my heart.

His breath disturbed the air between us. I held mine and listened to the beat of my heart, determined to follow its lead. Goose bumps spread up and down my skin from a combination of the cold glass he pressed me against and the potential igniting between us. My gut simmered, stirred by my desperation for more. But what? What should I do?

He touched a knuckle to my chin, and my skin heated under his hungry gaze. An awakening of sensual desire pulsed between my legs, moving in step with the way my heart swooned and dipped.

The dense fringes of his lashes swept across his impossibly beautiful cheeks as he admired my flesh. He was doubly graced by royal birth and impossibly good looks, and his powerful shoulders caged me in. He invaded my space until I barely knew where I stopped and he began. Raw desire pulsed between us. Then, he seized me again, fist tightening in my hair, and he parted my lips and staked his claim.

No coy nips and pecks. That wasn't what this was about. He

took me with brutal possession, and I surrendered as his tongue chased mine.

Where my lips were hesitant and unsure, his were aggressive and certain. The primitive hunger he possessed swept me away and had me whimpering, even as I clawed for more.

With his other hand palming my ass, he lifted me up, grinding against me with the hardness of his erection. I groaned as he drove his hips against me, needing him to shed the clothing that separated us.

"I want—" My voice broke, and I cleared it, embarrassed by the croaky sound.

"What do you want?" He released me and bent down until we were eye-to-eye.

Lust simmered in his eyes with something else as well. Despite the darkening of his pupils, mirth swirled in his gaze. As if his every desire had come true.

"I want you," I said, speaking the honest truth.

How I wanted him or how I wanted him to have me were questions I would struggle through later. For now, I merely needed him to begin.

TWENTY-FOUR

Kneel

RICHARD

My plans to slow things down flew out of my mind with an explosion of lust upon seeing Rowan in that crisscrossing of leather and chain.

I'd picked that piece off the rack more as a tease, never expecting she'd actually put it on. I'd envisioned her storming out or maybe even lifting her brow, challenging what the hell I'd been thinking.

Well, I'd been thinking something exactly along the lines of this.

A man could dream, right?

I had her shoved against the mirror, one hand palming her ass, the other wrapped tightly in her hair. I had full control over her head, but I needed so very much more.

Where had this desire come from? Did she bring it out of me? Or had it been there all along? How had this feral need to stake my claim, and mark a woman as solely mine been silent up until now?

These kinds of thoughts simmered in the back of my mind.

Propriety kept a short leash on a prince, but desire had brought me to explore possibilities in the clubs of New York where I was somewhat insulated from the incessant paparazzi.

It'd brought me to her.

Her eyes sought mine. The arch of her brow lifted, as if she was asking what I was waiting for. She was hesitant and unsure for certain, but something else lingered in that gaze.

She wanted this, and she'd given me the green light to do as I wished.

Don't fuck this up.

What did I want? My nerves rioted, rippling under my skin, and fired up my pulse. I had to make her mine.

I canted my head to the side, gulping breaths as a firestorm swept through me. Frustration flared because I wanted to kiss her lips and suck her peaked nipples into submission. I yearned to explore her gentle curves and lick my way to the treasure waiting between her legs. I needed to taste her essence and hear her cries as I drowned her in so much pleasure, she found herself awash in ecstasy. But I also needed to be inside her where I could feel the heat of her silken walls gripping my cock, plunging deep until there was no longer an ending to me and a beginning to her.

"Richard," she cried out. "Please…"

I grabbed her leg and settled it over my hip, and then I lifted her up. She wrapped her legs around my hips. The press of her pussy against my hardness had me groaning. My muscles tensed, easily taking her weight on my large frame.

A full-body trembling overtook her, something mirrored in the thrumming of my veins. Our combined need created a vacuum of sound with only the beating of our hearts to rush into the silence.

My pants were about to burst as my pulse went ballistic. All that blood racing in my veins had only one place to go.

There was no fear about Clara interrupting us. She had packaged every dress and had them waiting at the front of her shop. I'd explained who I was, and she had no problems with leaving me to lock the doors when Rowan and I were done.

I didn't think I'd ever be done.

Adrenaline surged through me, and my jaw ached with the tension girding my entire being. I could fuck her against the wall, but I needed more than a hasty shag.

My heart jackhammered. My cock pulsed with vitality. Breath surged in and out of my lungs. With my body on overdrive, I carried her out of the dressing room. No one could see us from the outside. I'd already checked. No need for innocent eyes or the lens of a camera to see what I had planned. My mind went to that raised dais and all the sinful things I could do. Her entire body tensed as I brought her outside the dressing room.

"Shh," I soothed. "Clara left."

"She what?"

I flashed my most devious smile. "Perks of being a prince. I have the keys, and we have all night."

I lowered her to the ground, holding her until she stabilized herself. She gave a slight nod, perhaps letting me know she trusted I wouldn't place her in a compromising position.

Her eyes betrayed the truth. Tight and terrified, her face paled. A raw, helpless feeling filled me because I didn't want to slow down, nor did I want to stop. My insides knotted with disappointment, but she hadn't yet told me no.

"You doing okay?" *How often do I need to check in?* I didn't know, and I hadn't read the manual. *Is there a manual? There has to be. Shit, I need to focus.*

She stole a backward glance to the dressing room, showing her uncertainty. My chest pinched, as I thought we would abort yet another attempt, but she turned back and pressed her finger to my chest.

An impish grin filled her face. "Maybe you should sit down, Sir."

Sit down? Why the hell would I—oh! Hell yes!

I allowed her to force me back a step and then another. It was a game because she was far too small to make me do anything. Looking over my shoulder, I shifted to the left and then plopped down in the chair. If she needed a little control, there was no way I would countermand her actions. For now, she was willing. I wasn't going to stop anything. Not when it was freely given.

And, while I craved to sample the essence of her on my tongue, the night had barely begun. As soon as I sat, she approached, looking a little turned on, and suddenly unsure. Or maybe I imagined those emotions flickering across her exquisite face.

Rowan lowered to her knees. With the briefest glance up for reassurance, she focused on my crotch. Without any hesitation, she reached for my belt and unbuckled it. The zipper of my trousers rasped as she dragged it down, opening my pants and freeing the unbearable pressure on my cock. Her silken hand reached in and gripped me, and a tiny gasp of her own echoed my sharp intake of breath.

Heaven.

Only one word fit the feeling. She began with a tentative caress, merely touching my shaft, but then her hand moved. I resisted the urge to come like a one-pump-and-done virgin. No pressure, right? I gritted my teeth and forced myself to hold on, to hold off, and to ride the edge of ecstasy brought by her amazing hand.

Freeing me, she ran her tongue over her lower teeth and then moistened her lips. Her gaze cast upward again, seeking my permission. Or so I hoped. I didn't mind if she took over completely, but there was a part of me that needed to regain control, even as she held my cock in her hand.

With a regal nod, I told her to begin. "It's dangerous to tease a prince."

"What about a Dom?"

"Even worse," I said.

"Hmm, then I definitely wouldn't want to tease you."

I hoped she meant what I thought. "I suggest you do something other than squeeze it."

"Oh!" She jumped a little, perhaps unaware that she gripped me tight.

Either she needed to move her hand or take me in her mouth. I was going insane with her holding me.

Screw this. I would take what I needed.

Leaning forward, I took control and pulled her to my cock. "Open," I said with a growl.

This was where I expected her to hesitate and pull back, but she inched forward, and settled into a more comfortable position. Her pert mouth opened and took me inside. I about died and came right then. Her rosebud lips wrapped around the flare of my cock, and her gentle eyes claimed mine. Full of nothing but trust, she waited.

While I might have enjoyed a teasing lick or a long, slow suck, the urge to fuck overcame me. I slammed forward, grinding my hips against her mouth, oblivious to whether she choked or not. The heat from her mouth encased me. My breath fled, rushing out in a ragged exhale. Locking my fingers around her head, I held her there, maybe for a little too long, but she didn't fight. Instead, the roughness of her tongue stroked the sensitive tissue under the head of my cock.

"Holy fuck," I said, pulling back.

As she locked her eyes on mine, our gazes bound us together with the force of destiny. Her lips curled around the skin of my shaft, and that wicked tongue of hers drove me insane. A shiver began at my nape and zinged down to the base of my spine, coiling there. I had a sneaking suspicion I would not last another drag of her lips down my cock. But, damn, I needed more.

With her trust held in the solidness of her gaze, I pressed forward, lifting again to bury myself deep within her mouth until the tip nudged the back of her throat. To my amazement, she never gagged, although her eyes did grow wide.

A tingle began in my balls, the sure sign of my impending release, but I wasn't yet ready for this to be done. My entire body was painfully aware and incredibly aroused with her on her knees, performing oral pleasure. If I didn't do something soon, I'd be unloading down her throat.

With a grunt, I pulled her off my cock, wanting nothing more than to ravage her amazing mouth. The look on her face, one of surprise, caught me off guard, but I didn't let it affect what I did next.

"Over there," I said, pointing to the raised dais. "Lie down, on your back, heels to your ass and knees spread."

Her eyes widened even further, looking like they would pop, but she scurried to obey, crawling the short distance to the raised platform. She positioned herself on her back, bent her knees, and scooted her heels to press against her ass. My heart came to a thudding halt.

The trifold mirrors afforded a view in nearly every direction, but my entire focus centered on the beauty displaying herself to my eyes.

"Fucking gorgeous."

Rising from the chair, I covered the distance between us in two strides. It was my turn to go to my knees, and I didn't mind that one bit. I intended to feast upon her flesh and worship this gift she gave. Only after I had her screaming my name would I unleash my fury and claim her as my own.

TWENTY-FIVE

Charter

ROWAN

Richard's fingers curled around mine as we boarded the charter for our flight back to New York.

Since we'd skipped dinner and hadn't checked into our hotel until after midnight, he'd ordered room service while I retreated to the bathroom, my mind in a tailspin. To my surprise, every outfit he'd had me try on made it to the trunk of our rental car. He'd busied himself with hanging the dresses, gowns, and even that black-and-white pantsuit into the closet in our hotel suite.

The question as to how compatible we might or might not be had been firmly and unequivocally answered in Clara's Boutique.

Two bedrooms? Something he'd arranged while I visited with Freddy. Now that our relationship had progressed, we would need only one, but it'd struck me hard.

Had he arranged for that before or after the fiasco on the plane? Had it been a show of respect or a concession of defeat?

The man had thought through every nuance and planned for every possibility. I found that admirable.

My return ticket had been canceled, and I supposed that meant Richard had firmly taken control of our next steps.

After taking separate showers last night, we'd polished off a late-night snack of sliders and wings and then crawled into bed. Was it odd how I found it funny that a prince would eat bar food? Something common and low class? I loved it, because Richard wasn't a pretentious ass. He was down to earth, even to the way he licked the wing sauce off his fingers. It made him normal, more approachable, and less intimidating.

His gentle snores might have kept me up any other night, but exhaustion had pulled me deep into slumber.

Early morning sunshine had poured through the windows and woken me first. Without knowing if he wanted room service or not, I'd packed my things, surprised to find a brand-new suitcase waiting in the living area of the suite. Even in that, he'd thought ahead. My treasure trove of designer outfits went into the suitcase and I waited for him to wake.

When he had, he'd pulled me from the couch, tossed me in bed, and made love to me until well past noon. I'd worried about missing my flight back, but he'd eased my fears, explaining the charter. We had taken a shower together. Explored every inch of each other's body. Then, we'd dressed for brunch and headed to the airport.

"Nice plane."

"Have you flown in a charter before?"

I had grown up wealthy and had rich friends, like Patrick. We flaunted our wealth.

"It's been a while."

His invisible security detail revealed themselves. They'd shadowed us the entire trip, but we would return to New York together. Richard did not introduce me, and the men all but ignored me. The only acknowledgment I received was their help in moving my luggage from the back of our car to the waiting jet.

Richard moved me to the rear of the plane. Overstuffed recliners waited there. Nestled into a private space, they would swivel and face each other once we achieved altitude. Up front, three rows of seats faced forward. His security detail filled those seats. Six large men, all who barely gave me a second glance. Although I suspected they were well paid for their discretion.

Richard buckled me in. "Once we're airborne, we can face each other."

I'd already figured that out but gave a gracious nod. This was much better than flying first-class and worlds apart from flying coach.

The single flight attendant approached Richard. "Your Royal Highness, may I get you a drink?"

He glanced at me. "Scotch on the rocks, and the lady will have a glass of champagne."

A tingle of arousal rose in my belly and settled firmly between my legs. Such a simple thing, him ordering my drink, shouldn't have this effect.

The woman moved to the front of the plane, took the drink orders of the men, and continued to the forward galley. She served Richard and me first and then passed out the other drinks as the plane taxied to the runway.

A few minutes later, we were airborne.

Twenty minutes later, Richard inducted me into the Mile-High Club in the back lavatory, one better appointed and much larger than the tiny lavatory on the flight down.

None of the men had turned around when Richard led me to the back or when we returned. Perhaps this was common behavior for their prince. My heart thudded with that thought. It was too easy to forget what he'd said about his playboy ways. Not that it should matter. We would be together for nothing more than the span of a year. Then, all this would be done.

A buzzing sounded from his jacket, and he pulled out his cell phone. I swiveled away, giving as much privacy as I could, and took the opportunity to gaze out the window.

I loved how the clouds streamed out below us. They obscured the ground and made me wonder if those below us enjoyed an overcast day or were in the middle of a deluge. From our altitude, the clouds had a darker coloring, which hinted at rain. Puffy peaks and valleys stretched out as far as I could see and made me wish, just once, that I could skim above their fantastical landscape.

When I turned back to Richard, a frown filled his face. He clutched at the cell phone, the tendons on the back of his hand rigid and taut.

"Is everything okay?" I asked although, from the look on his face, everything most definitely wasn't okay.

"What's your schedule this week?"

We hadn't really discussed my availability, and after our brief weekend, attending class was the last thing on my mind.

"I have classes from nine to three almost every day."

His jaw clenched. "And the weekend?"

"I'm free." It didn't escape me how he had not yet answered my question. I wanted to ask but had a feeling this wasn't the time to pry.

"This includes Friday?"

"That's an early day for me. I'm out by one."

"And your passport? Do you have it?"

There could only be one reason he'd asked about my passport. "If you need me to come to England, I can get out of my classes."

"No, you're to attend all your classes."

"If this is because of our agreement with—"

He gave a shake of his head and glanced at the men up front. They really were unobtrusive. I'd forgotten they were with us and almost breached the nondisclosure content of our Infidelity contract.

"I can skip out," I offered, growing more concerned.

"No. It's too easy to ask that of you, and once that starts, there will always be a reason."

"Richard…" I unbuckled and crossed the aisle to crouch in front of him. I lowered my voice. "Is everything okay?"

The muscles of his jaw bunched. It looked like he might explain, but his eyes closed, and he tilted his head against the headrest of his seat. "Nothing that concerns you, but I need to leave for England as soon as possible. I'll likely be there for more than a week."

"I can speak with my professors."

We'd just come together, and it was too early to be ripped apart.

"No," he said, "we honor our agreements, and that is a part of mine, but I need you to leave immediately after your class on Friday. I'll have a driver pick you up and bring you to the airport."

"And you?"

"I'll leave immediately."

Home? My tiny shoebox home with the dirty streets and sidewalks and a security door that was laughable at best.

"Okay," I said.

Lifting up, I kissed his brow and made to move back to my seat. His powerful arms wrapped around my waist and tugged me into his lap. Not caring about the men, he angled my face for a kiss. Not a slow, sensual thing. Not hot and hungry. This was a kiss of connecting and becoming one. Deep, passionate, and soulful, it was the stuff of fairy tales.

He pulled away, ending the electrifying contact, but kept me in his lap. Not knowing what to do, I snuggled against him. Together, we watched the clouds and the sunset. When we landed, he walked me to a waiting car. One of the security team carried my luggage and placed it in the trunk.

"I'll see you this weekend," he said, giving me one final kiss good night.

After our passion-filled weekend, this ending came far too abruptly. He didn't share, and I didn't pry.

"I'm going to miss you," I said, realizing the truth behind that statement.

He cupped my cheek and ran his thumb along my jaw. "Not as much as I'll miss you. Now, promise you'll attend every class and study extra hard."

"I will."

He leaned in, and our lips brushed chastely together. "I look forward to seeing you soon." Crooking a finger, he brought a security man over. "This is Mark Shepard. He's assigned to be your security while I'm gone."

"Hello, Miss Cartwright," he said. "It's a pleasure to meet you."

"I don't need a security detail."

"It's standard protocol, Miss Cartwright," Mark explained. "Anyone involved with a member of the Royal household requires security escort. I promise, you'll barely know I'm here."

"Well then, it's nice to meet you."

A black SUV rolled up. The remaining five men gathered bags and loaded up the rear. Richard's bag topped the pile.

He glanced over his shoulder. "That's my ride." Gripping my hands in his, he pulled me into a final hug. "I'll see you soon."

"I miss you already," I said, wondering what could possibly be pulling him away.

TWENTY-SIX

Hospital

RICHARD

ACCIDENT.
  Edmund at hospital.
  Need you immediately.
  No further details came with the message. Our individual phones had some of the most secure encryptions on the planet, but the Crown never took chances.
  What happened to Edmund? Why hadn't Mum given me more information? I hated heading into the unknown.
  "Are you ready, Your Royal Highness?"
  My security detail slipped back into proper etiquette now that we were headed home. No longer Richard, my title came to rest squarely on my shoulders.
  "I am."
  One week without tasting Rowan, touching her, making love to her—would I last? My heart said to make the call. Bring her back. Take her with me. But that wasn't how this worked. Contracts and stip-

ulations guided our actions. Her limits must be obeyed, and I couldn't violate them.

David and I had taken a few benders during our tenure at Oxford. My grades had tanked. For me, it hadn't mattered if I skipped long stretches of classes, but I'd spent many long hours making up what I'd missed under the stern eyes of royal tutors. Rowan didn't have that luxury. *And did I want that for her? Did I want her to give up her dreams to chase me around the world?*

The quick, and selfish, answer was most definitely yes, but my mother had instilled wisdom and an eye for the future in her younger son. My short-term needs weren't worth the long-term damage such a decision would make in Rowan's life.

One week. I could handle a week without her in my bed.

Seven hours of flight time brought me to London. Immediately, all the pomp and circumstance of my position smothered me. I hated every bit of it.

I missed Rowan.

The driver took me to King Edward VII's Hospital, nestled in an inconspicuous street in Marylebone. London's foremost private hospital, it played nurse to the royal family. With the presence of guards, there was no doubt my brother was inside. The car pulled up, and security detail flanked me as I entered. News hadn't made it to the populace because the streets outside were empty of pedestrian traffic. Soon, paparazzi would crowd the sidewalks.

The reception area was fittingly smart with stained glass windows and an open fireplace. A receptionist in a waistcoat and tie glanced up. Moving to his feet, he snapped to attention.

"Your Royal Highness." He handed me a ledger and then allowed me to pass after I signed.

With only fifty-six beds, the hospital catered to a wealthy and exclusive clientele. One of those rooms was reserved for the royal household. A short distance down a well-appointed corridor, a fully stocked library came into view. More fitting for a private members club than a hospital, it didn't faze me to see it here. I hadn't been kidding when I told Rowan I'd go head-to-head with her brother in a royal trivia match. My entire upbringing had been steeped in the history of my line. That library was where the Prime Minister had resigned his post back in the early sixties. Tons of trivia such as that rattled around in my head.

A yawn escaped me. Jet-lagged, my body had no idea what time it should be. Guards snapped to attention outside Edmund's room. With a rap of my knuckles, I entered. My security detail remained in the hall. One step in, and I came to a sudden and heart-thudding halt. Edmund lay in the bed, pale and wasted. Tubes and lines snaked from his body.

Mum stood beside him, cradling his hands. She looked tired and frail.

When had she grown so old? Where was her strength? Her vigor?

"What happened?"

"There was an accident," she said, blinking through her tears. "He lost control of his car and ran into a tree." She sniffed and dabbed a lace handkerchief to her nose.

"Mum," I said, "Edmund is strong. He'll get through this." I approached the opposite side of the bed and gripped his hand.

No response. He didn't react, and his limp hand lay, unmoving, in mine. A breathing tube had been inserted in his mouth and connected to a ventilator at the head of the bed.

"How worried do I need to be?"

She gave a long, slow blink. "Very."

TWENTY-SEVEN

Home
———

ROWAN

HEADING HOME TO MY POSTAGE-STAMP APARTMENT DIDN'T MAKE me happy. It wasn't that it was small. Or that there wouldn't be any food waiting. With everything that had happened, I would now have plenty of money to eat out. The check from Infidelity might or might not have dropped, but I'd be surprised if my bank account hadn't suddenly grown. My unhappiness stemmed from the realities of Richard's life.

He'd said nothing about what pulled him back to London. Not that I'd expected revelations of his personal life, but I wasn't an idiot. I'd seen that look before. It'd mirrored mine when the call came in about my father's suicide. It was a mixture of fear, desperation, desolation, and the end of the world, all mixing together in one massive holy-hell-no moment. Plastered on top of the devastation came the brave-face facade. The one I portrayed to the world. The very same one Richard had given me.

A quick search would reveal if something had happened to

any of the royal family, but my cell phone had died somewhere mid-flight. I had to wait until I got home to dig into that mystery.

But should I?

If Richard wanted me to know, he would've told me. Right?

Did I dare stress the fragile bond growing between us and ask for details? Or should I let him come to me in his own time?

These questions frustrated me. Instead of searching for answers, I turned my attention to the city outside.

"Excuse me." I tapped on Mark's shoulder. "This isn't the way to my apartment."

"Miss Cartwright," Mark said, "you're being taken to your new apartment."

New apartment? But then it hit me. Infidelity had mentioned that living expenses, accommodations, and even a daily allowance would be provided by the client.

Is it odd that I felt a pang of loss for my tiny home?

Several minutes later, we pulled up outside a steel-and-glass marvel with not one, but two doormen standing outside. One went to the trunk of the car and retrieved my bags, and the other opened my door. Mark exited as well and gave instructions while I tilted my head back and gawked.

"This way, Miss Cartwright," Mark said, leading me inside an opulent lobby.

"I live here?"

"Yes," he said, handing over a key card. "Top floor. His Royal Highness will be calling you tomorrow."

"I'm in class until three. Is there a number where I can reach him?"

Not once had Richard given me the number to his cell phone. Mark hesitated, and I understood.

"I'm sure he'll call when he can."

Evidently, I was at his disposal and not the other way around.

The elevator dinged and opened into the foyer of a luxury apartment with million-dollar views of Central Park.

Mark placed my bags down. "If there's anything you need, just call the front desk."

"I need my things from my apartment."

Richard might have bought me a new wardrobe, but it lacked the essentials, like sensible clothes for school and clean bras and panties. I'd only packed for the weekend, and I had nothing to wear. Not to mention my school books and laptop.

"All your things have been brought from your apartment," Mark said. "If there's anything else?"

"Where will you be?"

He was my security escort. Didn't that mean he needed to be nearby?

"I will be close. Rest assured, these accommodations are secure. What time do you need to be at Pratt in the morning?"

"My first class is at nine, but I like to be there about eight thirty."

"Your driver will be waiting." He pointed to a phone. "If you will call downstairs a few minutes before you're ready to leave, I will meet you here and escort you to the car."

"Thank you."

"Good night, Miss Cartwright."

"Good night."

With Mark's departure, I explored my new home. One room flowed into the next. Clean lines formed the core of the modern design. Off-white couches made of buttery-smooth leather would be great places to curl up with a book. Stainless steel appliances formed the backbone of a chef's dream kitchen. A six-burner stove wasn't something I would use. Although my culinary skills had improved in the past four months. A full-sized refrigerator and subzero freezer came stocked with prepared food. There was a list on the counter with a request for my food preferences. The open living room opened into a dining room with stark white chairs and a glass top perched on a bleached white coral pedestal. Tiny elements of the sea were everywhere. Hints of aqua blue popped here and there. Mostly in the accents, like the large floral displays sprinkled about.

I moved to the windows, floor to ceiling, which formed the outer walls. There hadn't been numbers in the elevator, but the building towered over the city. For a moment, concerns over voyeurs had me taking a step back, but I remembered some of the architectural design elements I'd been learning at Pratt. No doubt, these windows were constructed with one-way glass.

A whole week alone? How would I survive when I ached for Richard's touch, for the warmth in his eyes, and for the demands he placed upon my flesh? Yielding to him came as naturally as breathing, and his absence made me feel empty inside.

My exploration continued into the bedrooms. There were three. One had been transformed into a workout room. Another into a small workspace, which would be a perfect place to study. Someone else had already thought of that. Whoever had packed up my things from my apartment had lined up my textbooks on the bookshelves.

I saved the master bedroom for last, uncomfortable entering it alone. That didn't make sense, but it felt like Richard should be with me. He wasn't, but I needed to see if my clothes, shoes, and other things had made it over from my apartment.

All my clothes hung in precise, ordered rows in the larger of the two closets. My breath caught when I saw the bathroom. The space had been designed as a spa, one I intended to make full use of, probably later tonight. *Maybe a glass or two of wine while I soaked in that tub?*

I envisioned many nights when Richard would be called back to England. Until the end of my classes, I would be stuck here even if my heart desired to be by his side.

Uncorking a bottle of red wine, I poured a glass and brought it, and the bottle, back to the bathroom. The jetted tub called my name. My choice of scented bath soap, bath bubbles, and dissolving bath salts waited for my pleasure.

Now, to find my charging cord.

Thirty minutes later, as my fingers pruned and my body relaxed beneath the soothing water, my phone rang.

My heart stuttered a little, as I hoped it was Richard, but caller ID said otherwise.

"Hey, Patrick."

"Hey, girl. How are things? I haven't heard from you in a while."

"I'm good."

"Good? I thought you'd have something else to say."

There really was only one thing he would pester me about.

"Like what?" I teased, pretending ignorance.

"How about what it's like, dating a prince?" he exclaimed.

My stomach did another of those half-flip, half-roll things. "How did you know that?"

"Um, where have you been? Never mind because it's all over the Internet. *Prince Richard of Wales Dates Miss Rowan Cartwright, a Southern Belle with a Lineage Suitable for a Prince.*"

The bathwater sloshed as I surged up. "What?"

"That's just one of the headlines. Do you want me to read you the rest?"

"Where are you getting this?"

"You seriously haven't seen?"

"No."

"Well, my dear, you seem to have made a splash on international news. And you know the press is speculating the hell out of things."

"What does it say?"

"Hmm, looks like I piqued your interest."

"Well, no shit, Sherlock."

He laughed. "Okay, let me pull one of the tamer ones up." He cleared his throat. *"Prince Richard of Wales was spotted with Miss Rowan Cartwright, daughter of ill-fated land and banking mogul, Daniel Cartwright, on a weekend excursion to Savannah, Georgia. Reliable sources say the Prince and Miss Cartwright have been dating in secret for months. When asked where the couple had met, the source revealed a local New York nightclub noted for its edgier crowd."*

"Oh."

"So, I have to ask…" he said, drawing out his question, toying with me now.

"Don't," I said, remembering something about paparazzi being able to tap phones. "I don't think I want to discuss *that* over the phone."

"How about in person?"

"It's a little late."

"It's barely nine. I feel like I'm the last one to know all the important things, and I have questions."

"Patrick, you of all people know—"

"I know, but come on. You owe me something."

"Okay, but give me a minute. I'm not sure where I am." I hadn't looked at the address of my new building.

"Don't worry about that. I'm in the lobby."

"The lobby!"

"Yes, it's amazing how intrusive the paparazzi can be. I recognized the building from the photo. Is he there with you?"

"I'm not saying anything else on the phone. Let me get out of the bath. I'll come down and get you."

"You know, you could just buzz me up. What floor are you on?"

"Top."

"You might want to call down to the desk and tell them to let me up. I can entertain myself while you make yourself decent."

"Are you alone?"

"Yes, Cy's out of town."

"Well, hang up then, so I can call the front desk." *How the hell do I do that?*

Remembering the landline in the foyer by the elevator, I wrapped a towel around myself and padded out. A simple call to the number marked *Front Desk*, and Patrick was on his way. I disappeared back to the bedroom and slipped on a comfortable pair of sweats and a cotton sweater.

When I returned, Patrick was raiding the bar.

"Nice digs, girl."

"Thank you."

"Got any snacks?" He lifted a stopper to a bottle and sniffed. "Ah, the good stuff. You want some?"

The crystal decanter looked like it held scotch or whiskey.

I lifted my glass and held up the bottle. "I'm drinking wine."

"Well, bring it over, and tell me all about your prince."

We settled on the couch, and I began with the disastrous hook-up in the club. A couple of hours later, Patrick called for a ride home, and I snuggled into bed. It felt good to have someone to talk with about Infidelity. I hadn't gone into details. As my sponsor, Patrick understood the complexities of our arrangement. He answered a lot of my questions, like how much time he spent away from Cyrus and how that affected their relationship.

Pulling the covers tight below my neck, I spiraled into dreams of kneeling before Richard and other delicious things.

One night.

One blissful night.

I prayed we would have many more.

TWENTY-EIGHT

Heir

RICHARD

Mum and I sat vigil. My eyes burned with fatigue, and I ached to crawl into bed, preferably one with Rowan in it. The few times I'd dozed off, memories of our night had drifted into my dreams.

"You're falling asleep again," Mum said, snapping me awake.

"I've had a long day." A sleepless night with Rowan, followed by a flight through the night, topped by vigil over my brother's broken body, and I'd passed exhausted hours ago.

"We've both had long days," Mum said, dismissing my exhaustion. "We need to discuss what happens next." The sharpness of her words snapped at me.

"No, we don't." I refused to believe Edmund wouldn't pull through.

"We need to talk."

"Why don't we wait to hear what the doctors have to say

first?" Her lack of faith made my jaw clench and my fingers curl tight.

"You know what they're going to say."

She'd cried through the night, and I had done little to offer comfort.

"I don't want to talk about it. Edmund will pull through." Maybe, if I said it with enough conviction, my faith would make it happen.

"You've always been too quick to speak when you should stay silent," she said, chastising me. "We're going to have this talk because I know what they're going to say. Even if Edmund survives this injury, the swelling on his brain—"

"Can get better with time." My voice threatened to crack, but I kept it steady and strong, even as I fell apart inside.

She blew out a breath. "I was here when they brought him in. I saw the initial scans. While you were flying home, I was talking with his physicians. If he survives, the brain damage will be extensive. He's no longer fit to rule. You need to prepare yourself."

"I won't!" I yelled. Then, lowering my voice, I continued in a whisper, "I can't."

Despite the distance that separated us, I truly loved my brother. When we were younger, he'd lorded his birthright over me. I'd hated him for it. To say it'd caused friction would be an understatement. I didn't deny that. With time and wisdom, I had come to accept my place and found happiness in the freedom of living without the oppressive weight of that obligation. After being the butt of all the jokes growing up and being dubbed Richard the Spare Heir, this couldn't be happening. I hadn't been groomed to rule. The crown wasn't meant to be mine.

"You will be the future King of England." She placed her hand over mine.

I leaned over the frail form of my brother. "How can you give up so easily?"

Her scowl was deep enough to darken the room, but I held her stare with a greater force of will.

"I have not given up. He's my son. I want nothing more than for him to open his eyes, but I'm also the Queen of England. I must plan for the future. You need to be prepared to do the same."

My place was beside my brother, supporting him as the future king, not stealing his crown.

"We won't have privacy for long," she said, "and we need to discuss succession."

"What's there to discuss?" My entire world tipped on its axis.

She tilted her head. "You need to think of your heirs." Pushing away from the bed, she walked to the window. "It seems news has finally broke." Glancing down, she pursed her lips. "It's time to come home," she said, making her statement a proclamation. "Your jaunt across the pond is at an end. We will present a brave and united face to the world. You need to settle down. You can't chase every pretty thing. I've seen the photos of your latest fling. You must to find a suitable bride. England needs to know the future of the Crown is secure."

Her words slammed into me with the full force of a regal command. My chest ached, and my breath splintered. I couldn't leave Rowan, not when she'd tunneled deep inside to become a part of me.

"You need to meet Rowan before you dismiss her that easily."

"She's an American."

"So?"

"Her father was an embezzler, and she has no—"

"Her family is one of the most prominent names in the South. Her heritage stretches back generations. You couldn't ask for a better lineage." If it was all about establishing bloodlines appropriate for the crown, Rowan had that in spades. "Sure, her father made mistakes. He paid for them."

"He took his own life, Richard. That's hardly admirable."

"I'm not interested in Rowan's father." I firmed my voice. "If you're concerned over her pedigree, look again, Mum."

"The crown needs the stability of a vetted union, one which strengthens the family. No matter her pedigree, the girl is destitute." Her lips pressed into a thin slit and then twisted with displeasure. Deep, linear lines furrowed my mother's face, making her look shrewish. "You will cut ties with her. There's no reason to return to New York. That relationship ends now."

I tempered the anger boiling to the surface. Thoughts of ending things with Rowan made my chest squeeze and my heart splinter. "You cannot decree whom I do and do not date."

"No," she said, her lips pinching even tighter, "but I do control who you marry. As long as I'm alive, I will not sanction that relationship. It's best to end it before she entangles herself any further in your life."

I turned to my brother, stunned by how fragile he looked.

Edmund had always been taller, stronger, smarter, more vigorous, and definitely more kingly than me. Despite the animosity lingering between us, I did not wish this upon him, but I had to accept the truth. He would not be recovering from this. That meant, my obligations to the crown had to come first from here on out, but I wasn't yet done with Rowan.

I gritted my teeth and faced my mother. "I decide when to end things with her, not you."

In a year, it wouldn't matter. In a year, Rowan would walk away, and I would head to my destiny.

TWENTY-NINE

One Week

Rowan

One week of class dragged for what seemed like an eternity. I barely paid attention and almost missed turning in two assignments. I couldn't concentrate and most certainly couldn't focus on studies. Not while ambling around that empty penthouse until all hours of the night. It was huge, lonely, and barren of any of Richard's things. There was nothing to remind me of him, and without that, it was as if he didn't exist.

What emergency pulled him home?

My gut fluttered as I thought about the first tentative steps we'd taken. My skin heated and burned while I trailed my fingers over my body, imagining they were him. But my ill-fated attempts to force my pleasure only left me needing for him more.

My footsteps thundered in the stillness that hung everywhere. I tried all the rooms, searching for a spot that didn't feel lonely. Even the tub with bubbles failed to soothe the ache I felt.

I missed Richard.

I missed his touch. The passion of his kisses and the sternness of his tone when he commanded me to kneel were constant partners in my dreams. I missed lowering down to please him. I missed hours of clawing at the sheets while he brought me to heights of pleasure I never knew existed.

Instead of studying, I combed the Internet and found hundreds of articles about dominance and submission and all manner of things associated with them. The one night we'd spent together barely scratched the surface of what others had experienced, but it'd left an indelible mark on my soul. I wanted to explore the desires burning within me. Richard would be my guide, coaching, leading, and becoming the pillar of strength I sorely needed him to be.

With each passing day, my yearning intensified. The desire to see, touch, and breathe him deep into my soul became a constant ache.

As Friday approached, my excitement brimmed to overflowing. Now, here I was bouncing on my feet, impatiently watching Mark load our suitcases into the back of the car.

Richard and I would soon be together, but I worried. I hadn't heard from him since he left.

The first account of the Prince of Wales's accident had been on the front page of a smattering of magazines on a sidewalk vendor's display on Tuesday. Since then, speculation had run through print, television, and even Internet sites. The palace remained quiet on the state of his health. The royal family had been seen going in and out of the hospital where rumor said Prince Edmund was a patient. I had seen the haggard expression on Richard's face. Maybe I'd read too much into what I saw, but he wore the same mask of grief I knew all too well.

Class had gotten out at one, and by five, Mark and I were heading over the Atlantic. I unfolded a blanket and spread it over my lap. I didn't think it was possible to arrive well rested, but I planned to try. I didn't want the specter of fatigue to ruin the few hours Richard and I would share.

With the time change, we arrived early Saturday morning, London time. I still had no direct access to Richard, but Mark assured me I would see him later that night. Despite catching some sleep, it surprised me how exhausted I felt. Not good.

In my years abroad, the one country I had never been to was England. My travels had brought me to Italy, Germany, Spain, France, and Greece. Mostly, I'd stayed where the temperatures were warm, the waters crystal clear, and where I could rub shoulders with others who were rich like me. Correction, rich like I had once been.

While I thought I'd check into a hotel, Mark took me to what he described was one of Richard's private residences. I didn't fail to catch that this was merely one of many. The well-appointed townhouse took up half of a block. I expected armed guards out front, but if there was security, I couldn't find them. Cameras pointed down all around the entrances, and our driver pulled through a covered entrance to a courtyard out back where we unloaded.

A butler approached. "Miss Cartwright, welcome to Templeton Place."

"Thank you," I said, a little overwhelmed.

He led me through the opulent estate, full of old-world charm and intermixed with modern touches, and up a sweeping staircase until we reached a suite of rooms.

"Your rooms." He gestured for me to enter ahead of him and then gave a brief tour of the four-room suite. "His Royal Highness will be here later tonight. Until then, you are free to do as you wish. Templeton is equipped with a library, if that pleases you, and I left the Internet passcode on the nightstand beside your bed."

"Thank you," I said, stunned by the linen-coated walls, the

falls of silk cascading down the windows, and the carved dark wood of the dresser, nightstands, and canopy bed. This was a place for a princess, not a washed-up Southern belle.

While late morning local time, my body insisted it was still the middle of the night. With a short weekend ahead of me, I didn't know if it would be best to accommodate to local time or keep to New York time. With the amount of yawning I was doing, a nap sounded divine.

"If you need anything, you may ring," the butler explained. "Any of the staff can assist you."

"I think I'll take a short nap."

"As you wish. I'll let the staff know."

"Thank you."

During that entire exchange, he never once introduced himself. If I wanted to head out of my room and ask for help, I'd have to shout, *Hey you!* Surprising for a butler not to give his name. Maybe my status had been measured, weighed, and found lacking? I was an American girl flown in for a booty call. What did that make me?

I needed to process that.

In the meantime, I would be well rested for when Richard did show up. There had been no further information about the Prince of Wales. I prayed for his recovery and hoped Richard would be able to get away. I was selfish like that.

I grabbed my bag and pulled out my toiletries. The envelope from Freddy's home fell out. I'd forgotten all about it, and I set it on the nightstand with the intent to look at it later.

A short shower invigorated me, pushing back some of my fatigue, but I needed rest. Since I hadn't packed anything but lingerie, I decided to sleep in the nude.

I ran my hands across the fine linen sheets, buttery smooth to the touch. A faint scent of rose and lilac filled my senses and relaxed my tired body. Although late spring, a chill hung in the air. Fancy as this residence was, Richard's staff appeared to be a little skimpy on the heat. It didn't matter because, once I crawled under the covers, I couldn't have been more comfortable.

Maybe I'd take a peek at those documents. The adhesive on the manila envelope fought me, and I wound up ripping through the thick paper.

Snuggling in, I scanned the documents. It said something about a trust and had little sticky tabs for signatures. Too tired to focus, I allowed myself to doze.

Concerns over Richard spiraled in my mind. Memories of the night my father had taken his life stabbed deep into my heart. I would never understand why he'd made that choice. Freddy needed him, and I missed him dearly. I floated in a fog until everything faded, and I slipped into troubled sleep.

Pillowy-soft lips pressing against my mouth woke me.

"Good afternoon, my sweet Rowan."

Peeking through sleep-laden lids, I grabbed Richard by the neck and chased that decadent kiss.

"Richard!" I tugged him tight. "I missed you."

"And I, you," he said, looking tired and worn. "How was your week?"

"Too long," I said and then hesitated. Did I ask about his? Or did I pretend I didn't know what the entire world had been talking about for the past week? "How's your brother?"

Pain filled his features. "Holding on. Thank you for asking."

I chose not to pry. He would either share or not, but for now, he was all mine once again.

THIRTY

Papers

RICHARD

I RAN MY FINGERS THROUGH ROWAN'S HAIR AND BREATHED IN HER light fragrance. I didn't know if it was her shampoo, perfume, or natural scent, but it sent signals straight to my cock, telling me to claim her now. My lips ghosted along her cheek, and I nipped a trail down her neck where I paused to linger in the hollow of her throat, nuzzling and remembering how she made me feel.

Complete.

The covers dropped and revealed the creamy expanse of a bare breast. My body reacted, vibrating with an unbearable need to devour until I'd tasted every square inch of her delicious body. I lifted the downy cover and peeked beneath the sheet. Her cheeks turned a wonderful shade of pink.

"For me?"

"I wish that answer were a yes, but sadly, it was more an issue of practicality."

"Really?"

"I didn't pack PJs, and they told me you wouldn't be here until much later."

I laughed. "Well, I'm pleasantly surprised."

Before she could cover herself, I cupped her ivory breast, loving the way it fit perfectly in my hand. Her nipple peaked into a tight little bud, encouraging my next move. I dipped down and took her nipple in my mouth, happy with her gasp of pleasure. Rowan thrust her breast into my hand. I licked and sucked and treasured our reconnection.

Staring down, I memorized her face. I couldn't bear an ocean separating me from this amazing creature. Her presence made my blood sing and heart swell with disparate emotions. Hope for a life forever entwined with her shouldn't bring such sorrow.

I pulled in a breath. That would come later. For now, my cheeks filled with a grin, and I nuzzled her breasts, breathing in her essence and making it mine. Then, I placed my hand on her hip, lightly stroking my thumb against her skin. My entire body stilled, wired and vibrating with an unbearable need.

"I've fantasized about seeing you again."

I kissed her midsection and ran my tongue around her belly button. Her body arched into me.

"It's been the longest week. I want to trace every inch of your beautiful skin. I should crawl beside you and make sure everything is as I remember."

Her light laughter warmed the room and filled my heart. Was it too much to wish for an endless future spinning out in front of us? One that didn't come with an expiration date? My mother's words ghosted in my mind, but for now, obligation would take a backseat to other more carnal desires.

Her body stilled, and I could barely tell she was breathing. I knelt and dragged the covers to expose her nakedness to my gaze.

"So fucking gorgeous."

"Richard," she said, breathing softly. The need simmering in her eyes met mine.

I shifted, positioning her until I was settled between her golden legs. Her trim mound beckoned to me, and her essence flooded my senses, driving an insatiable hunger. Sliding my arms beneath her legs, I buried my face between her thighs and took what was mine. Her hands tangled in my hair while I licked and sucked. The taste of her drove me insane. As she wove her fingers through my hair, I drove her to orgasm until she screamed. I held her through the aftershocks, loving the way her body shook with the pleasure I'd delivered.

She shifted, putting her weight on her elbows, and captured my gaze. "Now, that was one hell of a hello," she said with the fiery brilliance of a well-satisfied woman.

I'd put that look on her face.

I licked her juices off my lower lip and rubbed at her wetness coating my chin. "You're fucking amazing."

Her smile broke my heart, sundered it to pieces, but I didn't care. She would catch the shattered remains and weave them into her soul, right where I belonged, making me stronger than before.

She touched her neck. "I owe you an orgasm, Sir."

Her cheeky grin brought a smile to my face and then a frown. My breath caught, realizing what I'd done. What I was about to do. Wouldn't that be crass? To fly her in for nothing but a romp in the sheets? My actions confirmed exactly what my mother had thought about Rowan being nothing more than my American fling. Rowan deserved better.

"Come, let's get you up. Have you ever been to London before?"

Her brows furrowed, and her body stilled. "Don't you want…"

"More than anything in the world, but that's not why I

brought you here. I'm interested in you." And that was the truth. My needs would be met. I planned on fucking her later tonight with all the passionate fury caged within me.

My staff thought exactly what my mother did, but unlike her, they would stay silent and keep their disapproval to themselves. Rowan wasn't the first woman I'd brought here for an evening liaison. The courtyard and rear entrance had been built to shield the prying eyes of paparazzi from my intimate rendezvous. I didn't want that for Rowan even if that was exactly what this might be.

And that was the problem. I was paying for the privilege of having her all to myself, but I wanted something more. I wanted her to choose me, but I also knew she could refuse.

My staff knew what I did with the women I brought here, and I hated that they'd put Rowan in that same class. It mattered to me that they respected her as a person and not as the plaything of a prince.

"We'll have plenty of time later tonight," I said, coming to a conclusion.

With a slap to her ass cheek, she squeaked as I propelled her from the bed. A stack of papers fell to the floor, and I bent to retrieve them while she went to put on clothes.

The quick peek violated her privacy, but I couldn't resist, and then my eyes grew wide. I should have stopped, but I scanned the documents, growing confused. As I was accustomed to the legal language buried in contracts, my hackles rose.

"Rowan," I called out as I carried the stack of papers to the bathroom.

"Yes?" She peeked out from the bathroom, arms wrapped around her back as she latched her bra.

"What is this?" I held out the papers.

"Oh"—she ducked back inside, and her voice muffled—"those were dropped off for Freddy to sign."

"Your brother is allowed to sign legal documents?" Maybe I'd assumed too much about his mental faculties, but it seemed off for an autistic man living in a group home to be signing away his inheritance.

"Yes, and no. Father never wanted to take that from him. He's not supposed to sign anything without me looking at it first. Freddy knows this."

"Have you read these?"

"I forgot about them, to be honest. I was distracted by a prince. I've been moping ever since."

"Moping? Why were you moping?"

She poked her head out the doorway. "I missed you, silly." A few moments later, she emerged, wearing the pants and blouse I'd bought at Clara's Boutique. "Is this okay? I almost brought jeans, but I'm not sure how I'm supposed to dress. I've never dated a prince before."

I glanced at the ballet flats on her feet. "As long as you promise not to leave a slipper behind."

A tiny grin curved the corners of her mouth. "I promise."

Lifting the papers, I circled back to my concerns. "You need to read these."

"Oh, I will. Maybe on the flight back though. I don't want to waste any of the time we have together."

My lips pursed because I wanted the same. "I looked at the documents. Please forgive me for prying. I didn't mean to invade your privacy. But I thought you'd lost everything?"

A frown replaced her smile. She headed back to the bedroom. "If you're talking about my finances, the only things not repossessed were the funds in my and Freddy's accounts. Our trust funds took a beating with the legal fees, Freddy's expenses, my tuition, and rent. There's nothing left. Why? You know all this."

"Did you know you have another trust fund?"

"I don't," she said with absolute assurance. "Only the one."

Now, things really didn't make sense.

"You need to sit down."

THIRTY-ONE

Trust

ROWAN

Richard helped me sit. I perched on the edge of the bed and thumbed through the papers, but my eyes lost focus. Then, my grip slipped, and the entire stack fell to the floor.

Richard knelt and gathered the papers. He didn't hand them back because my hands were shaking too hard. Instead, he retreated to the living area of my suite and the large secretary desk. There, he meticulously put the papers back in order. I sat, stunned, and convinced myself that Richard had misunderstood.

"Come," he said. When I didn't move, his voice turned deep and commanding. "Rowan, come here."

His order had my feet moving of their own volition. My body floated between the bed and the other room, and somehow, I sat in the chair he held out for me. My mind remained back in the bedroom, swirling with confusion and denial.

Several neat piles sat on the desk.

"This is a standard introductory statement," he said. "Nothing important, except for instructions on where to sign."

My attention went to the smallest of the piles.

"This one"—he pointed to the next stack—"details a trust you and Freddy inherited from your mother. According to this report, it's far from empty."

"I don't understand. Henry told me the funds had been depleted."

"I'm not talking about funds. And who is Henry?"

"His firm provides legal and accounting services and has been involved in Cartwright business for generations." If there was an additional trust, why hadn't Henry mentioned it? "Who established the trust?"

He glanced at the second stack. "Your great-grandfather on your mother's side. Is that where your family's wealth came from?"

Most of the family land acquisition had been the direct result of my great-grandfather's efforts during the Depression. Back then, land had been cheap—at least, for those with money. Families had lost their farms. Cartwright banks had held the liens and taken ownership of the land when it defaulted.

"I don't know. My parents shared everything. I assumed it'd all gone to my father after my mother's death. What does the rest of it say?"

My mother's death wasn't something I generally thought about. She'd died when Freddy and I were infants. Other than pictures, I had no memories of a mother.

"Well, that will take some time, but it's a listing of land deeds. You and Freddy hold joint interest."

My stomach clenched, and I grabbed at my midsection. I didn't like the direction this was headed.

He flipped through the third and thickest stack. "We need to figure out how much this is worth."

"How? I can't ask Henry. Not when he's been keeping this from me."

"I might be able to help with that." He stroked my hair. "I mean, if you want my help. I don't want to presume."

"Thanks," I said. "I do, and thank you. I wouldn't know where to start." My stomach tumbled in my belly, light and unsettled.

This was big. Huge. If this was available to me, why had Henry pushed marriage as the solution to my problems?

He held up the third pile with the listing of holdings. "My friend David can help. He's a real estate attorney in New York. Anything he can't sort out, he knows someone who can."

"Thank you," I said, feeling a little more settled. "What's in the last stack?"

I pressed my fist against my midsection, fighting the nausea threatening to overcome me. Shady land deals? A secret trust? What else did Henry have up his sleeve?

"It's going to be all right."

My entire body shook. "What if he sends another copy? What happens if Freddy signs?"

He kissed the top of my head. "Let me get this scanned and sent to David."

"How much do you think is there?"

"Sweet Rowan, I don't know, but there are pages and pages."

"I want to shoot Henry." Anger bubbled to the surface, and I curled my fingers into a fist.

He laughed. "How about you don't shoot anyone? I don't want to have to visit you in jail."

I wiped at my tears. "I didn't mean to ruin our weekend."

He dipped down, bringing his eyes in line with mine. "It's impossible to ruin our weekend. We're together, and that's all that matters. You're mine to take care of, sweet Rowan. I want all of you, even the difficult parts."

I smiled at him. "I want you, too. Is that crazy when we barely know each other?"

"I've thought of nothing but the unforgettable woman I met in the club. I haven't stopped thinking about you, and it feels like I've known you my entire life."

My cheeks heated. I hadn't stopped thinking about him either. Only now, all I could think of was Freddy. I needed to protect him from a man I had thought to call a friend.

"I need to get home," I said.

"I know, but first…" He gathered up the papers and put them into one pile. "Let's take care of this. I'll get David working. He's going to need time. Then, let's enjoy what's left of our day. I hate to lose you so soon."

"Sounds wonderful."

He gripped my hand. "Now, scrub those tears from your cheeks. I'll meet you in the library."

I did just that. I shed my tears and wiped my cheeks. I even took time to apply makeup. After fifteen minutes, I emerged from my room and located the library after only two wrong turns. Determined to enjoy the rest of my evening, I put a smile on my face, and my steps lightened. When I walked into the library, I came to a heart-stopping halt.

Tears were streaming down Richard's face.

THIRTY-TWO

Wait

RICHARD

"What happened?" Rowan's words called out from the hall.

But I didn't react. I couldn't.

I'd explained her situation to David. He'd promised to look into Rowan's trust. I'd made a note to look into Henry Porter and sent a text to my security team. My butler had taken the documents to scan. Then, the call had come, and my world had crumbled.

Edmund had passed.

"Richard?"

Rowan's light fragrance flooded my senses. She sat on the arm of the chair, wiped my tears, and then wrapped her arms around my neck.

A dam broke within me, and I folded her into me, needing the comfort of her in my arms. I let out my pain.

She said nothing while choking sobs spilled from my lungs.

Her tiny arms gripped me hard. I took in a deep pull of air and blinked free of the tears. Now was not the time to be weak. Not when the country needed me to be strong.

My voice decided to abandon me, but with a swallow past my grief, I managed to clear my throat.

The concern in her huge bluebell eyes latched on to my heart and gave me the strength to find my voice. Her fingertips caressed the side of my face, and I leaned into her warmth and support.

I grabbed her hand and twisted my fingers with hers, needing a more solid connection. "My brother passed." The sharp pain in my chest crippled me, and it took several long moments to gather my thoughts.

What do I need to do?

Fortunately, not much. Like the death of a monarch, the death of the heir to the throne was a well-planned affair. The official news would be announced by Buckingham Palace in the morning. Obituaries had been drafted in advance. We all had one prepared for emergencies.

"I'm sorry," she said and then kissed my cheek. "I'm so very sorry."

"Thank you," I said, trying to take a breath. I didn't think this pain would ease anytime soon.

"What can I do?"

I hugged her tight. "Just sit with me for a moment."

A moment was all we would have. Protocol demanded I go to the hospital. The staff would prepare my brother's body for transport to Buckingham Palace where he would lay in rest until a full-state funeral. Rowan wouldn't be allowed by my side. My mother would never condone it, and I wouldn't insist upon it. Not yet.

It had taken months to find Rowan. Now, after only a couple of hours together, I had to send her away. The universe was conspiring against us.

Shock ripped through my body with a sudden realization. With Edmund's death, I was now the Prince of Wales and heir to the throne of England. The formalities would come later. I would tour Scotland, Northern Ireland, and Wales to officially meet my people as their future king.

Could Rowan's and my timing be any worse?

I didn't think it possible.

"I'm supposed to tell you it'll get better," she said, "but it doesn't. I promised not to lie to you. It hurts, and it sucks, and then it hurts even more. It's the worst possible thing. I'm here for you. Whatever you need, I'm here."

"Thank you."

She knew exactly how I felt. It hadn't been that long since she lost her father. *Who had stood beside her when the news of his suicide came?* I couldn't imagine having to go through that alone.

"What happens now?" she asked.

I explained protocol. It helped to go over the formalities of state because it made my brother's passing feel a little less real—at least for a moment. It gave me time to catch my breath and absorb the implications of how my life would change.

"I see," she said after my words came to a halting stop. "Is there any way we can keep in touch?"

The hesitation in her question hinted at her state of mind. I wasn't the only one whose life had been irrevocably changed.

Her place would not be by my side. It couldn't be. The status of my rank disallowed that. Even through the agony ripping through my soul, her pain slammed into me. It mirrored mine.

I needed her now more than ever, someone with whom I could be both strong and painfully weak. She slid into my lap. For the next few minutes, she held me while I mourned my loss—at least, until my butler, George, returned.

"Your Royal Highness," he said with a clearing of his throat. "Your car is waiting."

I lifted my hand, letting him know I'd heard but also giving a dismissal. I would leave when I was ready. A minute or two more with Rowan wouldn't matter.

"You have to go, don't you?" The sigh in her breath told me she wanted to say more.

I could guess what that might be. She was an intelligent woman. It was what I respected most, but I didn't have the strength to give her the reassurances she needed. We'd agreed there would be no lies between us.

"I do."

She brushed back the hair from my forehead and stared deep into my eyes. "We have a year. We still have time."

"You're amazing."

My previous plans for a city tour, dinner, and a passionate night in bed seemed trite and inconsequential when placed beside the death of my brother.

"Do you have your phone with you?"

"I left it charging upstairs."

My mind wasn't working on full capacity. The conversations I wanted to share wouldn't be possible on an unsecured line.

"Mark will provide you with an encrypted phone. We can talk using that. I don't know how long it will be before—"

Her pillowy lips brushed against mine. "Family comes first. You lost your brother, and you need to grieve. Official duties will make that challenging, and having me here while you juggle all of that is impossible. I'll be waiting in New York. I'm not going anywhere."

"No," I said, "you're not."

Now, how to convince my mother to let me keep her?

THIRTY-THREE

Sponsor

ROWAN

I waved to Richard as his car drove away. He'd asked if I wanted to keep my flight back to New York the following evening, but the last thing I wanted was to wander around his London residence alone. I could do that in the penthouse, and I could relax there. Even if there were no personal effects of his to remind me of him, I considered it our home.

I could cry there without the judgmental eyes of strangers and whispers behind my back.

How long we would be separated wasn't clear. I hadn't asked, and he hadn't said.

"Miss Cartwright," Mark said, "if we're to catch our flight, we must leave."

"Okay, it won't take me long to pack."

I climbed the long, sweeping staircase to my suite.

In half an hour, Mark and I were back at the airport. I'd been in London barely ten hours. A part of me wished to stay and comfort Richard as I could, but I didn't want him worrying about entertaining me when his focus needed to be on his family and country.

Another seven hours brought me to New York. In all, I had been gone less than a day, and I'd spent less than two hours with Richard.

Mark left me with an apologetic smile, perhaps understanding my tenuous role. Exhaustion from two transatlantic flights had me crawling under the covers, and I barely felt my head touch the pillow.

A harsh ring the next day brought me to sudden and painful awareness. Thinking it was Richard, I answered, too asleep to realize it was my cell phone, not the encrypted one Richard had provided.

"Hello?"

"Rowan Cartwright?" The voice was unfamiliar.

"Yes?"

"This is David, Richard's friend. I was wondering if we could meet."

"What time is it?"

He gave a soft laugh. "It's ten."

"Ten?"

"Yes."

"I'm sorry. You woke me from a dead sleep."

"Perhaps we could meet after lunch? I'd like to come to your place. I have a few things of Richard's to bring."

"Of course." If he was bringing Richard's things, maybe the echoing penthouse wouldn't feel so lonely.

"Is noon too soon?"

"That's perfect."

After hanging up, I worked out the kinks in my muscles. Hopefully, David would bring Richard's clothes. My nights would be much easier if I could cuddle in one of his shirts.

Two hours didn't leave much time, but I managed to shower and make myself look presentable a few minutes before David arrived. When he did, two burly men accompanied him pushing carts stacked with boxes.

"Is there someplace you want the boxes?" David asked.

I pointed to an empty space on the floor. "There is fine."

"There's more. I'll bring the rest over later."

David was dressed in a smart business suit and carried a satchel over his shoulder. He was a strikingly handsome man. After the two men unloaded the boxes, he gave them a tip and then turned to me.

"Miss Rowan Cartwright, I have to say, you're a breath of fresh air."

"I am?"

"Yes, Richard has not stopped talking about you—all good things."

Heat rose to my cheeks, and I hoped he didn't notice my blush. The twinkle in his eyes said otherwise.

"Can I interest you in lunch?" he asked.

My gaze latched on to the satchel. It looked full, and that made me nervous.

"Do you mind if we order in?"

The thought of facing the crowds of New York left me less than enthused, and I didn't know what David might share with me.

He gave a soft laugh. "Not at all."

We agreed on Thai.

David unslung the satchel from his shoulder and took a moment to look around. "Now, I know why he chose to stay at my place."

"Why's that?"

"This place feels…"

"Empty? Cavernous? Huge?"

He smirked. "Something like that. Look, why don't you let Evelyn and I take you around town while Richard's away?"

"You don't have to do that."

"Consider it my pleasure. Besides, it'll be great networking. Richard says you're a design student at Pratt?"

"Architecture, but I study interior design as well."

"Then, you'll want to meet Evelyn. She knows a lot of movers and shakers always looking for fresh talent."

My insides lit up with a tingle of excitement for my future. These contacts could very well lead to a promising career. Patrick had mentioned he would put my name out to some of his contacts in the industry, but this was simply one more foot in the door.

"Wow, thank you. Of course, I'd love to."

It was the first time I'd considered what might happen after Infidelity. I didn't like the twisting in my gut or the sharp pain in my chest.

"Now"—his voice turned serious—"how about we talk about what Richard sent over?"

"I appreciate your help."

"I'd do anything for Richard."

What had Richard said to his friend? After the past twenty-four hours, my position in Richard's life felt tenuous, but David's praise gave me hope.

He headed to the dining table and pulled out a thick stack of papers from his satchel. "I have a few questions before we begin. Who is Henry Porter?"

"He handled my father's business accounts."

"Richard told me about your father. I'm very sorry." He laid out the papers. "Why don't you sit down? I need to explain this trust."

By the time our food arrived, I was no longer hungry. In fact, I was sick to my stomach.

"I need to get to Freddy," I said, "before Henry sends anyone else over with more papers to sign."

"How about today?"

"Today? I can't manage a trip to Georgia on this short of a notice."

"Richard left specific instructions," David said. "I'm not allowed to take you away from your studies. This needs to be handled urgently. And I have carte blanche to use his resources. Now, try and eat a little food. The plane is waiting."

I'd forgotten about the plane. While David stepped away to make arrangements, I tried to eat. Perhaps I should have felt anger toward Henry, but I was too shocked by the magnitude of his deceit. His father and mine had been friends forever. Why did he betray me? It didn't make sense, but numbers didn't lie.

My accounts had been drained faster than they should have been. David had been exceptionally thorough. As for this hidden trust, Henry couldn't touch it unless my brother signed over the rights to his share. There were nearly two hundred million reasons why Henry wanted guardianship over Freddy. All those reasons were tied up in land curated by his company over the generations. Henry wanted control, and it twisted my gut knowing he intended to cheat Freddy and me out of our inheritance. He hadn't approached me yet, but I wondered if it was tied to the arranged marriage he'd proposed.

Two hundred million in real estate. The number boggled my mind. I'd gone from destitute to wealthy in the blink of an eye.

My cell phone buzzed with, of all things, an incoming text from Henry.

Brent Parker has expressed concerns, given recent media coverage. Call me as soon as you get this.

David glanced down and read the text. "Rowan," he said, his tone heightening with concern, "how do you know Brent Parker?"

"With my recent financial difficulties, Henry facilitated a… well, it's kind of embarrassing."

"I need to know."

"Henry arranged a marriage. My family connections are important to Brent Parker. It has something to do with development plans in Georgia. In return, he's agreed to ensure Freddy's expenses are taken care of, mine as well. I agreed to the marriage, but then I was matched…um, I met Richard. Why are you asking about Brent Parker?" Although I already knew; it wasn't hard to piece that puzzle together.

"That's one of the names that keeps coming up when I search the properties in that trust. Brent Parker is a major investor in the proposed development of that land."

"I need to talk to Freddy."

He gathered the papers. "Come, let's see your brother."

THIRTY-FOUR

Library

Rowan

Freddy didn't take well to the unplanned visit. It took two hours to calm him before he stopped flapping his arms and crying out, "No visit. No visit. No visit."

Only after I wrapped him in a hug and wrestled him to the ground did his outburst fade. He settled into his favorite reading chair and allowed me to perch on the seat of a bay window looking out over the grounds. Spring had come to the South, and the budding of leaves coated the trees with a light tinge of green.

"Freddy, has anyone asked you to sign your name on paper?"

He shook his head. "You're not supposed to be here."

"I know it's not visiting time, and I'll be back in three Saturdays to visit with Rex and Sally. I want to feed Rex."

"Rex can't wait that long to eat, silly."

"I know, but you feed them on Fridays. I was hoping you could feed them on Saturday when I see you again."

"Okay." His head bobbed. "Why are you here?"

"I appreciate you letting me see you. I know Sundays are your reading days."

His attention shifted to the stacks of books.

I pressed on. "I need to tell you something important."

David hovered nearby, which meant finding a chair as far away as possible and pretending to read while Freddy and I talked. The explanation about Henry wasn't easy, but I broke it down. Freddy was smart, but if I didn't present the facts in a logical line of cause and effect, he wouldn't understand. His world was very black and white. I had to keep it simple and tell him Henry was a bad man who did bad things and that Freddy didn't need to be speaking with him anymore.

"Who's your friend?" Freddy asked. "That's not the prince."

I smiled. "No, he's not. But David is a good friend of Richard's."

"Maybe you can bring Richard to your visit? He might want to feed Sally."

"He's in England. Did you hear what happened?"

"I don't watch the news. It's depressing."

"His brother died."

His mouth rounded with surprise. "That means, Richard will be king."

"Yes."

"Oh." His face clouded over with pain. "Tell him I'm sorry. Is that what I'm supposed to say? That I'm sorry?"

"Yes, it is, and I'm sure he'll appreciate you thinking about him."

"So, who's David?"

"He's the one who found out about the trust I told you about. Do you understand what that means?"

"I do. Mom had land and gave it to us when she died."

The clock in the library struck six o'clock, and one of the staff entered. "Miss Cartwright, visiting hours are over."

I turned, not with irritation, but with gratitude for the privacy she'd allowed. Out of the corner of my eye, I had caught her shuttling residents away from the library while Freddy and I talked.

"Thank you." Turning to Freddy, I ran my finger along his sleeve. "I'm going to miss you."

"Miss you, too," he said, mirroring my good-bye.

During the two-hour flight back to New York, David explained the conditions of the trust.

"What do we do now? What do I do about Henry?"

Henry's text sat on my cell phone, unanswered. There was no way to tell how long before he found out I'd subverted his plans, and I feared retribution. I adored Henry—or had. Now, I didn't know what to think.

"Don't engage with Henry."

THIRTY-FIVE

To-Do

ROWAN

BASED UPON DAVID'S ADVICE, I SENT A NOTICE TO FREDDY'S home, ensuring Henry and anyone from his firm weren't able to gain access to my brother. Legally, my guardianship sheltered him, but physically? Fear pricked at my gut, and I considered pulling Freddy out of the home. But subject Freddy to a move?

Richard's phone burned a hole in my pocket. Too many times, I pulled it out of my purse and flicked it on, needing his guidance. No message. My fingers danced over the keys while I struggled with whether to reach out. The need to feel his touch, if even through the phone, pulled at me. Rubbing my face, I tucked the phone away and let the ghost of a smile curl my lips.

David didn't miss much because his eyes angled to my purse. "Give him some time, Rowan," he said. "You mean more to him than you realize. More than I think even he realizes."

"I know." But it hurt.

David dropped me off at my apartment, and I headed

upstairs to the boxes with Richard's things inside. If I couldn't speak to him, at least I could unpack his things and add his presence to this empty home. Most of the boxes contained clothes. I hung them in his closet. There were few personal effects, which I kept in the boxes. The man owned no T-shirts, which was unfortunate because I'd hoped to sleep in one. Denied that, I took one of his dress shirts and put that on, inhaling the dark essence of him. It made a little of the loneliness go away.

Later that night, I reclined on the sofa and started reading a new book. His phone chirped from inside my purse. My lips twisted with happiness mingled with sadness, but joy won out. My insides quivered when I read his text.

Sweet Rowan, can you talk?

Yes!

The phone rang a few seconds later.

"I miss you." The deep notes of his voice filled my ear and soothed the ache in my heart.

"I miss you, too. How're you holding up?"

"I have good and bad moments. The official announcement was made early this morning. I wanted to check in on you."

"You don't need to worry about me."

"I do. You're a part of me."

And he was a part of me, one that grew more profound with every passing day.

"I wish I were with you," I said, blurting out the words before I had a chance to realize how needy that sounded.

"I'd like that." The strain in his voice broke my heart.

"I know you're busy. I just wanted you to know, I'm thinking of you."

"That helps more than you realize." He heaved a deep sigh. "I have to admit something very selfish."

"Yes?"

"If it weren't for Pratt, I'd have you here now. I don't care what my mother says. I don't care what protocol demands. I need you."

My breath caught in my chest because I needed that, too. An ocean and several time zones separated us. That needed to change. I rubbed my cheek as an idea formed in my head.

We talked for over an hour, first about inconsequential things and then about David's visit. There wasn't much that Richard didn't already know. Either David had spoken to him before our trip to Savannah or he'd caught him afterward. After some time, Richard opened up about his brother. He shared bits and pieces of their relationship—his love for his brother as well as the difficulties they'd shared. My heart ached with the rawness of his pain and the burden of guilt ghosting in his thoughts.

As I went to sleep, I made my decision.

The next two weeks, I raced around town like a madwoman. First stop was my bank. The trust held millions, but none of that was cash I could use. Fortunately, the first payment from Infidelity had cleared. That gave me plenty of options.

Scheduling time to speak with my professors took several days. None were thrilled with me taking time off, but once I explained my very unique situation, they helped work out a schedule that would allow me to complete the term.

There was an option to take a year off or delay one term. Without knowing what the future held, I sat with my adviser, and we settled on taking a semester off. I could have taken the full year, but the agreement with Infidelity ran out in the middle of the spring semester. If Richard and I approached the end of our agreement and decided things would end, at least my future plans could resume with minimal interruption.

Richard and I talked every night. Not once did I reveal my plans. He wouldn't agree, and by the contract he'd signed with Infidelity, he was bound to accept the limits I had placed at inception.

One of my stops on my to-do list involved a visit with Ms. Flores.

She confirmed the contract couldn't be changed. Various reasons were given, but it came down to concerns Infidelity had with clients pressuring employees to change the terms of the contract.

"Safety first," she said, repeating one of many Infidelity catchwords.

While this frustrated me, she had my best interests at heart. If Richard chose to discard me at the end of our year contract and I had requested the stipulation regarding my studies be lifted, it would have profound repercussions on my future.

There was little to argue against that even if the financial reasons behind seeking employment with Infidelity no longer existed. If I chose, I could quit Pratt and never return. The trust settled all of that.

And Henry?

During those first few days, a flurry of texts had flooded my phone. I'd mentioned it to Richard during our nightly talk and never heard from Henry again.

While I was pretty certain more was going on in the background, Richard refused to elaborate. I could have demanded answers, but I didn't. Bottom line, I loved having someone who watched out for me. If anything, Richard was highly possessive—or at least, as much as he could be an ocean away.

He kept me up to date with his affairs. Edmund had been put to rest on the tenth day after his death. His body had lain in state while the nation mourned. With that completed, Richard had a several months' long tour of the country scheduled.

I intended to surprise the hell out of him.

THIRTY-SIX

Downstairs

RICHARD

EDMUND'S FUNERAL COULDN'T HAVE BEEN MORE MAJESTIC. ONLY the heat of tears had pricked at my eyes during the solemn event. Crying betrayed weakness—something I reserved for the one person closest to me. Strange how Rowan drew out my strength when I felt the weakest. She was ever at the forefront of my thoughts and starred in my fantasies late at night and in the mornings during my shower. I invited her into my innermost thoughts, exposed my turmoil, and shared my dreams as well as my fears. Technically, she was the person I knew the least about, but we were slowly rectifying that fault.

It felt like I'd known her forever.

During all the disturbance and unrest of the past weeks, her steadfast support had carried me through the long nights when my insecurities whispered the loudest. Our phone conversations would stretch deep into the night where we exposed our secret selves to each other.

With my thoughts focused on Rowan, I ignored the half-dozen tailors who swarmed around me, making certain the pins and ribbons hung properly on my royal dress. My mother sat in the corner, regal and proper in her grieving black. She would wear the color for several months, whereas I, by necessity, divulged myself of the depressing color. My official tour approached with the glacial surety of fate.

"You look magnificent," she said. And, for the first time, the sparkle in her eyes wasn't from tears.

I believed she honestly felt pride in her younger son. Of course, I'd been nothing but dutiful these past couple of weeks. I bowed to her every wish. Every request, I treated like a command. Whatever I could do to remove her pall of grief, I viewed as my solemn duty—with one exception.

"Thank you, Mum," I said.

With a brisk wave of her hand, she dismissed the room. The tailors and waitstaff disappeared with barely a rustle of sound, leaving the Queen of England alone with her sole heir.

"You will be spectacular," she said, coming to brush nonexistent lint off my shoulder.

"And you're certain you won't be coming?"

The trip would be a good distraction, and it had been some time since she made an official tour of state.

Her lips pinched, and I regretted my words. Edmund's death had aged my mother faster than it should have. I no longer saw the regal monarch from my youth. Instead, a frail, older woman looked back at me, worn and exhausted.

"I shall remain in London. It's important for the people to see their Queen going on with normal things now that Edmund…" Her voice caught on his name, and a tear slipped down her cheek. She cleared her throat. "Now that you are filling his shoes, it's time to show your resolve." Her eyes narrowed. "You must be on your best behavior. This is not the time for scandal or speculation."

"Yes, Mum." I pasted a smile to my lips.

She'd remained resolute about Rowan. Despite my explanation of Rowan's heritage, one of a handful of prestigious founding Southern families, my mother wouldn't budge. My hope had been to sway her opinion, but I'd accomplished the opposite instead.

She saw nothing other than a destitute socialite desperate to reclaim social standing by attaching herself to the English monarchy. Her arguments revolved around Rowan's status as a commoner and her American citizenship. According to English law, neither of those mattered, but my mother didn't care. The biggest black spot against Rowan was the size of her bank account. Also something that shouldn't matter. Considering I paid for the privilege of Rowan's companionship, bringing her to me and not the other way around, I found my mother's reasoning flawed, but there was no way to use that for Rowan's defense.

It took everything not to share the truth behind Rowan's finances. Following David's advice, we kept that a tightly held secret. He had friends investigating Henry Porter while I placed several of my security team into looking into the details surrounding her father's death. Rowan knew nothing about my investigation or the depths of my mother's disapproval. It was a good thing an ocean separated them.

My phone rang, and my mother's lips twisted. "Her again? I thought you'd severed ties?"

"You judge too harshly. Once you meet her, you'll understand why she's caught my eye."

"I'm not certain it's your eye she's caught."

"Mum!"

"Oh, I may be Queen, but I'm not daft. I know what drives a young man."

"You have no faith in me?"

"In you, I have all the faith in the world. That girl is another matter. Have you even glanced at the list I gave you?"

"You mean, the list of desperate socialites who want to wed a prince? You judge Rowan when you should turn your attention to that list. Seriously, Mum, did you even look at it?"

"They come from respectable families." The twitching of her eyelids confirmed what I'd already guessed. Her advisers had compiled that list, no doubt being paid handsomely to add this name or that, in hopes that a suitable candidate found her way to a crown.

"As does Rowan." But my words fell on deaf ears.

"They're not soiled by scandal," she insisted. "The crown cannot be attached to—"

I couldn't handle it anymore and let my anger surge to the surface. "Enough! What happened to her father has no bearing on Rowan. Please agree to meet her before you cast her aside based upon the crimes committed by another."

"End it with that girl. The time you spend with her is time you're not securing the future of our family."

My phone rang again. "I'm going to take her call."

She *tsked* her disapproval.

I glanced at the phone.

Are you free to talk?

Those were the words we used to ensure privacy.

Mum is here, but she's leaving.

That's a shame. I'd love to meet her.

My heart slammed against my chest.

Meet her?

Yes. I'm downstairs.

THIRTY-SEVEN

Union

Rowan

My heart fluttered with the nervous energy it pumped into my veins. With no outlet, my skin buzzed as my body came alight. I barely held it together.

David and my bodyguard, Mark, had orchestrated this meeting, all without Richard's knowledge. I hoped my presence came as a welcomed surprise and not something else. I refused to consider what might happen if Richard said no.

Somewhere along the way, I'd endeared Mark to my cause—either that or David had roped him into the role of coconspirator. Mark had arranged our travel plans and greased my way through multiple layers of security. David had filled me in on royal protocol and regaled me with stories of him and Richard growing up. Limitations would be placed upon me, he'd explained, but I didn't care. If all I could do was sleep by Richard's side, I would happily stay in the background during the day.

A hopeless romantic, David had affectionately dubbed the trip Operation Royal Union. Without him, I never would have made it through the front door. He'd seemed able to gain intimate access to Richard, but then I'd come to find how close the two of them were. The snippets of Richard's life told through his best friend's eyes had filled my heart with joy.

The three of us waited in the parlor of a grand estate. Like most buildings belonging to the royal family, it carried a name weighted with history. Richard's world wasn't the place for someone like me, but that was okay. I only wanted the tiniest bit. David tried to soothe me, but I stuck out like a sore thumb with my American accent and dress. It didn't bother him. He had grown up in London as the son of an ambassador, but the haughty stares and suspicious whispers gnawed at me.

What the hell have I done?

"Did he answer?" David asked.

"Yes." I shouldn't feel the beating of my heart, but it pounded like a kettledrum and sent a roar of my blood surging past my ears.

"And?" His brow lifted, seeking more of an answer.

"Nothing."

"Nothing? He didn't answer, or he didn't see the text?"

"He saw the text."

Maybe coming here was too bold of a move. Maybe Richard had been debating on how to get rid of an overly needy woman he no longer had time for in his life. Because, really, wasn't that exactly what I was?

A commotion drew my attention out of the tangle of my thoughts. Taking two stairs at a time, Richard raced down the majestic staircase.

"Rowan!" His voice boomed.

Security and waitstaff snapped to attention, heads swiveling to see what the disturbance might be.

My heart swelled in my chest until I thought it would burst from joy.

"Richard." My voice came out a soft and tentative whisper.

His gaze swept the parlor. I stood in the middle, hands clasped tightly beneath my chin. I wanted to run to him, but David's fingers brushed my elbow, reminding me not to directly approach the Prince of Wales. Otherwise, I would activate his security shield.

My hesitation didn't matter because Richard closed the distance in ground-devouring strides. My cheeks filled with a grin, and my lips curved into a smile. I didn't know what proper decorum dictated, but it didn't matter. His strong arms wrapped around me and yanked me hard against his chest. Before I could take a breath, his lips crushed mine, and the urgency of our reunion drove all my insecurities away.

David took a step back, giving us space. I curled my arms around Richard's neck and let his passion carry me away.

This was where I belonged.

He cupped the sides of my face and bent his knees until our eyes were at the same level. His thumbs wiped the tears on my cheeks, and the intensity of his gaze stole what had been left of my breath.

"What are you doing here?" Thunderous joy brimmed in his eyes. "I have missed you." He glanced behind me, and a knowing look filled his expression. "I should've known David was in on this." He released me and embraced David. "It's good to see you."

"You, too," David said. Then, the tone of his voice dropped. "I'm sorry for your loss."

Richard's features clouded for a moment but then cleared when he turned back to me. "You made it a thousand times better. I hope we get more than a couple of hours this time.

Please tell me you're here until Sunday. Oh, but I leave early." He shook his head. "We have the worst luck."

We'd had two blissful hours our last visit. Memories surfaced—the scruff of his beard scratching my thighs and how he'd buried his face between my legs. Heat rose in my cheeks, and I ached with the need for more.

"We'll have more than an hour or two," I said, not willing to disclose my plans in front of so many.

"How long are you here?" he asked, pulling me hard against his chest.

The brocades and medals of his regalia poked my skin. "As long as you'll have me."

His brows drew together. "Come, let's go where we can speak privately." He glanced at David. "You, too!"

Mark followed on David's heels. I suppose my security escort didn't need an invitation. Two other men peeled off from those gathered and traveled a discreet distance behind.

With a hard grip on my hand, Richard guided me down an ornate hallway, passing a string of opulent rooms.

I'd missed him. I'd missed the overwhelming presence of him.

Finally, he brought me to a wood-paneled game room with dark huntsman-green walls. A pool table dominated the room, barstools were snuggled in the corners, and a dartboard occupied the far wall. He angled me toward a corner furthest from the door where two barstools sat. Mark along with the other two men took up positions in the hall, leaving Richard, David, and me alone.

He spun to David. "Care to tell me what's going on?"

David redirected that comment to me. "It's all on her," he said and then gave a wink. "Go get him." Without another word, he left. On his way out, he pulled on the heavy door, shutting it with a sense of finality, sealing Richard and me inside.

Richard's eyes sparked with excitement. "I can't believe you're here. How did you manage it?"

"Simple," I said with a cheeky grin. "I bought a plane ticket."

His eyes narrowed. "You know that's not what I meant."

THIRTY-EIGHT

Game Room

Richard

My sweet Rowan had something up her sleeve. The urge to force her to spill her secret rose within me. A good swat of her ass should do it. She did that to me. No other woman ignited the beast like she did. With Rowan, it wasn't about simply dating. I needed to possess every facet of her being.

A growl escaped me. "I think you should tell me now," I said, giving that light swat.

Her eyes widened, and that made my cock jerk, but then an impish grin spread across her face.

"And what will you do if I don't?"

My gaze riveted to her tight ass, and I licked my lips. "Right now, I'm thinking about putting you over my knee."

She took a teetering step back. Those riveting bluebell eyes of hers widened even further. "You wouldn't."

I crossed my arms, affecting a relaxed and confident pose, while my desires clawed to the surface. All I could think about was ripping off the pompous uniform caging me in, divesting myself of my pants, and bending her over that pool table where I could retake my rightful place—standing over her, sliding inside her, and pounding against that perfect ass.

"If you think I wouldn't," I said, "answer one question."

"What?" Her voice shook, either from fear or desire. At this point, it didn't matter.

"How are you feeling, my sweet Rowan?"

Her mouth gaped, and her eyes rounded with understanding. That smirk returned, and then something amazing happened.

Dropping to her knees, she glanced up at me. "Green, Sir. Definitely green."

It was my turn for my eyes to grow wide, and I reined in the overwhelming desire to strip her down and fuck her right then.

"Someone has been busy." My heart swelled with a new emotion. Desire and overwhelming happiness filled my chest, but pride edged to the surface. "I thought you weren't familiar with…this." I gestured at her perfectly submissive posture—the way her hands turned, palms up, and how she sat back on her heels.

The curtain of her lashes swept against the rise of her cheeks. "Turns out, the Internet is a great place for research."

"And is this what you want?" My question needed to be answered. And, holy hell, what would happen if she gave the right answer?

"If you lead." Her cheeks colored, and she dragged her tongue over her lower lip. "I don't know if this is what you want, but it feels…it fits us, don't you think?"

"And what about punishments?" Because, if she didn't tell me what the hell was going on, and soon, I would lovingly beat it out of her.

"A little light swat here and there is fine. Maybe something more, but I'm not sure about some of the other things."

Her hesitation gave me pause, but her words instilled hope.

"Well, if you don't tell me what's going on, I'm going to bend you over that pool table and smack your smart ass into submission."

Her eyes sparkled with a flare of arousal, which stirred my rapidly hardening member to stand at full attention.

"How about a compromise?"

"That's not how this will be. If we take this step, if you're willing to travel this path, you'll follow where I lead. I won't have you topping from the bottom."

Her brows pinched together.

"Do you know what that means?"

She drew her lower lip into her mouth and pressed her teeth into the soft flesh. "I know what it means, but I was thinking about how I left you last time, and I've been aching to taste you these past two weeks. I just thought a little *worship* might lift your spirits. I didn't mean to top from the bottom." Her gaze cut away, and she struggled with some of the words.

Her interest was cautious at best and not something I would force. I would take that as a precious gift.

My focus cut to the door, and my eyes narrowed in thought. Rowan and I didn't have much time before my duties took me away, but I did have a few moments to indulge. I also had the best wingman in the world guarding the door.

She glanced at the bulge of my pants. "It would be a shame not to, um..." She giggled. "That must be uncomfortable."

"Trust me, I'm used to it."

She made it easy to relax, drop all the formalities of my status, and simply be a man. That was, perhaps, the best gift she gave.

"Well," she said, glancing up, "may I?"

The correct response would be to deny her, if only because she was topping from the bottom. But that would deny us both this pleasure. The thought of her ruby-red lips wrapped around my cock made my head spin. With my course decided, I unbuttoned my jacket and draped it over the back of the barstool. Then, I slowly released the buckle of my belt. With a crook of my finger, I gave the command.

"Come and greet your…" Her what? Master? Was that too presumptuous? I liked the sound of it, but our journey had barely begun. Sir? She'd bestowed that name upon me, but it didn't feel appropriate. I hadn't earned it yet.

She scooted forward, and all further thought stopped when the heat of her lips wrapped around the tip of my cock. With her cheeks sucked in, she took me deep. All the while, she looked up with adoration, trust, and something much more profound. Faith.

I curled my fingers in her hair, pulling slightly at the roots. In this way, I guided her, chasing my pleasure until the telltale tingle gathered in my balls. I tilted my head back, opening my mouth, as my hips jerked, and my ejaculate shot down her throat.

"Holy fuck," I managed after my hips stopped bucking.

She licked me through my release and used her mouth to clean me off.

"Now, how is that for a proper hello?" Her wink brought a smile to my face.

I ran my fingers through her hair and helped her to stand. Kissing her, the tang of my essence coated my tongue.

"I definitely enjoyed that."

Her eyes crinkled with promise. "All you have to do is make it a command. I'll gladly obey."

"My only regret," I said with a pointed look to the pool table, "is that, now, I can't bend you over that and fuck you from behind."

It would be a few minutes before I could perform again, more time than we had left. Quickly, I put myself back in order, making sure to tuck my shirt in tight.

"How do I look?"

"You look like a magnificent prince."

"Do I look like a prince who just had his cock sucked? Or do I look like a prince who carried on a nice, respectable conversation with his American girlfriend?"

Her lilting laughter filled the room. "You look like you've been pressed into that suit, and the only thing on your mind is the private conversation with your American girlfriend. Now, how about me? Do I look like I just gave a blow job to a prince? How's my lipstick?"

I couldn't help it. Her filthy mouth surprised me. "Better not let the Queen hear you say that about her son, and you might want to reapply."

"Oh," she said, "I will definitely do that." She twisted her fingers together. "I hope I never meet your mother. I would have no idea how to behave."

"Well, don't expect a warm welcome when you do. She's not the cuddly type."

THIRTY-NINE

Decisions

Rowan

Being together again brought my world into alignment. The empty weeks faded to a distant memory, and I refused to consider spending more time apart.

Richard examined his image while I reapplied my lipstick.

I slipped my arms beneath his and wrapped them tight around his back. Laying my cheek against his chest, I closed my eyes and breathed him in. "You look very regal."

He cupped my head and kissed my forehead. "When are you going to answer my question?"

"Which one?"

I knew exactly what was on his mind. My attention slid to the closed doors and the sounds I might make if Richard followed through with his promise. Perhaps this wasn't the time to test his resolve. But I was tempted.

"I'm here for as long as you'll have me," I said. "All I want is to sleep in the same bed with you for once."

"What do you mean, for as long as I'll have you?"

His question brought an explanation of the arrangements I'd made with my professors. "I have to come back for my exams and to present my projects. So, you see, I'll be busy." I rushed through my spiel, terrified he would stop me and utter the words that would send me back. "You don't have to worry about me, entertain me, or any of that."

His features darkened. "I wish you had discussed this with me."

"I wanted it to be a surprise."

"It is, but I can't have you with me and hiding in the shadows."

My heart crumbled. He didn't want me.

"Stop," he said, his voice stern and disapproving.

"Stop what?"

"If you think for a second that I would ever hide you from the world…" He shook his head. "I won't cheapen what's between us. If you come with me, you are with me."

"But…"

David had explained protocol. I wasn't a welcome addition to a prince's life.

"There are some functions you can't attend, but I won't let the world think I'm ashamed of you, not when you're the first thought in my head when I wake and the last when I go to sleep." He tilted my face, and a smile graced his features. "Do you understand what I'm saying?"

"I just want time with you."

"Well," he said, his expression lightening, "you have all the time in the world." He lifted his finger in warning. "But your studies come first. We'll come up with a schedule. Miss Rowan Cartwright, your world has changed." He drew in a deep breath and took his time in blowing it out, as if fortifying himself for what he was about to say next.

My eyes shimmered with the threat of tears. This man meant more to me than my heart could handle, especially knowing that time was working against us.

His voice deepened, becoming firm and commanding. "I love that you surprised me, but if you ever make a decision of this magnitude without checking with me first, you'll find yourself draped over my knee and finding it difficult to sit for a week. I'm not giving up on what brought you to me. I can't."

"I don't want to give that up."

His finger pressed over my lips. "Be careful with your words. You've agreed you don't want to give up the D/s lifestyle. As of this moment, your life revolves around me because my position demands it and, most importantly, because it's what I want. Can you live with that?"

If it meant staying with him, I would take anything.

"Yes."

"Good. Now, bend over the pool table."

"Why?"

"If for no other reason than I said to. I'm going to smack that ass. Because you gave me that right. Because you failed to include me in a major decision. And, finally, because you promised to never lie, and while not telling me about this isn't technically a lie, it does fall under an error of omission. My sweet Rowan, show me that pretty ass."

FORTY

Departure

ROWAN

Our rendezvous delayed Richard's departure. His entourage waited patiently while their prince smacked my ass and then fingered me into oblivion. In my opinion, the wait was well worth it. There was something wrong with me because the ten swats from Richard might have hurt, but the sensation left behind, the one pulsing between my legs, stayed with me far longer than the sting of his hand. When it faded, all I had to do was look at him or sneak a peek at his hand, and that delicious feeling would flood my senses yet again.

I wanted more.

"Come, it's time to leave." He set me on my feet and helped me get dressed.

A glance at my pants, wrinkled blouse, and comfortable shoes had my belly doing the flipping thing again. I dressed for comfort on the seven-hour flight, but there was no way I was going to be seen with the Prince of England while dressed like a slob.

"Um, I can't exactly go with you, not when I look like this." I made a show of how I looked.

He looked every bit the prince, regal, commanding, and sexy as fuck. I looked sloppy and cheap at best.

Gathering my hand in his, he interlaced our fingers. "I can't believe you're here. And you're certain your studies—"

"My curriculum has been set for this semester, and I'm taking off next semester."

His fingers twitched, and his jaw tightened. "Yes, that makes sense, of course. So, I have you all to myself?"

"Every day, except the first Saturday of the month, plus travel time. That's Freddy's day, and I'm not going to miss it."

"I can live with that."

We approached the heavy oak front doors, and he pulled up short. "Are you ready?"

I rubbed my palms on the fabric of my pants, surprised at how clammy they felt.

"Follow my lead and smile. There are over a hundred cameras out there."

My instinct was to run back home. Instead, I lifted my chin and pretended this was my grand debut at my debutant ball.

Flashes sparked in my eyes from a hundred different lenses. Richard tightly gripped my hand and lifted his other to wave. The polite crowd shouted no questions about the stranger on his arm, but every camera zoomed in on me. My association with Richard wasn't a surprise. Our picture had been shot in Savannah, and news had spread about his latest American fling.

Richard leaned down and whispered, "You're doing great. Smile, but don't engage."

That was exactly what I did for the next four months. A permanent smile would fix itself to my face whenever Richard and I appeared in public. My wardrobe expanded. Exclusive personal shoppers purchased clothing more appropriate for the functions I attended. Evidently, it wasn't appropriate to be seen shopping for myself. For the more casual events, I would join Richard, never straying far from his side. When I wasn't with him, Mark would watch over me, keeping the press and their questions far away.

It was kind of fun—being kept in a bubble and protected from the rest of the world. Richard's protectiveness shadowed me during the day, and his possessiveness caged me in at night. He consumed my every waking thought and all of my dreams. The moment his royal engagements completed for the night, he would whisk me away to the privacy of whatever accommodations we held for the night. We rarely went out socially, spending most of our time behind the closed doors of the bedroom. There, I entered a completely different realm and became something else.

I learned to kneel, to obey, to please and be pleased. We drowned in the pleasure of each other's flesh, giving and taking, as we learned what we could about the other. As my comfort level increased, spankings took on a more prominent role. Richard released his restraint, delved into his fantasies, and dominated me with the sureness of his will.

I followed, willing, loyal, and obedient. One memorable evening found my voice hoarse after I disobeyed for the sheer pleasure of his hand punishing my flesh.

An understanding grew between us—limits defined, lines drawn, and roles determined. In public, we'd charm the populace and endear ourselves to the press. In private, I'd cry, beg, and bend beneath the unwavering steel of the man determined to steal my heart, claim it with his dominance, and bind me with his love.

There were days when my jaw would ache, when sitting would become a reminder to obey, and when the throb between my legs couldn't wait for the night to begin again. We soaked each other in and settled into our unique but complementary roles. Life couldn't have been more perfect—until the summons came.

"What do you think she wants to talk with me about?"

My entire body throbbed. He'd taken me with brutal aggression, amping up the intensity of our lovemaking with a feral hunger. The signs of tonight would linger on my flesh for days, if not longer.

After months of being ignored, his mother had finally admitted my existence, and I would go to her with the marks of her son imprinted on my ass.

"I think she wants to speak with you about me."

"Is that a good thing or a bad thing?"

He reached over my head and released the silk ties restraining my wrists. My jaw hurt from taking him deep in my mouth. Training, he'd called it, but I thought he loved the ferocity of a good face fucking. He intended to cure me of my tendency to gag. These were the moments I loved—when he came unglued and left all decorum behind. My ass throbbed—not from the power of his hand, but from the sting of his latest and favorite flogger. My pussy ached with terrible need, and I squirmed on the sheets, needing the barest hint of friction to send me over the edge. He had yet to satisfy me. Sometimes, I thought he enjoyed making me beg.

For myself, I didn't know the woman I'd become. This wanton thing found pleasure in kneeling, service, and sacrifice for a man who had wrapped dominance around a fragile heart and squeezed every ounce of submission from my soul. I feared and admired him, but I hadn't yet accepted this was what I'd become.

With a look, Richard would put me in my place or send my heart soaring. From across the room, a single arch of his brow would let me know if he intended to abuse my mouth, punish me, or lick and fuck me into oblivion. Some nights, he would do all and more, always pushing my limits and testing my tolerance for pain.

Twisting toward him, I draped a leg over his hip. "Please," I begged, "you can't make me face her alone."

He slapped my ass when I humped his leg. Just a little friction.

"Stop!" He flipped me on my back. "What do you want?"

"I want to come," I said, pleading for relief.

"And I want more of that sweet ass. Watching your body twitch drives me insane."

He'd just emptied himself down my throat, which meant it would be a few minutes before his cock hardened again.

"I don't know if I can…"

His eyes narrowed to thin slits. "Is it ever your place to deny me what I want?"

I bit my lower lip. My ass throbbed, and while I enjoyed a good spanking, it took time before the endorphins morphed pain into pleasure. I was horny as fuck and not willing to wait. My hesitation didn't go unnoticed, and he took any choice from me with a quick flip to my belly. As he straddled my thighs, the first smack fell on my tender flesh. My yelp spurred him on. My body twitched and jumped, dancing to the fury of his open hand.

Two fingers slid between my thighs and found my wet pussy. I clenched when he shoved them deep inside, and my screams turned to moans. He stroked me through my first orgasm and then bent my knees until he could shove his fully erect cock into my walls.

"I think I've found heaven," he said and then slammed deep inside.

The smacking of our flesh replaced that of his hands, and I came again, screaming out his name. He finished a few seconds later and then collapsed on the bed beside me.

He pulled me to him. "Don't worry; you're not going anywhere."

I had no intentions of leaving, but in the morning, I would face the full force of the Crown. The Queen didn't approve of the woman who shared her son's bed, and I feared for the worst.

FORTY-ONE

Tea

ROWAN

Tea at Buckingham Palace.
Nervous?
I wasn't nervous.
Terrified?
Maybe.
Petrified?
Most definitely.

I threw up once. Used the bathroom twice. A quick shifting of my feet had Richard grabbing my arm. Protocol defined limits to our public displays of affection. Hand-holding fell on the list of prohibited things. Richard broke that rule often, but in Buckingham Palace, nearly a foot of open space separated us, except his light touch.

"Stop." He released my arm and smoothed down his suit jacket. "You're going to be fine."

"I'm going to throw up again."

"No, you're not. Make me proud." He couldn't have picked more powerful words.

"And you're going to be there, right?" Despite his words of comfort, my voice shook.

"Absolutely."

A steward approached. "Miss Cartwright, Her Majesty the Queen will see you now."

Richard gave a nod of encouragement and stepped with me.

The double doors of the tea room opened, and the steward coughed. "Her Majesty will speak with Miss Cartwright alone."

"Alone?" The catch in Richard's voice put me on high alert.

"Yes, that is what she specified." The man clicked his heels and stood even straighter.

The muscles of Richard's jaw clenched. "Rowan…"

"It's okay," I said, sounding far more confident than I felt.

I'd already gone over all the scenarios in my head. A challenge waited beyond those doors, and no matter what happened, I would make Richard proud.

The doors closed behind me with a soft thud. The Queen sat at a small round table set with a linen-and-lace table topper. A full tea service with raised plates full of confections, finger sandwiches, and what looked to be scones sat before her. She did not look up but read from the newspaper clutched in her hand. This left me to wait, and while I told myself I wouldn't fidget, my feet moved, and my fingers twisted together. She left me standing well over a minute before slowly adjusting the glasses perched on her nose. Her assessment took me in from head to toe, and her frown told me she saw nothing she liked.

"Miss Cartwright," she said, her voice cold and unwelcoming. "Thank you for coming."

"Thank you for the invitation, Your Majesty." Hopefully, my pleasant tone could salvage this meeting. "I have been looking forward to meeting you. Richard has said nothing but lovely things."

I was to wait for her invitation to sit. Instead, her lips twisted with distaste.

"About my son…" She lifted her teacup and took a dainty sip, drawing out her next words.

Not about to be intimidated, I took in a breath and met her disapproval head-on.

"Richard is wonderful. We're very happy." In the past few months, I'd allowed myself to dream of a future with him in it.

"That is of no concern," she said. "You will stop this charade. End things with my son, and disappear back to where you came."

The world stopped beneath my feet. At least, that was what the sudden gut-wrenching felt like. With nothing to steady myself, I swayed on my feet. My breaths pulsed in, too fast and too shallow. I was going to faint. My mind went blank, and my jaw dropped.

Disappear? Had she really told me to disappear? Like a piece of trash she could sweep out of the way?

Indignation rose within me, and I snapped. "I'll do no such thing."

"You'll do as you're told, child. You have no future here. If you care for Richard, you'll do what is right."

Who the hell did she think she was?

"Richard will determine what is and isn't right."

She placed the teacup on the table and trained the full force of her imperious gaze on me.

My spine stiffened, but I wasn't going to back down. Evidently, neither was she.

"Americans are so testy. I admire your grit, common as it is, but you don't understand. I have spoken, and my word carries the weight of law. You are excused."

FORTY-TWO

Conversation

RICHARD

Perhaps I shouldn't be surprised my mother wished to speak with Rowan alone, but I didn't like sending Rowan in without my support.

The past four months had been nothing but extraordinary, a melding of two halves becoming one soul. It was too early and too close to Edmund's death, but my decision had been made. Rowan would be mine—not for the span of a year, but for the rest of my life.

The e-mail had gone to Infidelity this morning, exercising my buyout option. After Rowan's official summons, the time approached to discuss our future with my mother. My nerves rioted with anticipation of the conversation occurring behind those doors. My hopes went to Rowan on making a smashing first impression.

In the middle of my contemplating, my phone rang. I was

tempted to ignore it, but there weren't many reasons for David to call.

"Hello?" I said, lowering my voice to avoid the ears of the staff. I moved to a chaise by the window and sat with my back facing the corner.

"Can you talk?" David's terse voice broadcast his concern.

"I can."

"This won't take long." He rarely minced words.

"Go on."

"The holdings in Rowan's trust are undervalued."

"By how much?"

"It's easily over three hundred, maybe more."

I arched my brow, surprised. "Why the change?" I expected a ten or twenty percent increase, but over half? It didn't make sense.

"The value of some of the land was underpriced, set for a quick sale by Henry Porter. Several contiguous parcels run along an undeveloped portion of the coastline, right where Parker's company has plans for development. It's a land grab."

"But her assets are protected?" I studied English law, not that of the United States, but the basic tenets were similar.

"Yes, for now. However, if Porter succeeded in pressuring Rowan to marry Parker, then the doctrine of transmutation would've applied. All that needs to happen is the commingling of property. Once that occurs, the property in the trust becomes marital assets. Considering Porter kept the trust secret, it's clear he and Parker intended to gain control once she married Parker."

"What about Porter?"

Following my orders, Rowan had cut off all communication. Concerned over retribution, I'd placed a security detail on her brother. I didn't trust the prick. Not when over three hundred million was at risk.

"Steps are underway to remove him as the trustee. It's a lengthy and complicated process."

"What about the other matter? Her father?"

His entire arrest, sentencing, and suicide felt wrong.

"I have no doubt Porter was involved, but her father broke the law."

"And his suicide?"

"There's no evidence of foul play."

Not unexpected, but I held hope I'd be able to clear his name. I wanted to give that to Rowan and ease her pain. Another more selfish reason sat beyond that door in the judgmental mind of my mother interrogating the woman I loved. I prayed it was going well.

The double doors to the tea room whispered open on nearly silent hinges. Rowan stepped out and scanned the room. Her hand flew over her midsection, and it looked like she was about to get sick.

I vaulted out of my chair and rushed over, grabbing her elbow. Steering her out of the room, I took her down the hall and into a vacant room where I slammed the door behind us. Her entire body trembled, and her complexion paled.

"What happened?" I said, concerned she was going to get sick.

Nerves had been her enemy earlier, but this pointed to something different. The skin of her arm felt clammy, and she didn't respond to my question.

"Rowan!"

Her gaze lifted to mine and then slid away. "She told me to go home." Rowan's legs gave way.

I caught her in my arms. Taking a knee, I lowered her down, propping her back against the wall. Her eyes brimmed with tears.

"You're not going anywhere."

"Your mother's exact words were, 'End things with my son, and disappear back to where you came. My word is law.'"

I folded her into my arms. "I decide when we end things, and there's no way I'm sending you back unless it's to see Freddy. You're mine, irrevocably and always *mine*." The last word came out as a growl.

With a rap to the door, I signaled Mark. He would've taken up guard outside the door.

I kissed Rowan and wiped the tears from her face. "Mark is going to wait outside that door. No one will come in, except me." I hated leaving her in this state, but I had words to share with my mother.

"Don't leave me," she said, clutching at my chest.

"I will never leave you, but I need to have a conversation with my mother."

Her eyes widened, and she gave a slight nod. "I must look miserable."

"You've never looked more amazing."

To know losing me had put her in such a desperate state angered the hell out of me, but it told me something else. Her feelings mirrored mine.

FORTY-THREE

King

RICHARD

On a rampage might not be the best way to confront my mother, but this wasn't a conversation between mother and son. As heir apparent, my demand would be heard.

The doors to the tea room were closed. Two doormen stood to either side, men I ignored, men whose eyes widened as I shoved the doors open and marched inside where my mother sat, daintily sipping tea.

"I expected a response, but theatrics? This behavior is quite unbecoming."

"If you think for a second—"

"What I think is you've dallied enough. My patience is worn out. I will see you wed and a son on your knee in less than two years."

"That's preposterous." I wasn't ready to become a father. The other? My future belonged with Rowan. "You can't dictate that."

Her brow lifted. "You'd be surprised what I can *dictate*."

"Not this."

"You don't expect me to believe you care for this girl?"

"I do."

"A destitute child you paid to be your companion?"

My mouth gaped.

She flicked her napkin off her lap and dabbed at her mouth. "You think I didn't know? You think the best secret service agency in the world couldn't find out?"

"You had me investigated?"

"I had her investigated, and of course, with thirty thousand pounds disappearing from your account and reappearing in hers…"

"You have no business interfering in my personal life like that."

"You don't understand how your life has changed. A little indiscretion here and there was fine when it didn't matter, but you're to be England's next king!" She slapped her napkin down on the table. "Really? Paying for sex!"

"I never paid for sex. I paid for companionship." Paying for sex was beneath me, ludicrous to consider, disgusting even, but it made perfect sense. Technically, I paid for Rowan's companionship, never for sex.

"Is that what you're calling it?" A sneer pinched at her face. "She's not fit to be in the same room with you, let alone your bed."

"Who is in my bed is none of your business."

"No, but it's the business of the Crown. You must associate with a woman worthy of becoming your queen. Not a desperate creature who sold her body—"

"Enough!" I said. "Your intelligence network seems to have missed a thing or two." I ground out my words, struggling to retain my dignity and not sound like a petulant child.

"The girl's father was a thief. He embezzled millions and took the coward's way out. She has nothing but debt and the morals of a whore."

The skin of my neck heated, and my fingers clenched. None of this was going the way I had hoped. Hugs and kisses weren't my mother's thing. I hadn't been kidding when I told Rowan not to expect a warm welcome, but this?

While I fumed, my mother continued, "That's not the kind of woman my son will associate with. She's not the kind of woman worthy to be the future queen. Your arrangement ends today. I've been more than patient, believing you'd come to your senses, but clearly, you need me to step in. A king is not a man ruled by passion, and you're wasting your time when you should be looking for a suitable bride."

"I'm not ruled by passion, but my heart has spoken. Rowan isn't going anywhere. And her family is one of a very few prestigious Southern legacies. And"—I lifted my finger, emphasizing my point—"not that it matters, but she's far from destitute."

My mother scoffed. "Not with the money you've thrown at her to be your private plaything. I'm certain her finances look quite nice now."

"You might want to look again. You missed about three hundred million of them."

Her eyes widened. "Nonsense."

"How our relationship started has no bearing on where it's headed."

"And where is that?"

"You know exactly what I mean."

She shot up from her seat. The fine china chattered and shook. "I'll never allow it. I won't sign—"

"Then, I'll never marry." The threat left my mouth before I realized what I'd said.

It wasn't my intention to break my mother's heart. She trod a fine line between Queen and mother. Her eyes widened, and all color drained from her face. Hands trembling, lips quivering, she swayed. I barely got to her before she collapsed back in her chair.

"Mum," I said, "I'm sorry."

She fanned herself and gripped the edge of the table. "This is not the behavior of a king."

Good thing I wasn't king yet.

"Does she mean so much to you that you'd defy your Queen?"

"More than life itself."

My mother took in a deep breath. "You will not marry that girl."

"That is exactly what I intend."

Her lower lip quivered. "I will not allow it. You require my consent, and I forbid it. That woman will diminish the status of the royal house, and you won't marry her while I draw breath."

Privilege granted many rights, but it took many more away. I peered into her eyes, only to see the resolute determination girding her countenance. My mother's mind was made up.

But so was mine.

FORTY-FOUR

The Rules

ROWAN

THE NEXT FEW MONTHS PASSED IN A DAZE. RICHARD AND I SPENT our nights wrapped in a tangle of limbs, buried beneath the pleasures of the flesh, and enraptured with each other. We explored mutual fantasies, took tentative steps, and built something entirely ours.

This man held my heart in his hands. I'd freely given it, knowing how this would end. I'd fallen completely and irrevocably in love with a man I could never have. He purchased the privilege of my time and stole my heart, and it was only a matter of time before he utterly destroyed me.

"A penny for your thoughts," he said, kissing my shoulder.

I rubbed at the rope indentations encircling my wrists.

My journey into bliss began with the strike of his hand and ended with the fury of crop and cane. He took without mercy and fucked with fury.

My jaw ached. My pussy throbbed. I'd been gloriously fucked

into oblivion, and I never wanted to leave this place of contentment. I snuggled against his hard body and drifted, at peace.

"My mind's a blank," I murmured, lying to him.

He flipped me over his legs and struck my ass ten times—hard and without concern for my screams. Those screams morphed into a low, reedy moan with the arrival of the delicious heat that followed.

"Richard…" *Do I dare beg for relief?*

"What happens when you lie?"

"I get spanked." I hated when he forced the truth.

"Did you lie just now?" His hand caressed the tender flesh of my ass.

After the cane, fresh welts lined my ass and thighs. The burn had faded, but the deep, aching throb persisted.

I bit my lip. "Yes, Sir."

"And what are the rules?"

"No lying."

"Then, tell me what you were thinking."

I didn't want to ruin our moment. With his busy schedule, we had precious little time alone, and after his mother's decree, I spent even less time with him in public. The press still followed us around, interested in the woman he kept by his side, but that was where the speculation ended.

"I was thinking about next year."

My break from my degree would end with the arrival of the spring semester. My time with Richard would end then, too.

He rubbed my ass, soothing the burn, but I needed more. His fingers dipped between my legs and found my aching clit. My body responded, racing too fast toward orgasm. With a flick of his thumb, my climax slammed into me, stealing my breath and making me forget our vacant future.

He flipped me, dropping me to my back. Lifting my legs over his shoulders, he positioned his erect cock at my entrance. The slow slide of him inside me had my fingers clutching and my back arching off the bed. He rocked into me and then dragged his cock out. Not in any hurry to come again, he drove me over the edge. His hips bucked while the aftershocks of my orgasm ripped through me.

"You're mine," he said, nipping at my throat. "Never forget it."

"But your—"

The firmness of his lips silenced anything I'd had to say. "What did I say?"

"I'm yours."

With his body once more wrapped around me, I sank into his embrace, but my mind spiraled into a lonely future.

FORTY-FIVE

Last Month

RICHARD

I concluded my dealings with Infidelity, buying out my contract. I would no longer pay for the privilege of Rowan's company. She would no longer be an employee.

She would find out later what that meant.

Perhaps it wasn't fair to keep my plans secret, but I couldn't risk a leak—at least, not until I'd sorted out the obligations that bound me and my crown.

Christmas came and went—time she spent alone while I attended state functions. Mum remained resolute, and a chill settled over our interactions. Her refusal to reconsider my relationship met the steel of my determination. We found ourselves at an impasse, and I saw no way around it.

The week after New Year's found Rowan in my arms. We were back in Savannah for her visit with her brother. Mark drove the car to Freddy's home, and I clutched her against my chest.

The crunching of gravel announced our arrival. I exited first and then gave her a hand to help her out.

"I'll wait for your call," I said.

We appeared to be alone, but I never knew when a telephoto lens might be aimed at us. Decorum dictated our behavior. I would not irritate my mother by being anything less than circumspect—at least, in the public eye.

"It shouldn't be that long."

"I hope not."

"I'm going to tell him," she said.

"About?"

"He doesn't handle change well. I need to tell him about us." The smile on her face slipped, invaded by a frown.

"What are you going to tell him?"

Had she figured out my plan? I'd say yes, except for the melancholy in her expression.

"I'll start small, mention we won't be seeing each other—"

"Whoa, what do you mean, won't be seeing each other?"

"When I see him next month, we won't be together. No lies, right? I can't lie to my brother."

No lies. That was my rule. One I'd broken with the decisions made without her input. It was time to rectify that error, but first, I had a phone call to make.

"Can you hold off on saying anything?"

"I'd rather not."

"Consider it a request. Ask him if I can meet him when I pick you up. Can you do that?"

"Why?"

"I think we should tell him together."

She breathed out a sigh. "I suppose."

"Promise?"

"I promise."

Wrapping her in my arms, I hugged her tight, damn any lenses trained on us. She was my past, my present, and my future. My forever belonged with her.

Rowan went to visit her brother while I had a conversation with my mother.

"Good evening, Mum."

"It's late to be calling."

With the difference in time zones, she would be getting ready for bed, exactly when she was most vulnerable. No one would be with her, all the servants dismissed for the night. I needed to speak to my mother, not my Queen, and I needed her alone when I ripped out her heart.

"I apologize."

"This couldn't wait for morning?" The terseness of her tone reflected her irritation.

"Not this."

"Well," she snapped, "get on with it then. I don't have all night."

Marrying without the Queen's consent would disqualify me from succession. The law couldn't be clearer. Faced with a life with Rowan and that without, my decision had not come easily. England would have its king. It just wouldn't be me.

"I'm with Rowan, visiting her brother."

"And this required a phone call?"

"I'm going to ask for her brother's blessing."

Silence greeted me on the other end of the line. "Richard—"

"If there's one thing I've learned, some burdens are too heavy to bear. You taught me to lead with wisdom but never forget to rule with my heart. Rowan is my heart. I'm sorry to disappoint you, Mum. I'm sorry what this will do to England, but this is my decision. If I can't have your blessing, I pray, one day, you'll understand the choice I made. I hope you can forgive me."

A click sounded.
"Mum?"
No answer.
"Mum?"
The call had disconnected.

FORTY-SIX

Contract

ROWAN

I SHOULD HAVE HEARD SOMETHING. AT LEAST TEN TIMES A DAY, I would open my inbox and then click it closed. My contract with Infidelity had taken a beating, too, the papers crinkled as I pored over the legalese. The client had to exercise their notification within one month of the contract's anniversary date. I had no notification of renewal.

Perhaps I'd been foolish to believe our time would never end. I'd been well paid. At forty thousand a month, nearly half a million sat in my bank account. After Henry's betrayal, I had no confidence in lawyers. It wasn't smart to leave that money sitting in an account, but I had no idea what to do with it.

I could always add to the land trust, but the problem with land was that it didn't pay the bills. Half a million in the bank, three hundred million more sitting in a trust, and I didn't want a penny of it. I wanted to turn back time and beg my father to make better choices and not leave Freddy and me alone. If that had happened, I never would have found myself at Club Infinity. I never would have met the love of my life. I never would be faced with saying good-bye.

A month had passed since my last visit with Freddy. This time, Richard didn't accompany me. He was in New York with David and left me to fly to Savannah alone.

"Sis," Freddy called out, "stop squeezing Rex. He's full."

Despite my request to change feeding day to Saturday, Freddy had kept Sally and Rex on his Friday schedule. I was surprised he'd let me handle Rex. The cool scales of his skin chilled my skin as Rex coiled around my forearm. His forked tongue tasted the air, flicking out too fast to follow. Freddy cleaned the cage. Sally wound herself into a knot on his chair.

We spent many of our visits doing mundane things. Generally, the monotony soothed me. Seeing Freddy happy in his home made it easier to bear the institutional necessity of his life.

"I thought Richard would be here," he said.

"He couldn't make it."

"He's nice."

Theirs had been an odd interaction. Freddy had reacted well to Richard, talking animatedly about the line of succession. Freddy had recited some fifty-odd names, and Richard hadn't missed a beat. Before I had known it, Freddy had pulled Richard aside, leaving me to read in the library. Where they had gone or what they'd talked about wasn't something either of them had shared with me. What Richard and I hadn't done was break the news to Freddy, which left me to do it alone.

"Yes, he is." I pulled Rex off my arm, cradling his long body with ease. "Is it ready yet?"

"Almost," Freddy said.

"I want to talk to you about Richard."

"You love him." Freddy cracked a grin.

This wasn't going how I wanted. "Sometimes, things don't

work out." It was best to put the truth out there and pray Freddy understood. "Richard and I aren't going to be seeing each other anymore."

Freddy gave a big grin. "You don't know the secret."

My brows pulled together. "What secret?"

His gaze zeroed in on the clock. "Tank's clean. Give me Rex."

Freddy put Rex in the tank, and then he gathered Sally and deposited her inside. Covering the top, he clicked on the heating lamp to keep them warm. With his task complete, he turned to me. "You need to leave. Richard is here."

"Remember, I told you Richard is in New York?"

"Richard's outside."

I arched a brow, confused.

"You need to go," he said.

I was dismissed.

With my head down, I wandered outside. It would take time to make Freddy understand.

Outside, a black car pulled up, and the man of my dreams stepped out of the car.

"Richard!" Even knowing the end was barreling down on us, I leaped into his arms.

"My sweet Rowan," he said. "I have missed you."

His lips crushed mine, and I dissolved in one of the few remaining kisses we had left.

"You didn't tell me you were flying down!" I wrapped my arms tight around his neck, uncaring of royal protocols. I had one week left with this man, and I didn't care if my actions weren't proper.

"How are you feeling?" he asked, triggering me to his state of mind.

"Green," I said, laughing. "Green all the way."

He settled me back on my feet and held open the door to the car. I crawled in the back, and he slid in beside me.

"You look amazing," I said.

He was dressed in a dark suit, pressed white oxford, and narrow black tie. The suit was barely a step below a tuxedo, and I'd seen him in plenty of those. The man wore a suit like a second skin.

"What's the occasion?" I asked.

"I'm going shopping," he answered and then flashed a grin.

"I see. *You're* going shopping."

"Indeed, I am. Now, sit back, and behave."

I needed no encouragement. Nor was I surprised when we pulled up outside of Clara's Boutique. Our adventure had begun here. It might have started at Club Infinity, but this was where I'd made the decision to stop running.

He climbed out and offered his hand to help me exit the car. Clara met us at the door, a huge smile on her face. This time, she greeted me with a hug and kisses to my cheeks.

"It's so good to see you." Clara turned to Richard and dropped a set of keys in his hands. "Everything is set up exactly as you asked. Good luck."

Good luck?

"Come," he said, pulling me inside. "Stay there, and don't you dare move."

No problem. There wasn't anywhere to go.

He spun around, locked the front door, and lowered the shades. He gave a wink. "To keep prying eyes out."

"I guess you don't want them to see what you're *shopping* for," I remembered the leather and chain outfit I had worn last time we were here.

"Most definitely." He came to me, more of a prowl than anything else.

Between one step and the next, the entire tone of our evening changed. This was no longer Richard the Prince. This was the man I loved and the uncaged beast inside.

He held my hand and took me to the sitting area. "Strip."

My eyes widened, but I obeyed without hesitation. If he had a mind to play, I would follow. I kicked off my shoes, a smile lifting my cheeks. Then, I pulled off my blouse, shimmying out of it as I began my striptease. There wasn't anything sexy about me taking off my clothes. Grace was not one of my gifts, but Richard didn't seem to mind. My pants came next, and I peeled those off in a disastrous mess of hopping around. I couldn't help giggling. Finally, I kicked them off, and his laughter spilled into the room, mingling with mine. That warmed my heart and hurt it, too.

Putting my hands to my hips, I stared him down. "If you're going to laugh, I'm stopping right here."

His head shook, slow and purposeful. "If you don't strip out of your bra and panties, I'm going to rip them off myself."

"Don't tempt me," I teased.

"You really don't want to spend the next few minutes over my knee." He gestured with an imperious wave. "Now, strip."

I removed my bra with much more grace than I'd taken off my pants. Hooking my thumbs under the band of my panties, I made a show of stripping out of them nice and slow, knowing exactly what that would do to him. A quick glance at the tenting of his pants, and my work was done.

He approached me but stayed a foot from the dais as he walked around, taking me in from every angle. It took everything not to fidget or squirm.

"I will never get tired of this. You're amazing."

If he didn't think he'd ever get tired of me, why the hell hadn't he renewed our agreement? My pride kept me from asking that question.

"Now," he said, "listen carefully."

My spine stiffened, as I knew we were transitioning into our private roles.

"I want you to go into that dressing room and put on the dress I picked out. Understand?"

"Okay." That seemed like a simple request. Why was he acting weird about it?

I swore, his eyes never left me.

"I'm serious."

"I think I can handle that."

He huffed a low laugh. "We'll see about that."

Great. He had something up his sleeve. Didn't matter. He gave an order, and I obeyed.

Rolling my shoulders back, I puffed out my chest and enjoyed how his gaze angled to my breasts, tightening my nipples. I marched off the stage, turned the corner into the dressing room, and pulled up short. My hands covered my mouth, and tears poured out of my eyes.

All satin and lace, the cornflower-blue Cinderella dress boasted layers and layers of tulle in a petticoat that seemed to float on air. Gems were embedded in the layers that shimmered beneath the lights, and a corset framed the top of the sleeveless gown.

The solid tread of feet had me spinning around. I took a step back and gasped when Richard took a knee. He held up none other than a glass slipper. His grin spread across his entire face, reaching to the corners of his eyes where the lights overhead reflected and sparkled.

"I have a ring, but I couldn't resist becoming a cliché. Now, are you going to put on your dress, or am I going to have to spank that pert little ass?"

"What is this?" My cheeks hurt from the smile on my face. "Your mother forbid—"

"If you dare mention my mother while standing naked in

front of me, I'm going to smack that ass until you can't sit for a month. Now, Miss Rowan Cartwright, will you do me the honor of being my bride?" He rose and came to me. Reaching into his pocket, he pulled out a ring and then knelt again. "Will you marry me?"

"How…" My mind splintered in a million different directions. "You can't. What about…" I knew we didn't have his mother's blessing and exactly what that meant.

He bowed his head and then gripped my hand. Before I knew it, the ring slipped onto my finger. "I can't imagine a life without you."

"What about Infidelity?" I hadn't heard anything from them. Not one peep.

"I bought out the contract. I want you for the rest of my life." Standing, he went to the dress. "Now, I really need you to put this on."

"You intend for me to actually wear that?"

"What else would you get married in?"

"You can't be serious."

"I've never been more serious."

I wrapped my arms around his neck. "I haven't said yes."

"You don't need to." He poked my chest. "Your answer is in your heart. I'm in there, just as you're in mine. Now, let's get you dressed. Everyone is waiting."

"Everyone?" I had no everyone.

Turned out, I was wrong.

Richard helped me into the dress and enjoyed tying me into the corset a little too much. I could barely breathe. Our wedding took place in the library of Freddy's home. My brother had been in on the whole thing. David and Evelyn as well. Freddy must have told Richard about Patrick because he was there, too. He'd brought Cyrus. And Mark! Mark stood by the door, a silent and ever-present sentry.

"How did you arrange all of this?"

"Perks of being a prince and having kick-ass friends."

A prince who would never wear the crown. My heart ached for what he'd lost, and I prayed I would be enough.

The small, intimate ceremony wasn't the one in my dreams, but the dress made me feel like a princess, and the love radiating in Richard's eyes made all the rest unimportant.

I had everything I wanted.

But I wanted something more.

FORTY-SEVEN

Tea

ROWAN

"Rowan!" My brother trotted up as Richard and I were getting ready to climb inside the car. "You forgot your phone!" He jumped up and down.

I gave Richard a short kiss. "Let me see what's got Freddy riled up."

Richard squeezed my hands and stepped back while I navigated the drive in my voluminous Cinderella dress.

Freddy held out my phone. "It's for you." A smile spread across his face. "I spoke to her."

My brows pinched together. "Spoke to whom?"

His eyes rounded. "The Queen."

I glanced at the phone, my stomach dropping. The top bar of the phone flashed green with *Call in Progress* showing.

"Freddy...is she on the line?" I pressed a hand over my belly, feeling suddenly sick.

"Yes, silly." He thrust the phone at me. "She wants to talk to you."

This can't be good.

My hand shook as I took the phone and pressed it to my ear. Richard had explained his last conversation with his mother, which removed him from the throne.

"H-hello?"

"Rowan." The curt voice of the Queen of England jarred my senses.

"Yes?" I had no idea how I was supposed to address the Queen, especially now that she was my mother-in-law.

She might not be speaking to her son, but that didn't change the fact that they were family. I intended to spend the rest of my life mending that fence.

"Is my son with you?"

"Do you want to speak to him?"

"No. I want to talk to you."

"Me?"

"Yes. I expect you to be at tea on Thursday."

"Um…" *What the hell is happening?*

Richard's brows lifted. "Who is it?"

I mouthed, *Your mother.*

His eyes rounded with surprise.

"Oh, don't be daft," she said. "Not many people receive a standing invitation for tea with the Queen of England."

"Excuse me, but I'm a bit confused. Richard and I—"

"I know all about that. You need a proper wedding. Preparations are already in place."

"I don't mean to be rude, but Richard told me about your conversation."

"Richard is impetuous and runs off, half-cocked, most days. I'm counting on you to be a moderating force."

"Okay…" *What is going on?*

A *tsk* sounded through the phone. "My son reminded me of something important. He reminded me that I'd taught him to rule with his heart. You hold his heart, my dear girl, and I expect you to rule with him. Temper his recklessness. Now, we'll meet every Thursday for tea. Time to learn what it means to be a queen."

What?

"Tell my son he has my blessing. If you're worth walking away from the crown, then you're worthy to be queen. Now, about tea?"

"That depends on Richard." I had no idea what Richard had planned for our honeymoon, but I didn't care. My place was by his side. "I follow wherever he leads."

"Then, he's made a brilliant choice. Tell him, I expect you this Thursday." The woman didn't mince words. She disconnected and left me gaping.

"Are you going to tell me what that was all about?" he asked.

I cocked my head. "Evidently, the Queen has invited me for tea."

***

If you enjoyed reading about royal billionaire H.R.H. Richard, you'll love reading about Hawke Sterling; a billionaire in paradise.

HAWKE: Billionaire in Paradise, is a Steamy, Holiday Billionaire Romance that will heat up the sheets and keep you warm on a cold winter's night.

Grab your copy today. Click HERE.

Christmas in paradise turns out to be way more than she bargained for...

Quinn Hayes had it all and lost it all. Her picture-perfect relationship, the venture capital she needs to launch her fledgling company…gone. All she has now is the vacation she planned to take with her ex-fiancé—and there's no way she's letting that go. The last thing she expects (or wants) to find in Euphoria is love. But the sexy, confident man she meets there has her wondering if a rebound is precisely what she needs.

Hawke Sterling doesn't do romance. He's far too jaded for that. Fairy tale, happily ever after endings just aren't for people like him. But there's something about Quinn that has him questioning everything. She's smart, charming, and entirely too gorgeous for his piece of mind. Too bad the only thing he has to offer her is heartbreak.

When it turns out that Hawke holds the key to Quinn's professional success (or ultimate failure), he'll have to decide if the cost of being with her is more than he's willing to pay—and Quinn will need to decide if taking a second chance at love is worth the risk…

Hawke, a steamy, billionaire, holiday, contemporary romance, is book 1 in the Billionaire Boys Club. It features an arrogant alpha male hero and the smart, feisty heroine who steals his heart. Get your copy today and let the binge-reading begin.

Grab your copy today. Click HERE.

***

Keep current with Ellie Masters.
CLICK HERE
Receive news of her writing and new releases.

Please consider leaving a review

I HOPE YOU ENJOYED THIS BOOK AS MUCH AS I ENJOYED WRITING it. If you like this book, please leave a review. I love reviews. I love reading your reviews, and they help other readers decide if this book is worth their time and money. I hope you think it is and decide to share this story with others. A sentence is all it takes. Thank you in advance!

ELLZ BELLZ

ELLIE'S FACEBOOK READER GROUP

If you are interested in joining the ELLZ BELLZ, Ellie's Facebook reader group, we'd love to have you.

Join Ellie's ELLZ BELLZ.
The ELLZ BELLZ Facebook Reader Group

Sign up for Ellie's Newsletter.
Elliemasters.com/newslettersignup

Also by Ellie Masters

The LIGHTER SIDE

Ellie Masters is the lighter side of the Jet & Ellie Masters writing duo! You will find Contemporary Romance, Military Romance, Romantic Suspense, Billionaire Romance, and Rock Star Romance in Ellie's Works.

YOU CAN FIND ELLIE'S BOOKS HERE:
ELLIEMASTERS.COM/BOOKS

Military Romance

Guardian Hostage Rescue Specialists

Rescuing Melissa

*(*Get a FREE copy of Rescuing Melissa when you join Ellie's Newsletter*)*

Alpha Team

Rescuing Zoe

Rescuing Moira

Rescuing Eve

Rescuing Lily

Rescuing Jinx

Rescuing Maria

Bravo Team

Rescuing Angie

Rescuing Isabelle

Rescuing Carmen

Rescuing Rosalie

Rescuing Kaye

Cara's Protector

Rescuing Barbi

Military Romance

Guardian Personal Protection Specialists

Sybil's Protector

Lyra's Protector

The One I Want Series

(Small Town, Military Heroes)

By Jet & Ellie Masters

EACH BOOK IN THIS SERIES CAN BE READ AS A STANDALONE AND IS ABOUT A DIFFERENT COUPLE WITH AN HEA.

Saving Abby

Saving Ariel

Saving Brie

Saving Cate

Saving Dani

Saving Jen

Rockstar Romance

The Angel Fire Rock Romance Series

EACH BOOK IN THIS SERIES CAN BE READ AS A STANDALONE AND IS ABOUT

A DIFFERENT COUPLE WITH AN HEA. IT IS RECOMMENDED THEY ARE READ IN ORDER.

Ashes to New (prequel)

Heart's Insanity (book 1)

Heart's Desire (book 2)

Heart's Collide (book 3)

Hearts Divided (book 4)

Hearts Entwined (book 5)

Forest's FALL (book 6)

Hearts The Last Beat (book 7)

Contemporary Romance

Firestorm

(KRISTY BROMBERG'S EVERYDAY HEROES WORLD)

Billionaire Romance

Billionaire Boys Club

Hawke

Richard

Brody

Contemporary Romance

Cocky Captain

(VI KEELAND & PENELOPE WARD'S COCKY HERO WORLD)

Romantic Suspense

EACH BOOK IS A STANDALONE NOVEL.

The Starling

~AND~

Science Fiction

Ellie Masters writing as L.A. Warren
Vendel Rising: a Science Fiction Serialized Novel

About the Author

ELLIE MASTERS is a multi-genre and Amazon Top 100 best-selling author, writing the stories she loves to read. These are dark erotic tales. Or maybe, sweet contemporary stories. How about a romantic thriller to whet your appetite? Ellie writes it all. Want to read passionate poems and sensual secrets? She does that, too. Dip into the eclectic mind of Ellie Masters, spend time exploring the sensual realm where she breathes life into her characters and brings them from her mind to the page and into the heart of her readers every day.

Ellie Masters has been exploring the worlds of romance, dark erotica, science fiction, and fantasy by writing the stories she wants to read. When not writing, Ellie can be found outside, where her passion for all things outdoor reigns supreme: off-roading, riding ATVs, scuba diving, hiking, and breathing fresh air are top on her list.

She has lived all over the United States—east, west, north, south and central—but grew up under the Hawaiian sun. She's also been privileged to have lived overseas, experiencing other cultures and making lifelong friends. Now, Ellie is proud to call herself a Southern transplant, learning to say y'all and "bless her heart" with the best of them. She lives with her beloved husband, two children who refuse to flee the nest, and four fur-babies; three cats who rule the household, and a dog who wants nothing other than for the cats to be his best friends. The cats have a different opinion regarding this matter.

Ellie's favorite way to spend an evening is curled up on a couch, laptop in place, watching a fire, drinking a good wine, and bringing forth all the characters from her mind to the page and hopefully into the hearts of her readers.

FOR MORE INFORMATION
elliemasters.com

facebook.com/elliemastersromance
twitter.com/Ellie__Masters
instagram.com/ellie_masters
bookbub.com/authors/ellie-masters
goodreads.com/Ellie_Masters

Connect with Ellie Masters

Website:
elliemasters.com
Amazon Author Page:
elliemasters.com/amazon
Facebook:
elliemasters.com/Facebook
Goodreads:
elliemasters.com/Goodreads
Instagram:
elliemasters.com/Instagram

Final Thoughts

I hope you enjoyed this book as much as I enjoyed writing it. If you enjoyed reading this story, please consider leaving a review on Amazon and Goodreads, and please let other people know. A sentence is all it takes. Friend recommendations are the strongest catalyst for readers' purchase decisions! And I'd love to be able to continue bringing the characters and stories from My-Mind-to-the-Page.

Second, call or e-mail a friend and tell them about this book. If you really want them to read it, gift it to them. If you prefer digital friends, please use the "Recommend" feature of Goodreads to spread the word.

Or visit my blog https://elliemasters.com, where you can find out more about my writing process and personal life.

Come visit The EDGE: Dark Discussions where we'll have a chance to talk about my works, their creation, and maybe what the future has in store for my writing.

Facebook Reader Group: Ellz Bellz

Thank you so much for your support!

Love,
Ellie

Dedication

This book is dedicated to you, my reader. Thank you for spending a few hours of your time with me. I wouldn't be able to write without you to cheer me on. Your wonderful words, your support, and your willingness to join me on this journey is a gift beyond measure.

Whether this is the first book of mine you've read, or if you've been with me since the very beginning, thank you for believing in me as I bring these characters 'from my mind to the page and into your hearts.'

Love,
Ellie

THE END

www.ingramcontent.com/pod-product-compliance
Lightning Source LLC
LaVergne TN
LVHW040134080526
838202LV00042B/2907